UNDETERMINED DEATH

LAURA SNIDER

UNDETERMINED DEATH

Severn River Publishing
www.SevernRiverBooks.com

This is a work of fiction. Names, characters, businesses, places, events and incidents are either the products of the author's imagination or used in a fictitious manner. Any resemblance to actual persons, living or dead, or actual events is purely coincidental.

ISBN: 978-1-64875-394-7 (Paperback)

ALSO BY LAURA SNIDER

Ashley Montgomery Legal Thrillers

Unsympathetic Victims

Undetermined Death

Unforgivable Acts

Unsolicited Contact

Unexpected Defense

To find out more about Laura Snider and her books, visit

severnriverbooks.com/authors/laura-snider

For my sisters and strong women everywhere.
Others call you bossy, cold, and aggressive.
I call you what you are.
Inspiring.

PROLOGUE
RACHEL

100 days before trial

Alone. It was such a strange word to her. When broken down it was one letter, "a" followed by the word "lone." Its meaning, *without others*, was somewhat of a dream to her. It made her think of The Lone Ranger. A man and his horse out there on the wide range, surrounded by miles and miles of land.

But that was not how *she* was alone. Her alone came from within. A malfunction in her brain—in her life—that separated her from everyone around her. It detached her even from herself. She didn't choose it. She didn't even like it, but it was the only way to survive in her world. And that was all she was doing. Surviving.

That was how she found herself in a motel room in the tiny town of Brine, Iowa. Alone. Scared yet determined. She'd made a plan, and it was already in motion. There was no way out. She reminded herself that she was prepared. She had a bag full of supplies. One bottle of vodka. One pair of scissors. One bag of snacks and one bottle of Ibuprofen.

So, this is it, she thought. Who was she kidding? She was not prepared. There was no point in lying to herself anymore.

Her eyes traveled around the room, sparsely furnished but containing the basic necessities. A bed with two end tables, each holding a single dusty lamp. A decade-old television atop an ancient dresser. Weatherworn drapes that clung to a paint-chipped curtain rod.

The room was shabby, she had to admit, but she didn't begrudge it for its condition. For she knew its true beauty lay in the freedom that came within. She knew better than anyone that beautiful surroundings could never replace the independence that this room provided, even if only for a couple hours. She set her bag of supplies on the bed and pulled the curtains closed, blocking the small fingers of light cast out by the setting sun.

The bathroom was tiny, but it contained all that she needed. A sink, toilet, and bathtub, which would become vital in a matter of hours. Or would it be minutes? She had no idea how long it would take. She flipped off the light and returned to the bedroom, sliding the top dresser drawer open. It made a scraping noise, wood on wood, and moved slowly, jerkily. Inside the drawer, she found the TV remote and a copy of the *Holy Bible*. She grabbed the former and left the latter. She had no need for a Bible. Her soul was not worth saving.

She lay on the bed and clicked the remote's power button. It was the first time she had complete power over a remote. Her father, Isaac, was the only one permitted that kind of control. The TV screen sprang to life. Voices permeated the room as three talking heads filled the screen. A news anchor and two guests, bickering like cats from rival territories. She changed the channel, flipping from one station to the next until she found something worth watching. Cartoon Network. An episode of *Scooby-Doo* was on, and she settled in to watch the show.

Rachel watched the group of teenage crime solvers. Velma, the supposed dumpy one, always caught her attention. The girls at school had always preferred Daphne. Not that any of those girls would talk to Rachel. But she was an expert at hiding in the shadows. Becoming invisible. Listening. That was how she overheard many conversations over the years. Most teenage girl conversations were garbage. Nonsensical discussions about boys and teachers. But sometimes the girls spoke of her.

None of it was kind. She probably shouldn't have bothered to listen, but part of her wanted to know how they felt about her. In that way, she could belong to those cliques of girls, even if it was only through insults. So she listened as they called her a *freak*. A *whore*. A waste of good genetics. She listened when they said that she was sleeping with the school counselor, Mr. Frank. She listened as they claimed her frequent absences were because she worked the streets at night.

Rachel hated them. Not for their words, but because she envied them. She coveted their plainness. Their normality. She'd give up her beauty any day. Trade her face with another's. Any one of them would do. Jessica, whose skin was almost entirely consumed by freckles. Michelle, whose deep acne scars marred the lower half of her face like craters on the moon. Emily, whose underbite had all the boys calling her "bulldog."

Rachel would trade faces with any of them—all of them—in a heartbeat. Take that which they loathed and give them what they desired. Beauty. But she'd give them the option that nobody gave her. She'd warn them first. She'd say, *be careful what you wish for*. For Rachel's beauty was the source of her problems. Without it, she wouldn't be in her current predicament.

She shook her head, dispelling thoughts of school, and refocused on the television. In this episode of *Scooby-Doo*, the Gang was trying to solve the mystery of the Creeper. The villain was a green, goblin-like creature with a hunched back and a very unfortunate haircut. Rachel liked how the bad guys in *Scooby-Doo* committed their crimes by pretending to be ghosts and ghouls that scared people away. It was unrealistic, and that was precisely why it was so refreshing. For Rachel knew true villains; they were not so kind as to scare others away first. True villains kept their victims close, held onto them, and never let them go.

A sharp pain, almost like a pulse, drew her attention away from the television. She wrapped her arms around her rounded belly and moaned. *These are the early contractions?* she wondered. *How will I get through active labor?*

Rachel shoved herself into a sitting position and grabbed her bag from the end of the bed, unzipping it in one fluid motion. Several towels tumbled out along with a large bottle of Hawkeye vodka that belonged to her father. She stole it from his liquor stash. He would notice its absence—he noticed anything out of place—but Rachel didn't plan to return home.

Another contraction rocked her body. She curled into a ball, moaning, until it passed. Then she unscrewed the top of the bottle and took a large swig of vodka. She coughed and almost spat out the vile-tasting liquid, but she forced herself to swallow. The liquor burned its way down her throat, warming her from within.

Can I do this? Rachel wondered.

She shook her head, forcing the thought from her mind. It wasn't a question of *can*. She must. Her plan was foolproof. She'd had nine months to prepare, and she knew what to do. She would give birth, then she would leave. It was a good scheme. One that would work in most circumstances. Except, like everything else in Rachel's life, it didn't quite work out as she had planned.

1

ASHLEY MONTGOMERY

76 days before trial

The girl did not look like a killer. She was tiny, insubstantial, sitting there across from Ashley in her jail jumpsuit. Her clothing was a faded green with no design or wording except *Brine County Jail* printed in heavy black block lettering across the back. The outfit was meant to dehumanize. To show ownership. To say that this girl was something less than human. A criminal. A piece of property owned by the county. It disgusted Ashley.

Shackles wound their way around the girl's feet. A chain ran between her legs and up her waist, connecting her leg restraints to the manacles twisted around her wrists. *That's not necessary*, Ashley thought. The restraints created a barrier between Ashley and her client. Differentiating them. When, in truth, they had quite a lot in common.

The girl kept her head down, her hands folded neatly in her lap, shoulders rounded. Her fingers were long and elegant, but her nails were bitten to the quick. A disgusting habit that didn't appear to be new judging by the size of her nailbeds.

"Rachel," Ashley said softly.

Rachel lifted her head but did not meet Ashley's gaze. She stared at different portions of Ashley's face—her forehead, chin, and cheeks—dusty

brown eyes darting around in quick, awkward shifts but never making eye
contact. Rachel's eyes were haggard and worn, like they belonged to a
woman five times her age.

"Rachel," Ashley repeated.

"Yeah."

Rachel focused on Ashley's forehead so intensely that Ashley had the
urge to cover it with her hand. It made her feel uncomfortable, self-
conscious, reminding her of the way kids used to call her "forehead" when
she was a teenager.

"How are you?"

Rachel blinked several times, surprised by the question. Like she didn't
know how to answer. It was a dumb inquiry, Ashley supposed. Rachel was
in jail, charged with murdering her newborn baby. She was probably
feeling pretty shitty. How else was there to feel?

"Who are you?"

"My name is Ashley Montgomery. I'm your attorney. I've been
appointed to represent you."

The girl's expression did not change. Her facial features remained still
as a statue. Eerily calm. Those high cheekbones protruding as though chis-
eled out of stone.

"I'm your public defender."

"Oh," Rachel said.

Ashley was one of only two defense attorneys local to the small town of
Brine, Iowa. All other attorneys came from Des Moines or Carroll. The
latter was also a small town, but not Brine small. It was large enough to
have two Subway sandwich shops. Brine had one, but it closed years earlier.
There weren't enough sandwich eaters in a town of only six thousand
people.

"I'm here to help you."

The girl shook her head, slowly and deliberately. A denial made in slow
motion. "Nobody can help me."

"I disagree."

Ashley was the best defense attorney in the region, maybe even the
state. In the past two years, she tried two high-profile cases. A murder and a
sexual assault. One ended in an acquittal, the other in a near acquittal. Of

course, both of those men were later murdered, but that had nothing to do with Ashley's representation.

Rachel shrugged as if to say, *maybe, but maybe not.*

Ashley was a public defender. She understood the stigma that came with that title. She could spend the rest of the meeting outlining her stellar credentials, but that would be a waste of time. It never changed any minds, and Rachel would see Ashley in action soon enough. There was no point in belaboring the issue. Time was limited, and they still had some basic questions to get through.

"How old are you?"

In Ashley's initial client meetings, she always started with the easiest questions. It was a way to develop a rapport before getting into the difficult details that would come later.

"Eighteen."

"Still in high school?"

The girl looked around. The walls were cement, heavy and impenetrable, the doors made of steel. The jail was a giant cage, built to confine the dangerous, the criminal.

"Not anymore."

Fair enough, Ashley thought.

Rachel would not complete her second semester of her senior year. She would not go to her senior prom or receive her diploma along with her classmates. She would be in jail. The magistrate had set her bond at one million dollars cash. No judge was going to change that, not with the interest in the case rising to national levels. It was too political. Iowa judges had to answer to voters in retention elections, and Rachel's story had made the front page of every newspaper, the headline of every broadcast. She was a star. And not in a good way.

Ashley would see about arranging an in-jail GED program for Rachel, if for no other reason than to keep the poor girl occupied. Ashley knew what it was like to be behind those bars. She had been wrongly accused of two murders a year earlier, and her time in jail had almost broken her. All charges were dismissed, but Ashley's incarceration had stolen a small piece of her soul. She knew how it felt to be in Rachel's position, and she would do everything she could to help ease the girl's stress.

Ashley pulled a legal pad and pen out of her bag, writing *Rachel Smithson Notes* on the top line.

"Where did you go to school?"

Rachel was not from Brine. Everyone knew everyone in a town so small. But Ashley had never seen Rachel before. A girl with that kind of beauty did not go unnoticed.

"Waukee."

Waukee was a small town in Iowa that had been swallowed years ago by Des Moines's ever expanding population. Large, luxurious houses had replaced the endless acres of cornfields. It was not a cheap place to live. Rachel had grown up with money. Ashley wondered why her parents hadn't hired one of the large criminal defense firms in Des Moines. People with money did not leave their children's representation up to public defenders.

"Have you spoken to your parents?"

Rachel flinched. Her shoulders twitched and she ducked her head lower.

"I'll take that as a no," Ashley said. It was a bizarre reaction, but it was too early to understand the meaning behind it. "You're eighteen, legally an adult. We don't have to involve your parents. But I can give them a call at your request."

"No."

Rachel's voice was tentative but firm. She did not want her parents involved. It didn't necessarily mean anything. If Rachel was from a well-to-do family, she may not want them to know that she had been criminally charged. Considering that her face had been flashing across all the news stations, though, that ship had sailed.

"I won't contact them, but can you tell me their names?"

"You won't call them?" Rachel sounded suspicious, like promises made to her had a history of being broken.

Look into the family, Ashley jotted on the second line of her notepad.

"I work for you, Rachel. Not your parents."

"You do?"

Ashley sighed. "You are an adult now. That comes with consequences"

—she gestured to the room around her—"like jail instead of juvie. But also benefits, like attorney-client privilege, that doesn't extend to your parents."

"Are you saying that you can't repeat anything I tell you?"

Ashley shook her head. "Not unless you want me to."

Rachel looked down at her hands, picking at her fingernails. It was a stalling tactic, a way to gain space to think when space was something that had to be taken rather than freely given.

"Isaac and Lyndsay Smithson." Rachel's full lips barely moved, but the words were clear.

Ashley scrawled the names on the third line of her notepad. As she did, the sleeve of her shirt pulled up toward her elbow, exposing her forearm.

"What happened?" Rachel said, leaning closer to Ashley.

Ashley followed Rachel's gaze and saw a smattering of bruises running along her hand and up her forearm.

"I don't know…" Ashley said, confused.

The bruising hadn't been there earlier that day. Nobody had grabbed her around the wrist, and she didn't remember hitting it on anything.

"I do," Rachel said in an oddly distant tone.

The bruises were strange, but Rachel's reaction to them was even stranger. How could she possibly have any idea what happened to Ashley's arm? Ashley shook her head, dispelling the thought. It did no good to doubt a client's intentions.

"So, Rachel." Ashley pulled down her sleeve and folded her fingers together, placing her intertwined hands on the old, scuffed desk that separated her from her client, suddenly grateful for its presence. "You are probably wondering why I have not asked you about what happened in that hotel room."

A row of wrinkles rippled across Rachel's forehead, then vanished as quickly as they had appeared.

"I haven't asked about it because I don't want to know." Ashley paused. "At least not yet. But maybe never."

Rachel's jet-black hair shimmered in the florescent lighting.

"The burden is on the State to prove you guilty beyond a reasonable doubt. You and I"— Ashley gestured toward Rachel and then back to herself—"we don't have to prove anything. All we have to do is sit back and poke holes in their story."

One dark eyebrow rose. A question. To what, Ashley wasn't entirely sure. So she forged on.

"I will request the evidence from the prosecutor. We will go through it. If we are lucky, there will be suppression issues and other things to work with. My goal is to get as much of their evidence thrown out as possible. That could be a lot, or none, depending on which officers were involved."

Ashley hoped her friend, Katie Mickey, had not been part of the investigation. Katie was an officer with the Brine Police Department. At one point, Katie had been sloppy, making mistake after prosecution-shattering mistake, but that was in the past. She had learned her lesson and was now meticulous, careful to follow every rule. It was great for the general population's constitutional rights, but unhelpful for Ashley's purposes.

Rachel nodded slowly, but the action didn't feel like it was meant to be an agreement.

"What I am telling you is that I don't care if you did it. All I care about is what the prosecution can prove. The State is the one that has to worry about good and bad, right and wrong. My focus is on winning."

Rachel bit her bottom lip. It was red and chapped in a way that made it look as though she were wearing lipstick. "What do you mean by 'winning?'"

That was the million-dollar question. A "win" could mean all sorts of things. Usually, it meant a better outcome than the State's offer had been. Here, she doubted any offers would come from the prosecutor's office. Not with the current political environment. So, a "win" for Rachel meant anything less than a life sentence.

"Honestly," Ashley said with a sigh, "you will probably end up with some sort of conviction. Our best chance is probably going to be a child endangerment conviction with a ten-year prison sentence."

Ashley had braced herself for an outburst. A shocked, *Ten years? Ten whole years?* Which was a lot to someone Rachel's age. More than half her life. But Ashley saw no concern in Rachel's eyes. No reaction. Rachel was devoid of emotion, like she'd been the entire meeting.

"Do you hate me?" Rachel asked. Her tone was flat, but not entirely uninterested.

Ashley patted the girl's hand. It was pale and ice-cold. Rachel didn't flinch away from Ashley's touch, but she did meet her gaze for the first time. Something hard, something unyielding, lurked behind those breathtakingly beautiful eyes. They were a shade so light brown that her raven hair drew out the shreds of yellow and green within them.

If Ashley were younger, she might have envied Rachel. But she had long ago learned that Rachel's kind of beauty came with a cost. It drew attention, and not always in a good way. Murderers were a dime a dozen, but a gorgeous girl accused of killing her baby, well, that was a case worth following.

"No," Ashley said, "I don't hate you." Ashley didn't judge her clients, no matter what the State claimed they had done. They got plenty of criticism from the public.

Something in Rachel's detached exterior wavered, like a tiny door of trust was begging to open. But in that moment, Ashley's phone began to buzz inside her bag. Rachel's mouth closed, her eyes darting toward the bag. Ashley sighed deeply and picked her beat-up laptop bag off the floor, digging in it for her phone. The screen read *Tom Archie.*

Tom was the former jail administrator and Ashley's current boyfriend. He had moved to Des Moines in the fall to study psychology at Drake University. She missed him. He had only been gone for a few months and he visited every weekend, but Ashley still felt like part of her was missing.

Rachel's eyes widened at the sight of Ashley's phone.

"It's not your parents," Ashley said, holding the screen at an angle so Rachel could read it. "I said I wouldn't call, but that also means I won't answer their calls. I'm not backdooring you like that."

A muscle twitched in Rachel's jaw.

The phone buzzed several more times. Ashley looked down at it longingly. She wanted to answer. It had been days since they last spoke, and the last call hadn't ended well. Tom had been upset, claiming that she worked too much. That she "wasn't making their relationship a priority." Ashley understood his concerns, she really did, but she didn't know how to fix them. Her clients, including Rachel, needed her. Ashley reluctantly pressed the silence button, thinking, *I'll call him in a minute*. The meeting was almost over anyway.

"Your arraignment is at 1:00 this afternoon."

Rachel furrowed her brow. A small dimple appeared between her eyes. It was adorable, which was a real problem. Juries were made up of people, and Rachel's appearance was a detriment. Women did not generally like other women, especially ones as striking as Rachel.

"Arraignment?"

"It's a hearing where we enter a plea. A formality. Usually, it's done in writing, but the judge wants us in court. Judge Ahrenson likes to put on a show for the cameras."

Rachel nodded like she had expected as much.

"It will be a short hearing. We will walk into the courtroom, Judge Ahrenson will read the indictment, and we will enter a plea of not guilty. We will then demand a speedy trial and the hearing will be over."

"Speedy trial?"

"Yes. It means they must start your trial within ninety days from the date they filed the trial information, the formal charging document. That was filed a couple weeks ago. So, as of today's date, our ninety days is down to seventy-six." Ashley raised her hands in surrender. "I know it isn't ideal, but it has its benefits. I demand speedy in all my cases. It puts pressure on the State. If, for some reason, we need more time, we can waive. But that also means you sit in here longer."

Ashley paused to study Rachel's expression. Still no change, no outrage.

"I will tell you that jail is far worse than any prison. At least prisons let you outside your cell for meals, work, and yard time. Not that you will end up in prison. I hope to avoid that as well, but we also need to keep this realistic. A prison term is the most likely outcome."

"Okay," Rachel said, her words a Ben Stein monotone.

"We have to do something about the way you look before your arraignment."

"We do?"

Ashley studied the girl. "You need to look more..." She paused, chewing on her lip. "Frumpy."

Rachel looked down at herself. "This isn't frumpy?"

"No." Ashley shook her head. "I mean yes, on most people. But you look like a character on *Orange Is the New Black*. The Hollywood version of a defendant. We need you to be unattractive. Maybe the hair..." She snapped her fingers. "That's it. I'll come back before your arraignment with a pair of scissors and some dark purple eyeshadow. We are going to paint bags under your eyes and cut you some uneven bangs. You should try to limit your sleep if you can. That should help for future hearings."

"I'll need help staying awake. There's nothing to do in here."

Ashley tapped a finger against her lips, thinking. "Do you like to read?"

"Yes." Rachel's face lit up for the first time. It was like the sun coming out from behind a layer of thick clouds.

"I think there are a few books around here. I'll ask Kylie, your jailer, and see if we can't get you a few."

"Oh, thank you." Rachel's eyes began filling with tears.

"Don't mention it." It was such a small thing. Ashley was unsettled by Rachel's sudden change in demeanor.

"I'm not sure about the hair idea." Rachel touched the ends of her straight hair. "My *father* likes it how it is."

Rachel said the word "father" in a lilting, sarcastic way. An accusation, like Isaac Smithson carried the title but had never lived up to it.

"Fuck him." It was an automatic reaction. Probably not the most professional thing she could have said, but Ashley didn't think any man had the right to dictate his adult daughter's appearance.

A small smile crept onto the corners of Rachel's lips. "Okay."

"Try to relax," Ashley said, patting Rachel's hand. "The next couple months are going to be a shit show. I'll do my best to protect you from the brunt of it, but there will be cameras. Lots of them." There was no avoiding it. Rachel's trial was going to be a media circus.

Rachel nodded and Ashley stood, the plastic chair scraping against the floor as she rose from her seat. Rachel stood, too, her wrist and leg restraints jangling.

"I'll make sure they take those off for our next meeting." Ashley nodded to the chains binding the girl's hands and feet.

Rachel posed no danger to Ashley. Ashley was small, but this girl was practically skeletal. She had birthed a baby only weeks earlier, but it looked as though Rachel had not eaten a proper meal in months. Ashley pressed a small silver intercom button.

"Are you done?" asked Kylie, the jail administrator.

"Yeah," Ashley said. She always felt strange speaking into the jail's intercom system. Like she was talking to a wall.

"I'll be right there."

Ashley and Rachel were silent until Kylie arrived.

"You ready?" she asked, motioning to Rachel.

Rachel nodded and rose from her seat.

Ashley watched her client shuffle through the iron door and into the maw of the jail. The door slammed shut, swallowing her whole.

2

KATIE MICKEY

The air in the interview room was cold. A few degrees lower and Katie felt sure she would be able to see her breath. The whole police station was the same. Chief Carmichael was trying to save every dime, pinch every penny, so that he could keep all his officers. They only had six. One fewer would matter.

Budget cuts, Katie thought bitterly.

It was all thanks to the damned "shortchange the cops" movement. It started as a small group of misfits but gained traction after the arrest and conviction of John Jackie, a former Brine police officer, for bribery and murder. The group had even convinced Forest Parker, a Brine city council member, to join. Now they seemed virtually unstoppable.

Forest Parker, Katie thought.

She had once found him captivating, even handsome. Now she couldn't believe she'd ever considered him moderately attractive. Katie blew into her hands and rubbed them together. She was waiting for Detective George Thomanson. *Detective*. A new addition to his name. He was the only one on the Brine police force. A year had passed since George's promotion, which came after he and Katie solved the triple homicide that led to Officer John Jackie's arrest. Katie had been the lead on that case, yet she had been passed up for the promotion.

Chief Carmichael was not intentionally sexist. His failure to choose her wasn't purposeful or malicious. She knew that. He was a good man who tried to be fair. His bias was implicit. He was of a generation that thought police officers ought to be men, and nursing was a woman's job. It was based in the misguided belief that men were protective and women nurturing. It was bullshit. Katie knew plenty of women who couldn't nurture a houseplant, including herself and her friend Ashley Montgomery, and there were scores of cowardly men.

"This way." Katie could hear George's voice echoing down the hallway.

She stood just as he entered the room.

"Katie," George said with a nod.

"George," Katie replied through clenched teeth.

A tall, thin man with a wiry build and clean-shaven face followed closely behind George. The man stood erect with his shoulders back and his head held high. If Katie had to estimate his age, she would guess he was somewhere between fifty-five and sixty-five.

A woman came next, following three or four steps behind the men. She, too, was thin, her build petite. Heavy creases were etched across her face, creating two identical crevices around her mouth. Premature worry lines, Katie guessed. She wondered if it was genetics or life. Considering the reason for the interview, Katie guessed the latter. The woman held herself in a very different fashion from the man. Her shoulders were rounded, her head down. A woman trying to hide. From what, Katie didn't know.

"Mr. and Mrs. Smithson," Katie said, extending her hand. "So nice to meet you."

The man eyed Katie's hand, then stepped past her into the room. The woman shook it. She had a weak grip, and her palms were cold and slick with sweat.

"This is Officer Katie," George said, gesturing toward Katie.

"Officer Mickey," Katie corrected.

Mr. Smithson gave Katie a cool nod and Mrs. Smithson flashed a small, tentative smile.

"Right, right. My mistake." George cleared his throat and straightened his suit jacket. Detectives didn't have to wear the traditional blue uniform.

There was no dress code, so George had started wearing suit jackets with jeans, an attempt to visually elevate himself above the rest.

"Have a seat wherever you'd like." George motioned to the chairs on the opposite side of the table.

The conference room contained one long table surrounded by ten faux-leather rolling chairs. The chairs were worn, but they were high-backed and had that soft, broken-in feel. Detective Thomanson dropped into the chair next to Katie, and Mr. Smithson chose one directly across from George. Mrs. Smithson waited until her husband was seated and comfortable before choosing the chair across from Katie.

Katie watched the two interviewees closely. People often said plenty without even uttering a word. A few minutes around the Smithsons were plenty to start sketching a picture of the family dynamics. They had what some would term a "traditional" marriage. Mr. Smithson was the head of the household. He held the control. To Katie, that meant the buck stopped with him. All the glory, all the blame. But judging by his demeanor, she doubted he took a shred of the blame. That was left for Mrs. Smithson.

"Mr. Smithson," George said, threading his fingers together and placing them on the conference table. "Your first name is Isaac, right?"

Mr. Smithson nodded.

"Mind if I call you Isaac?"

"That's fine." His voice was gruff but not outwardly intimidating. Deep with an almost hypnotic component to it. The kind of voice that seemed all-knowing, trustworthy. Easy to convince others to do things they might not have done without his encouragement.

"And Mrs. Smithson." George turned his amber eyes to the woman. "You look lovely today."

Mrs. Smithson smiled and patted her hair.

Katie blinked several times in rapid succession, annoyed.

"Her first name is Lyndsay," Isaac said, hooking his thumb toward his wife. "You can call her whatever you want. She answers pretty well to 'woman,' too."

Katie bristled. If the man was this disrespectful in front of police officers, Katie shuddered to think how he treated Lyndsay behind closed doors.

"Lyndsay it is," George said, smiling broadly.

Of course, George would ignore Isaac's maltreatment of his wife. He tried to pretend gender equality was important to him, but his actions told a different story. He didn't care unless there was benefit in others believing that he cared. That benefit certainly didn't reside anywhere within the vicinity of Isaac Smithson.

"I'm sure you know why you are here," George said.

Isaac nodded. Lyndsay shifted her weight, staring down at her hands folded neatly in her lap.

Katie pulled a notebook and pen out of her pocket. She clicked the end of the pen and looked up at Isaac. She and George had discussed their approach before the meeting and decided it was best for George to handle the questioning. At least, George had decided it would be best for him to take the lead. Katie, as the inferior officer, didn't have much of a choice in the matter.

"You have come to the police station of your own accord. You are not under arrest. You know the way in and out of this place, right?" George nodded toward the door.

"Yes. Same way we came in," Isaac said.

Katie doubted Isaac knew the way out, but he wasn't the type of man to ask for directions. The hallways in the police station were deliberately confusing, especially the one leading to the interview room. It wound around several cubicles and down two separate hallways. The walls of the building were all the same unadorned cinder block, leaving no clues, no breadcrumbs to mark the way out. Every turn was identical.

"You are free to leave at any time."

It was something they told all interviewees unless the person had already been arrested. Not that Isaac and Lyndsay's interview was expected to implicate them in any wrongdoing. The baby was their daughter's, not theirs, and all evidence indicated that Rachel had been alone in that hotel room. Advising them of their rights was just standard procedure. It allowed all questions, even inculpatory ones, without first reading Miranda warnings. Miranda put people on edge. It made them guard their words. It was something best avoided during an investigation.

"We understand," Isaac said.

"I'd like to get a little background on you and your family."

Isaac nodded.

"How many children do you have?"

"None anymore."

The guy had disowned his only child. Even before her conviction. Katie was struck with a sudden pang of empathy for Rachel. The girl truly was alone in the world. Much as Katie had been ever since she was sixteen. Rachel was eighteen, but in today's world, that still felt like a child. Katie shook her head, reminding herself of Rachel's horrendous actions. The girl was nothing like Katie had been as a child. Katie had to make tough decisions, but she never physically harmed anyone. Rachel had. She'd killed a helpless baby.

George tapped his fingers on the table. "Rachel was an only child?"

"Yes."

"By choice or circumstance?"

Isaac's eyes drifted toward his wife. "Circumstance. My wife couldn't have more than the one. We tried. I wanted a boy, you see. But something is wrong with her body."

"Miscarriages?" Katie asked.

Isaac ignored Katie entirely, directing his answer to George. "The babies all died in the first trimester. Something about a hostile environment."

"Did that upset you?" Katie stared right at Lyndsay as she spoke, but the woman made no move to answer.

"It bothered me back then," Isaac said to George as though they were the only two in the room. "Miscarriage after miscarriage. But knowing my wife, they would have all ended up as girls anyway. Seeing how Rachel turned out, I wish I would have stuck with no kids."

Me. I. My. The world revolved around Isaac Smithson, at least in his eyes. Katie's gaze traveled toward Lyndsay, who was sitting so still she looked petrified. Her eyes remained trained on her intertwined fingers, cast downward in a demure fashion. Deference to her husband. Katie would get no answers from her. At least not while her husband was around.

"So, just the one child," George said. "Do you want grandchildren?"

Isaac shook his head. "We won't have any. The only chance was that one sitting there in the morgue. Rachel won't get knocked up where she's going.

I hear she has a public defender representing her. A woman. There's not a snowball's chance in hell that girl is getting out of jail."

Isaac was underestimating Ashley. A mistake that far too many had made in the past. But Katie wasn't going to correct him. He'd find out once he came face-to-face with the local public defender.

"Did you know Rachel was pregnant?" George asked.

Isaac sat up straighter and Lyndsay twisted her hands in her lap. This was the million-dollar question. One asked in all the news coverage and debated in the rumor mill down at Genie's Diner. Everyone wanted to know the parents' role in Rachel's crime. If they knew, they could have done something. Found a doctor and provided prenatal care for Rachel. Kept closer tabs on their girl. Any small change might have resulted in the birth of a healthy baby.

"No," Isaac said, slowly yet firmly. "We knew nothing."

Katie could hardly believe that an eighteen-year-old could hide a full pregnancy, but it was possible if Rachel hadn't gotten very big. It was approaching winter, the season for large, baggy clothes.

"Who is the father of the child?"

"I don't know for sure."

"You don't have any ideas? No boyfriends? Friends who might have turned into something more?"

"None that I knew about. But she was in school. Who knows what kind of trouble she got up to while there?"

The school would know, Katie thought, but did not say.

"If you ask me, that school counselor was a little too interested in her. He kept pulling her out of class. Talking to her. She didn't have anything to say, but he kept trying."

School counselor? Katie wrote on her notepad.

That was easy enough to follow up on. There should be records at the school. She hoped the school counselor didn't turn out to be the baby's father. Or any adult, for that matter. Rachel was seventeen when she conceived. A minor. An adult paramour would complicate the prosecution. Create sympathy for a girl who didn't deserve any.

"Anyone else?"

"No." Isaac pressed his palms into his eyes. "Well, actually, yes."

"Who?"

"There was a guy who spent some time hanging around the house. He was in his twenties." Isaac paused to think for a moment, then nodded. "Early to mid-twenties. He would stroll by the house around the time that Rachel was walking home from school. I told him to stay away from her, but he kept turning up."

"Who was it?" George asked.

Katie sat up straight, pen poised and ready to jot down the name.

"I don't know his name. He was a police officer from one of the Des Moines suburbs."

"Do you know which suburb?"

"No. But like I said, he was young. In his twenties."

It was a hint, but it didn't narrow the field all that much. Des Moines was a city of suburbs. There was Ankeny, Clive, Urbandale, West Des Moines, Waukee, Pleasant Hill, Altoona, Norwalk, and Grimes. And those were just the names that instantly came to mind. There were more. Thousands of police officers in the Des Moines area would fit Isaac's limited description.

"How about clubs or after-school programs?"

"None. Rachel went to school and came home. She was a loner."

Katie clicked her pen, then leaned forward. "How about other people? Did anyone else visit your house regularly?"

Rachel's baby had a father. It wasn't immaculate conception, that was for sure. The lab would test the baby's DNA, but unless the father was a felon or his DNA was already on file for some other reason, there was little chance they'd match it to anyone.

Isaac's cool gray gaze slowly slid toward Katie. His lip curled into a sneer. For a moment, Katie thought he wouldn't answer. But then he did.

"Nobody," Isaac said. "I keep everyone off my property. Even cops."

Katie narrowed her eyes. "Why cops?"

"I told you one has been hanging around my house, waiting for Rachel. I heard what happened around here with that John Jackie fella. The guy worked for you and he was a serial killer. I'm not letting the devil in through my front door. Especially if they are hiring people like *you*."

Katie knew that he meant women. She had more talent and intellect in her pinky finger than he did in his whole body. And women, including Katie, were perceptive, a gift that Katie used to her advantage in investigations. It often took a while with witnesses, but she could differentiate between lies and truths.

Katie's instincts told her that this man was lying. But why? It could be something as simple as a desire to make himself look better. Or it could be something far worse.

3

ASHLEY

"Hi, Elena," Ashley called as she stepped through the front door of the public defender's office.

Elena was the office manager, a new hire who was already proving invaluable. She was in her early twenties, tall with long, flowing dark hair, and a high-school graduate with no college training. But Ashley hadn't been looking for degrees on a resume when she'd made the hiring decision. What Ashley needed was smart and discreet. Elena was both of those things.

"Hey, Ashley," Elena said in her sing-song voice.

Ashley had never quite understood how Elena could manage so much happiness. Her life had not been easy. She lived in constant fear of losing her parents. She was born in America, but her parents were undocumented. Their lifestyle was entirely dependent on a president they didn't get to choose.

Ashley wished she could do something for the family, but immigration was an extremely specialized area of the law. She had never done that kind of work. It was probably best for Elena's family to continue hiding in plain sight anyway.

"Any mail?"

Elena pointed to a side table. A stack of envelopes lay beside a stunning bouquet of flowers and two unopened boxes. "From your fan club."

The gifts had been coming every few days since Ashley had participated in an interview with Iowa Public Radio. The interview was mostly about her wrongful incarceration and attempted murder by a Brine police officer last year, but Ashley had also used it as a springboard to fundraise.

Her efforts had paid off, literally. She'd received enough donations to hire Elena and keep her on indefinitely. But as Ashley's mother used to say, *Nothing is free*. The cost of the interview had been the flock of men who heard her story, looked her up, and decided that she was the woman for them.

Ashley groaned and grabbed a pair of scissors, heading toward the pile of mail. The flowers had no note, which Ashley appreciated. If she read one more *I love you* from a stranger, she might just lose her mind. These men were infatuated. It was not love. Tom hadn't even told her that he loved her yet and they had been dating for ten months. But that relationship had been rocky lately, so maybe he never would.

She turned her attention to the boxes and ran scissors along the tape of the first one. Inside were two heart-shaped boxes of assorted chocolates, store-bought and sealed.

"One for you." She handed a box to Elena. "And one for me."

"Thanks," Elena said.

Ashley turned to the second box. The return label listed an address and name that she recognized. *Tom Archie*. A smile spread across her lips. Two weeks had passed since Tom had learned about the gifts from her admirers. It was the basis of another—she wouldn't call it an argument—passive-aggressive exchange of words. He was bothered by other men sending her gifts.

This was the second box he had sent this week. Apparently, he'd decided to add himself to her list of suitors. It was a kind gesture, she supposed, even though it was motivated by jealousy. It didn't make up for all the weirdness that had been settling between them, but it helped.

Ashley ran the scissors along the packing tape, slicing it in two, then popped the top. Inside, she found a second box, smooth and white. A box made for gifting. She lifted the lid, and the sweet scent of homemade candies filled the air. An envelope fluttered to the floor.

"Is that another box of candies?" Elena said, coming up to Ashley's side.

Ashley nodded. Tom had never baked anything for her. The fact that he had now meant something. The first box of chocolates had been fantastic, but she would have appreciated the gift even if the candy tasted like ashes.

"I didn't realize he knew his way around a kitchen," Elena said.

Elena hadn't known Tom while he was the jail administrator, back before he and Ashley got together, but she had gotten to know him over the past several months. He was in Brine every Friday afternoon. Ashley was always busy until closing time, so he would sit out front with Elena and chat.

Ashley shrugged. "Me neither."

"They look delicious."

Ashley held the box toward Elena. "You're welcome to try one."

"No." Elena raised her hands. "I couldn't possibly. He made those for *you*. Not me. Besides." She patted her flat stomach. "I'm watching my figure."

"You're ridiculous." Ashley didn't understand why girls Elena's age couldn't see themselves clearly. Even the thin ones found fault with their bodies.

"I just need to lose a couple pounds."

Ashley shook her head and crouched to pick up the envelope that had fallen from the box. There was no point arguing sense into Elena. Girls her age had been brainwashed by a lifetime of stick figures in "beauty" magazines. "I'll open this one in my office," Ashley said, holding up the envelope.

"I would, too," Elena said, waggling her eyebrows.

In the short span of time that Elena and Ashley had been working together, they had developed a friendship. Ashley welcomed it. Elena had scores of friends, so one more probably didn't mean much to her. She was an open book that everyone wanted to read. Ashley, on the other hand, was like a lockbox.

"Before you go," Elena said, "I wanted to tell you that I have that new case file ready."

"Rachel Smithson?"

Elena nodded. Due to the volume of cases, their office was always running a little behind with the creation of files. "That's the one. It's sitting on your desk."

"I just saw Rachel."

"What's she like?"

"She's...ummm..." Ashley searched for the right word to describe Rachel. "Odd."

"That's to be expected, right? I mean, normal people don't have babies alone in a hotel room, then check out and return home like nothing happened."

"True," Ashley said.

Elena had worked for Ashley long enough to know better than to assume a defendant's guilt. But the facts she had outlined were incontrovertible. Rachel's behavior was strange, whether she was the cause of her child's death or not.

"Thanks for getting the file ready," Ashley said, patting Elena on the shoulder. There was no use focusing on unanswerable questions. "You've been doing some good work here. I don't know how I ever managed without you."

A year earlier, Ashley had no support staff. She didn't have the budget. The public defender's office was an arm of the government, which meant that the legislature held the purse strings. Funding for criminal defense was unpopular in good years, but the economy had taken a downturn and Ashley watched helplessly as her funding disappeared. But she had found a way to outsmart the legislature. Thanks to Iowa Public Radio, she'd been able to cut out the middleman and go straight to the people.

Ashley turned toward the hallway leading to her office. "I'll be in my office if you need me."

"Right-o," Elena said, making the *okay* sign with her fingers.

Ashley headed toward her office, positioned in the back of the old building. Several empty offices lay ahead of it, spots Ashley hoped to eventually fill. There had once been another defense attorney in the employ of the Brine public defender's office, Jacob Matthews, but he had left for a corporate counsel position several months ago.

When Ashley reached her office, she collapsed into her old but extremely comfortable chair and placed the box of treats from Tom on her heavily scratched desk. Taking two candies from the box, she popped one in her mouth and chewed. She groaned with pleasure. It was so good. Just like the first box of candy he had sent. She popped a second one in her mouth and turned to Tom's letter. It read, *I will do better*, in Tom's familiar, slanted scrawl.

Oh, Tom, she thought with a sigh. They both needed to "do better," but the question was how? The box of chocolates, while an appreciated gesture, wouldn't solve anything. She needed to talk to him. Glancing at the clock, she decided it was time to try his cell again. She dialed Tom's number and waited. It rang two times, then went to voicemail.

"Hi, it's me," Ashley said. "Call me back." She tried to keep her voice breezy but failed miserably. Could he blame her? He was the one complaining about her failure to make time for him, but he hadn't been answering her calls either. It was hypocritical.

She tossed her phone aside and turned to Rachel's file. The arraignment was later that day. The first page of the file was the indictment. The caption read "State of Iowa, Plaintiff, vs. Rachel Smithson, Defendant." Rachel's mug shot was below her case number, FECR015987. In the picture, Rachel's head was tilted down, her eyes shifted away from the camera. Her ruby lips were frozen in something between a smile and a frown.

Ashley flipped the page and turned to the Minutes of Testimony. The Minutes were a list of witnesses and a short excerpt of their expected testimony created and signed by Charles Hanson, the lead prosecutor in the county. The Board of County Supervisors appointed Charles as county attorney after Elizabeth Clement's arrest a year earlier.

The list of names in the Minutes of Testimony was expected. A clerk at the hotel where the body was found. Several members of the night cleaning staff. A seemingly endless list of officers, including Katie Mickey and George Thomanson. A medical examiner. Rachel's father. But not Rachel's mother.

Ashley made a notation on her legal pad. *Mother sympathetic?* It was a longshot considering Lyndsay Smithson hadn't attempted to reach her daughter since her arrest.

Turning back to the Minutes of Testimony, Ashley noticed a second obvious and glaring name missing from the list. The father of Rachel's unnamed baby. It wasn't by accident. Nobody knew his identity, yet everyone was speculating. A few Waukee high school students appeared on the national news, claiming he or she knew someone who knew someone who said Rachel had a boyfriend. There were rumors about teachers, but no names had surfaced.

A few days ago, several female students who lived near Rachel started mentioning a police officer. None had been able to describe him past, "He was hot, that's why I noticed him." This mysterious officer raised questions that nobody seemed interested in answering. Nobody except Ashley.

It could be a dead end, or it could lead to a viable defense. Either way, Ashley couldn't ignore it. She would start with the Waukee Police Department, which kept records of all dispatched officers. It would be easy to find out who might have gone to the Smithson residence in an official capacity.

4

ASHLEY

"Hold still," Ashley said as she sectioned off a chunk of Rachel's long hair. It was 12:45, and there wasn't much time before they needed to leave for Rachel's arraignment hearing.

Rachel squeezed her eyes shut as Ashley brought the scissors close to her face.

"I'm not going to hurt you," Ashley said in the most soothing tone she could muster. "Just a little snip and we'll be done."

"Okay," Rachel said. The word rasped from her throat, barely above a whisper. She stilled her movements, but her body continued to shake. Tiny, involuntary spasms.

"Are you ready?"

Rachel's eyes popped open, and she tracked the scissors with them. Her gaze held naked fear. It filled the room, palpable in its density.

"Ready?" Ashley asked again.

This time Rachel answered. She squeezed her eyes shut again and said, "Yes."

Ashley slid the scissors across Rachel's hair in a quick, fluid motion, careful to slice at an angle. Long strands of hair fluttered to the floor, leaving a row of short, jagged bangs.

"Perfect," Ashley said with a smile.

One of Rachel's eyes opened slowly, and a few seconds later the other followed suit. She looked down at the pile of hair, her expression smooth and unperturbed.

Next, Ashley pulled out a makeup kit and dabbed a mixture of dark purple and deep gray under Rachel's eyes.

"In the next couple of weeks, I'd like you to try to limit your sleep."

Rachel nodded. "Kylie gave me some books to read."

"Good," Ashley said, then stepped back and admired her handiwork. "It's better, but you're still too pretty. There isn't much we can do about that now. Maybe a bad dye job will help. I'll have to run it by Kylie first, though. I can't imagine the jail will like me bringing chemicals into their facility."

"May I?" Rachel reached for the scissors, her voice tentative but determined.

"I really shouldn't," Ashley said, looking down at the twin blades.

Scissors were sharp and dangerous. A weapon. But Ashley knew that Rachel wasn't going to hurt her. She had years of experience with criminal defendants and could sense danger like a drug dog could sniff out cocaine. This girl didn't have an aggressive bone in her body. If Rachel wanted to cut her own hair, who was Ashley to stand in the way?

"Okay," she said, handing the scissors to Rachel.

Rachel's long, elegant fingers encircled the handle, and she brought the scissors to her unblemished ivory cheek, pressing down hard enough to draw blood.

"Whoa." Ashley pulled the scissors from Rachel's hand. "What's wrong with you? Why would you hurt yourself?"

Tears welled in Rachel's eyes. She had always seemed small, but she shrank further into herself, a beautiful girl lost in a world full of cruelty.

"You said I was too pretty..." She paused, tears spilling down her cheeks. "It's not my hair. It's my face." She gasped, choking on her sobs.

It was Rachel's first display of emotion, and it caught Ashley off guard. Ashley's jaw dropped and her mind grappled for the right words to say, but her thoughts moved sluggishly. Much like they had over the past couple days. It was like a deep fatigue had settled into her body and mind.

"You're right. I am too pretty. It's always been the problem. I don't want to be pretty. I want scars." Her stony exterior had dissipated, devoured by blind desperation. "All over my face." Rachel beckoned for the scissors.

Ashley cradled them against her chest and took another step backward. "I'm sorry, but I won't. I didn't mean it so, so…literally."

Rachel dropped to the ground, hugging her knees and rocking back and forth. Tears streamed down her face, making tracks through Ashley's carefully applied makeup. "It doesn't matter what you meant. It's the truth. I don't want to look like this anymore."

Ashley watched Rachel, too stunned to say anything. This poor, broken girl. So many women would sell their soul to have a face like that, yet for Rachel, it had been a curse. What had happened as a result of that curse, Ashley didn't know. But she guessed it had something to do with that baby found in hotel room 101.

Ashley crouched beside Rachel. "Hey, hey, hey," she said, gathering the bawling girl into her arms and dabbing at the blood on her cheek with a Kleenex.

Rachel sank into Ashley's embrace. It wasn't the first time Ashley had seen a client teetering on the edge of despair, but Rachel's raw emotions were more intense than most.

"Shhhh," Ashley said, rocking back and forth. "Shhhh, now. You're safe. Everything is going to be all right." The words tumbled from Ashley's mouth, but she didn't know if they were true.

Slowly, ever so gradually, Rachel's tears subsided, and she was able to sit back and wipe her eyes. As she did, she looked down at her hands, streaked with blueish-purple eyeshadow.

"Oh, no," she said. "I ruined it."

"It's fine, Rachel." Ashley helped the girl to her feet. "It wasn't that convincing anyway. Besides"—she gestured toward Rachel's blotchy, tear-stained face—"this is better."

A small, almost imperceptible smile flashed at the corners of Rachel's lips. Then the door flew open and Kylie stepped into the small room to retrieve Ashley and Rachel. It was showtime.

"Are you ready for your arraignment?" Ashley asked, placing both hands on Rachel's shoulders and looking her square in the eye.

Rachel's dusty brown eyes were slick with unshed tears and red-rimmed from crying. She nodded, a small, almost undetectable bob of the head.

"You'll be fine," Kylie said, twirling her key ring around her finger. "I'll keep you safe."

Kylie was young, in her mid-twenties. Short and strongly built. She had a deep, booming voice that could sound almost severe, but Ashley had known her since her first day as a jailer. Back then, she had been tentative. Her demeanor changed as she gained more experience on the job. These days she was a force to be reckoned with. Intimidating, but kind at heart. Ashley had no doubt that Kylie would make good on her promise.

"There are a lot of reporters out there..." Kylie's voice trailed off when she saw Rachel. Her eyes darted from Rachel's bangs, to Ashley, then to the floor, where heavy chunks of hair lay spread out like a platoon of dead soldiers. "I see you've been working on your appearance. It, um"—she cleared her throat—"looks nice."

Ashley laughed and tucked the scissors into her laptop bag. "Don't lie. It's supposed to look bad."

"You're right. It looks terrible. You okay with it, kid?"

Rachel smiled. A quick flash of teeth and crinkle at the corners of the eyes, but it was enough to light up the room. "Yes."

"What happened to your face?" Kylie asked, staring pointedly at the small cut on Rachel's cheek.

"Nothing," Rachel said in her small voice.

Kylie's gaze swung to Ashley, who only shrugged. She trusted Kylie, but she had no intention of telling her about Rachel's breakdown.

"Let's get you over to the courthouse. I hate to do this, but..." Kylie held up Rachel's shackles. "I have to chain your feet and hands. The prosecutor is worried you are going to run."

Ashley rolled her eyes. "He would."

There was nowhere for Rachel to run. Charles Hanson, of all people, should know that. Rachel was public enemy number one. Not just within the state of Iowa, but nationally. If she ran, she'd likely find herself on the business end of a shotgun followed by two bullets and a shallow grave. Rachel was far safer in jail than anywhere else.

It only took Kylie a few minutes to attach Rachel's chains. The girl shivered when the cold steel touched her skin, but otherwise remained still throughout the process. Then they were off to the courthouse.

The shackles made it difficult for Rachel to walk, each step more of a shuffle. Ashley stayed on one side while Kylie took the other, each gently taking the young girl's arms, steadying her. They took an elevator down to the first floor, pausing just before the doors that led to the outside world.

"Are you ready for this?" Kylie asked Rachel.

Rachel sucked in a deep breath and turned to Ashley. A sheen of tears sparkled in her eyes.

Ashley felt for the girl, but there was no way to shield her from this. "We are going to have to face the cameras sooner or later. Keep your head down. I'll try to block you as much as I can from this side. Kylie will do the same from her end."

Ashley paused to look at Kylie, who nodded.

"We just need to get through this crowd and to the courthouse. Whatever you do, don't say anything to any reporters. Okay?"

Rachel nodded and bit her bottom lip.

Kylie placed her hand on the door. "It'll be like ripping off a Band-Aid. One. Two. Three." She shoved the door with one strong arm, and it flew open.

Light stung Ashley's eyes. She blinked several times and focused on the path between the jail and the courthouse. There were so many people. All of them shouting. Cameras flashed with blinding light. Several rookie police officers stood in the middle of the path, making way for the jailer, defendant, and attorney. Ashley took several steps, then noticed a wetness below her nose, trickling down toward her mouth. Instinctively, she reached up, touched her face, and looked at her fingers. They were red with blood.

"Shit," she said as she leaned forward and held her free hand under her nose. She didn't know the cause. Maybe it was the dry late autumn air. Maybe it was stress.

"Are you okay?" Kylie said, peering over Rachel's head, concern evident in the furrow of her brow.

"Yeah. I just need to find a Kleenex."

Ashley stopped, swung her laptop bag around, and dug until she found a tissue. She pressed it to her nose and nodded to Kylie that she was ready to continue. She knew there would be some unfortunate photographs and even more unfortunate rumors circulating around Brine after the images hit the evening news, but there was little Ashley could do about it.

The three women moved slowly, methodically through the crowd of press and local gawkers. It was pandemonium. Everyone jostling toward the front to get a good look at Rachel, who they believed to be a sadistic killer. Reporters shouted questions as they held their microphones out toward Rachel. Everyone talked at once. Their words twisted together, turning into a garbled roar of noise. The onslaught seemed to go on forever, but all they needed to do was cross the street.

Moments later, they were through the courthouse doors. With a whoosh, the heavy doors slammed shut behind them, instantly muffling the sound of the crowd. Ashley issued a heavy sigh of relief as a hush fell over the three women. She'd never been so relieved to be inside a courthouse. Then they made their way up the stairs to the second-floor courtroom, which would no doubt be full of onlookers and even more cameras.

5

RACHEL

They walked. Kylie to her left, Ashley to her right. Like a Salem witch on her way to the gallows. A long walk toward a short drop. The chains around her feet and hands weighed her down, dragging behind her. They clinked and jangled, growing heavier with each step. A burden. A punishment.

Kylie held Rachel by the arm, firm but not rough. Her hands were calloused, scratching against Rachel's skin as she tugged her along. At Rachel's other side, Ashley was less solid. A small woman who carried herself with confidence that Rachel had never seen in a female. There was a naked power in Ashley's strides. She guided Rachel along, gliding across the floor as though walking upon water. Ashley was not pretty, but she was striking. Handsome, almost, but in a softer way than men.

"Right through here," Kylie said, pulling Rachel out of her thoughts. Kylie's hand rested on the courtroom door. "You ready?"

Rachel swallowed hard and nodded. She was not ready, but she didn't know how to properly express herself. She'd never had the opportunity.

The courtroom door swung open and the three women took several shuffling steps inside. Two male police officers stood stiffly just inside the doorway, their arms at their sides and their backs straight.

Rachel did not make eye contact with them as she passed, but she could feel their gazes roving over her body, taking what they could. They knew they held power over her, and they weren't inherently *good*. Not like children were led to believe. They were men. Like every other man, they were crude, needy, angry, and aggressive. If they had met her in another way, they would treat her in the same way as that other officer.

Kylie and Ashley guided Rachel forward, passing the gallery packed with onlookers. Rachel wasn't fazed, at least not until she saw them. The woman—*mother*—would not look at Rachel. But the man glared at her in that characteristic way. Those eyes that held her like a possession. A piece of property. A disobedient animal in need of breaking.

Rachel's heart banged against her chest and her gaze darted to the floor. The attorney, jailer, and defendant continued forward. All eyes were on Rachel. She could feel the intensity of the gazes slithering along her skin. A hush had fallen over the crowd, leaving the courtroom silent aside from the clink of Rachel's chains.

When the group neared the front of the courtroom, Rachel heard the familiar clearing of a throat. A deep rumbling of phlegm coming up and then back down. Out of instinct, her eyes darted up. And there he was. Mr. Frank, the school guidance counselor. The man who watched her as she made her way through the school hallways. Calculating. Considering.

Rachel's mind froze and her knees locked, unable to move. It was too much. She thought she could do this, but she couldn't.

"One step at a time," Kylie murmured into her ear. It was a kindly cooing, like she was talking to a newborn baby. "It will be okay."

Rachel allowed Kylie and Ashley to lead her past a small barrier—a short railing that separated the gawkers from the lawyers. In that moment, Rachel believed Kylie. That she would be *okay*. The *men* were out there, behind those barriers, and she, Rachel, was surrounded by two strong women. Those men would never get their hands on her again. She was safe.

Ashley guided Rachel to the defense table and pulled her seat out for her. Rachel thanked Ashley and sat down. Chivalry was not dead after all. Kylie pulled up a chair and sat behind Rachel. It was meant to look like Kylie was her keeper, but Rachel was grateful to have one more body separating her from the outside world.

"All rise," a man in all black shouted from the back of the courtroom.

The chains made it hard for Rachel to stand, but Ashley helped her struggle to her feet. They stood side by side in solidarity.

"You may be seated," the judge said as he strutted into the courtroom. His black robe billowed behind him, like Lord Voldemort.

The benches creaked as the onlookers sat back down.

"We are convened today in Brine County case number FECR015987, State of Iowa vs. Rachel Smithson," the judge said in a booming voice. He was tall and wiry with a hooked nose and a thinning head of gray hair. His sharp blue eyes darted around the room like a bird.

"Today is the date set for arraignment. Are the parties ready to proceed? Mr. Hanson?" The judge's gaze shifted toward the prosecutor.

"Yes, Your Honor," the prosecutor said in a silky voice.

"Ms. Montgomery?" The judge's eagle eyes settled on Ashley.

"Yes, Your Honor."

"I presume you are the defendant, Rachel Smithson," the judge said, his words echoing throughout the cavernous room.

Rachel did not look at him. She knew better than to meet a powerful man's gaze. "Yes," she said in her meekest, most deferential tone.

"What was that?" the judge said.

"Yes." Rachel tried to speak up.

The judge leaned forward and placed a hand behind his ear. "I'm old and hard of hearing. You're going to have to speak up."

"She said, 'yes,' Your Honor," Ashley said.

The tightness in Rachel's chest—the feeling that came when she had done something disappointing—eased. She wondered how Ashley could take such an authoritative tone, especially with a man who clearly held power over her.

The judge cleared his throat. "Rachel Smithson, you are charged by Trial Information with two counts. Count one, murder in the first degree, and count two, child endangerment causing death. Both are Class A felonies punishable by life imprisonment."

Life in prison did not bother Rachel. It was life outside of prison that had been the problem.

"How do you plead to these charges?"

Rachel opened her mouth to respond, but she couldn't bring herself to form the word "not" before the "guilty." For she had done what was alleged. She had a baby. That baby was dead. It was her fault.

"She pleads not guilty on all counts," Ashley said.

"Do you waive formal reading of the indictment?" the judge asked.

"Yes. And we demand speedy trial."

"Very well," Judge Ahrenson said with a disapproving grunt.

It was all gibberish to Rachel. She just wanted out of that courtroom. Away from the intense gazes that cut through her skin and straight to her soul. Rachel tucked into herself like she always did when she wanted to disappear, allowing her mind to go blank. To forget all that was around her. All that she had done. Erase the lack of weight in her belly. The emptiness that tiny body left inside her.

The judge banged his gavel and Rachel flinched.

The hearing was over, and Ashley and Kylie ushered her past the crowd. This time the faces blended together, merging from the many to one huge mass. It was disconcerting and comforting at the same time. For she did not see the judgment, the accusations. She did not have to remember her past, the one created by the men in her life. She hoped that she would never see any of them again, but her wishes rarely, if ever, came true.

6

ASHLEY

The cameras followed Ashley and Kylie as they steered Rachel out of the courtroom, trying to catch every movement, every expression. Footage for talking heads to analyze later in the day. Undoubtedly, Rachel's haircut would be a topic of conversation. But that was better than the alternative, an unending onslaught of condemnation of the mother who did the unthinkable.

Ashley was careful to stick close to Rachel, shoulder to shoulder. Partially to assist her in maneuvering in those damned chains, but also for another, larger reason. Solidarity. She wanted people to see that they were a team. That Rachel was a girl. Human. Just like everyone else.

Kylie guided Ashley and Rachel down the stairs and through the crowd of media and onlookers filling the space between the courthouse and the jail. The two buildings were next to one another, so they only had to shield Rachel for a few minutes. Then they were safe inside the jail where reporters were not allowed.

Rachel sighed deeply once the heavy iron door slammed behind her, locking her inside.

It was a sigh of relief. Ashley couldn't imagine anyone feeling that way about a jail, but then again, the reporters had been tenacious. Far more than they had been when Ashley was in chains. She turned toward her client, studying her. Rachel wasn't quite like anyone Ashley had ever met. She was like an empty shell, lost beneath the waves of the roaring sea, waiting to be discovered.

"Hey," Ashley said, speaking softly. "You did fine in there."

A tear slid down Rachel's cheek, but she nodded.

Rachel's wrist and ankle restraints clattered to the floor as Kylie unlocked them one by one.

"Thank you," Rachel said, rubbing her wrists.

"Sure. I wish I didn't have to put them on you at all. But rules are rules." Kylie shrugged as if to say, *what is there to do about it?*

Rachel nodded, keeping her head down. Eye contact was rare for Rachel. The exception, not the rule. It was a lack of confidence. A young woman trying to make her way in a man's world.

"I have something for you," Ashley said, digging in her bag.

"You do?" Rachel's voice was flat, uninterested.

"It's nothing special," Ashley said as she pulled out a stack of papers and handed them to Rachel.

Rachel accepted the documents with tentative hands, pulling them snug against her body, pressing them into her bony chest. "What are they?"

"Your formal indictment as well as the Minutes of Testimony. There are a few preliminary police reports attached to the Minutes. You should read through them and make notes on questions you might have for me. I'll be back to discuss your case as soon as I can."

Rachel nodded, looking down at the stack of documents uncertainly.

Ashley turned to Kylie. "Does she have something to write with?"

"Nope. I'll get her set up, though."

Rachel was silent. A tear slid down her cheek. A single, lonely soldier threading its way toward the unknown.

Ashley wanted to wrap her arms around the girl, pull her close, ease her pain. But she restrained herself. Comforting a client during a full-blown panic attack was one thing, but it wasn't appropriate for Ashley to continue doing it. She couldn't get too close, emotionally or physically, although Ashley was starting to struggle with that propriety. Rachel was like a baby bird that had fallen from the nest. Featherless. Motherless.

Defenseless. Looking for a way back home. The question was, what was home to Rachel?

Ashley shook her head, pulling herself out of her thoughts. There was work to do. Not only on Rachel's case, but on those of her other clients. She had mountains of paperwork to go through. Time was a commodity that could not be wasted.

"All right," Ashley said, clapping her hands together. "I'm out of here. See you two tomorrow."

As she made her way down the stairs and out the front door, she was greeted by flashing cameras and shouted questions. *Damn it*, she thought. *I forgot about the reporters.* She had planned to go through the back way to avoid them. There wasn't much for it now but to push her way through them. She headed toward her office, straight into the crowd. She squeezed past some and elbowed others who were unwilling to let her through.

"Ashley," a reporter shouted as he shoved a microphone in her face, "is it true that Rachel hid her pregnancy from her parents?"

"No comment," Ashley said in the flattest, most uninteresting tone. They would not get tonight's sound bite from her.

"The prosecutor says that Rachel drowned her baby and threw her in the hotel trash can. Is that true?"

"No comment."

"How is Rachel handling jail? She looks terrible."

"No comment," Ashley said. Inwardly, she was pleased with the question. It meant her little hair trim had worked.

"Who is the baby's father?"

"No comment," Ashley said. Truthfully, she had no idea, but she fully intended to find out.

Ashley was growing frustrated. The crowd was jostling around her, and it was hot there in the center of it all, despite the chill in the air. Ashley pulled at the collar of her coat, loosening it from her throat, but it didn't help. A row of sweat formed along her forehead and she was starting to feel lightheaded. She tried to shove past a burly man, but he wouldn't let her through. She was trapped.

A circle had formed around Ashley, reporters noticing her presence and stepping back to give her space. People surrounded her, like a dance circle or a wolf pack. Nobody moved for a few seconds, then someone from behind Ashley reached out and grabbed her arm. Ashley swung around to see a man close to her age with brown hair and plain features. He was not wearing a press badge. He smiled crookedly as Ashley tried to yank her arm away. He pulled her closer to him, surprisingly strong for such a slim build.

"Did you get my letter?" he said. He was close enough for Ashley to smell his breath, a mixture of garlic and onions.

Ashley leaned back. "No. I mean, I don't know."

"I've been watching you. Heard you on Iowa Public Radio."

"Please let me go," Ashley said as gently as possible. There was something wild in his expression. An insatiable hunger, and she was his bait.

"I love you."

A fluttery, panicky feeling made its way into her chest. What was wrong with this man? He looked so normal on the outside, but the glint in his eyes screamed *crazy crazy crazy.*

"Let me go," Ashley begged, but he only tightened his grip. He wasn't going to release her.

"Hey," a woman nearby shouted. She wore a black puffer jacket with *Des Moines Register* stitched above her heart.

Ashley braced herself for more questions about Rachel, but they didn't come.

"She said to let her go," the woman from the *Register* said, taking a step closer. She was stocky like Kylie, with strong shoulders.

Ashley's stalker released her arm so suddenly that she fell backward. She stumbled and almost fell, but the woman caught her arm, pulling her back upright.

"Thank you," Ashley said, and she meant it. This woman was the only person in the entire crowd brave enough to intervene.

"Name's Carley," the woman said, handing Ashley a business card. "I'm a staff writer for the *Des Moines Register*. That, what just happened there"—she nodded toward the stalker's retreating figure—"was messed up."

"Yes," Ashley agreed, but she was hesitant. She didn't know where this was going.

Now that the danger had passed, several other reporters were moving closer to Ashley, shoving Carley from both sides. Carley didn't budge, not even when a man twice her size tried to edge her out.

"I'd like to talk to you," Carley said, "but not here." She tapped the card in Ashley's hand. "Give me a call and we'll set something up if you're willing."

Ashley shook her head. "I can't talk about Rachel's case. Not while it is pending and probably not afterward."

Carley shrugged. "Who said I wanted to talk about Rachel Smithson?"

Ashley gestured around her. "Everyone wants to talk about Rachel."

Carley chuckled. "Just give me a call." Then she turned and disappeared back into the crowd, leaving Ashley to fend for herself.

Questions were hurled toward Ashley from every direction. But then, thankfully, the prosecutor, Charles Hanson, exited the courthouse. The attention swung toward him as he stood on the courthouse steps, straightening his tie and smiling brightly. The wind whipped at the collar of his shirt, but his hair did not move.

As the throng of press moved toward Charles, leaving Ashley alone in the street, the prosecutor met her gaze and nodded at her, his smile widening. His expression said *ha ha, they like me better than you.* Which was just fine with Ashley. He could go ahead and think he'd stolen her limelight. Ashley gave Charles a mock salute and slowly began backing away.

When she finally made it to the edge of the crowd, she turned and sprinted to her office. She was almost to the front door when she saw a familiar person walking down the street. Officer Katie Mickey.

Ashley and Katie were close friends. Maybe even best friends. But they had an unwritten rule when it came to cases like Rachel's. They steered clear of each other throughout the pendency of contentious cases. They were on opposite sides of the law, and spending time together while a case like Rachel's was unresolved led to arguments. That had happened during a particularly violent domestic assault six months earlier. Ashley and Katie had such a row over drinks one night that they didn't speak for nearly a month. After that, they decided it was best to keep their distance until cases like that came to a resolution.

Katie smiled at Ashley, who returned the gesture, waving before ducking inside her office and out of sight. As Ashley stepped past the threshold, her toe caught on the doorframe and she stumbled. She hadn't lifted her foot high enough. Her arms pinwheeled as she tried to regain her balance, but she felt so weak. Weary in a way she had never been before. Perhaps it was from the hectic day and the run-in with the psychotic man. Perhaps it was something else.

"Whoa," Elena said, standing from her desk. But she was too far away to intervene.

Ashley fell hard, crashing to the floor.

Elena rushed to her side. "Are you okay?"

Ashley lay there for a moment, regaining her strength, before allowing Elena to help her to her feet.

"What happened? Was it the paparazzi?" Elena cast a dark look at the front door.

"No," Ashley said with a groan. "I mean I don't think so. I'm just clumsy is all."

Elena furrowed her brow like she didn't quite believe Ashley's explanation.

Ashley dusted herself off and moved farther into the office. "I hope none of them got any pictures of that."

"They probably didn't," Elena said uncertainly. "I'm sure the pictures will come out well. You always look so glamorous."

Not a chance, Ashley thought.

If Rachel was public enemy number one, Ashley was number two. She was sure that, at the very least, the conservative members of the press would choose the worst picture of her, blood dripping from her nose, sweat beading along her brow, lips dipped into a firm scowl.

After all, she was the villain in their story. The magician trying to manipulate Rachel's way out of chains. That was precisely what Ashley intended to do, but she liked to think of herself as the protagonist. The underdog fighting for her client's freedom.

"Anyway," Ashley said, "I've got work to do. If you see a lull in the crowd out there, feel free to sneak out early. I know all this attention isn't good for your family."

"Thank you," Elena said.

"Don't thank me," Ashley said. "It's mostly for selfish reasons. I can't lose you."

Ashley headed back to her office, pulling her phone out of her bag as she walked. Still no missed calls from Tom. No messages either.

Sighing irritably, she removed her laptop from her bag and gingerly placed it on her desk. She set her phone next to it and turned to the case files stacked neatly in the corner of her desk. Other cases that needed her attention. The work was never-ending.

She grabbed the top file and dug in. As she flipped a page, a droplet of red blood fell from her nose, splashing onto the paper.

"Damn it," Ashley said aloud. She held her hand under her nose and grabbed several tissues from a box sitting on her desk.

What is going on? she wondered as she pressed the tissues against her nose.

Stress had weird effects on the body, she knew that from experience, but bloody noses were new. Maybe she was more stressed than she thought. She popped another one of Tom's homemade candies into her mouth and chewed. Comfort food.

The nosebleed eased after the first five minutes and Ashley was able to refocus on work. Hours passed as she made her way through the stack of files. Finally, after what felt like a lifetime, her phone buzzed. A text message. She jumped and grabbed it.

Saw you on the news. You look lovely.

It was Tom. The knot in her chest began to unravel. She glanced at the clock. 6:30. Rachel's story must have been on the afternoon news.

I very much doubt that, but thanks anyway. Do you have time to talk?

No. I have a study session with Harper tonight. I'm already running late.

Harper?

She's in some of my psych classes. The only one my age. Us old people have to stick together.

He was spending the evening with some other girl. Ashley's gut twisted. She wasn't a jealous person by nature, but it didn't sound good for their relationship. Especially since Tom and Ashley had spent very little quality time together over the past couple weeks. This was how it began. The beginning of the end of a long-distance relationship.

Okay, Ashley said.

She wanted to sound cheery. Calm, cool, collected. She trusted him, didn't she? If she was honest with herself, she'd admit that her faith in their relationship was not perfect. It was hard to trust anyone wholly and completely when so much separated them. Their lives these days felt too detached. But she wouldn't say any of that. Not now, at least. That was a conversation best had in person.

Thanks for the candy, BTW, Ashley texted.

Sure?

A question mark. What did that mean? He had sent the candy. She recognized the handwriting in the letter. It was the same scrawling script that she'd seen on the little notes he used to leave around the house before he moved away. She had no doubt that he'd written it. So what was with the question mark? Was he mad at her again? If he was, he had no right to be.

Ashley shook her head and tossed the phone aside. She wasn't going to placate him with messages saying, *what's wrong, honey?* and *are you upset with me?* If he had something to say, he should come right out and say it. She was tired of Tom's passive-aggressive bullshit. For the first time, she wondered if their relationship could handle distance and the rigors of her life as a public defender.

7

KATIE

Katie glanced at her watch. 2:35 p.m. She was five minutes late for her meeting. She hurried down 8th Street, toward Genie's Diner. Ashley was in front of her office, on her way inside, no doubt to avoid the crowd of reporters. The public defender's office was at the corner of 8th and Central, directly across the street from the diner.

Ashley turned to look over her shoulder just in time to see Katie. She waved, and Ashley returned the gesture before hurrying through the front door. As she did, Ashley's toe caught on the curb and she stumbled.

Katie stopped, eyeing the space where her friend tumbled out of sight. Then her gaze drifted toward the pack of reporters hot on Ashley's heels. They were like hunters chasing a cornered fox. Should Katie do something about it? Tell the reporters to leave Ashley alone? But, then again, they were within their rights. They weren't on private property or harassing Ashley. They were merely doing their jobs.

Besides, Ashley's fall probably had more to do with her sleep patterns than the stress of reporters. Ashley was like a border collie when it came to her clients. Loyal and determined. Willing to work herself to death if that was what it took to succeed. Someone had to be there to keep Ashley in line. Usually, it was Katie, but that wasn't an option now. At least not until Rachel Smithson's trial had ended.

Something crashed into her, cutting through Katie's thoughts and knocking her off balance. She almost fell, but she caught herself before she hit the pavement.

"Watch where you're going," a man said.

"I'm sorry. I was..." Katie trailed off when she looked up. Her eyes narrowed. "You," she said, her tone darkening.

"Forest Parker. The one and only," the man said, brushing dirt off the knees of his slacks.

Forest was a member of city council. He was the youngest of the three, in his early thirties. His dark hair was wild and wavy, adding emphasis to his remarkably pale blue eyes.

"Thank God," Katie said with a snort. "This town can't handle more than one of you."

"Ditto, Katie," Forest said. He paused for a moment. "Actually, I take that back. One of your kind is far more than Brine can manage."

For some unfathomable reason, Forest Parker hated the police. Which was a shame since the city council set the budget for the Brine Police Department. Since Forest's election, the purse strings had slowly grown tighter, closing in around Chief Carmichael, and Katie by extension.

"What is your problem? Why do you hate us so much?" Katie growled.

One of the few lessons of any value that Katie's mother had taught her before abandoning her was that she should always seek to understand her opponent. A form of *keep your friends close and your enemies closer*. Of course, Katie's mother had been speaking of high-society gossip circles rather than real life. But, then again, those women were like crocodiles. Dangerous in their own right.

Forest smiled in an infuriatingly pleasant way. His features were even, symmetrical. Attractive if not for his personality.

"You," Forest said. "Not to worry, though. Not for long."

"Sure, sure," Katie said with a scowl. He meant his whole "shortchange the cops" movement. "And what, exactly, do you plan to do once you succeed and there are no police officers in Brine?"

"That's for me to worry about."

"You better get to worrying about it, then. That, or buy yourself a new pair of Nikes. Because you're going to be running from a lot of criminals without our help. Run, Forest, run."

"Very original, Katie. That's a junior high insult. But, then again, you aren't all that different from a teenage bully, now are you? All brawn, no brains," Forest said before spinning on a heel and marching away.

Katie grunted, clenching her fists into balls as she watched him disappear around a corner. She kept her mouth clamped shut and shook her head, fuming. She didn't trust herself to respond.

"Katie."

Katie looked up. George was peeking his head out the doorway to Genie's Diner.

"Are you going to stand out there in the cold or are you going to get in here? It's 2:44. You're fifteen minutes late for our meeting."

Great, Katie thought.

She groaned inwardly and trudged inside, following George to a booth in the back corner of the diner. She was in for another lecture. George thought his promotion to detective made him her supervisor. It didn't. Or at least it wasn't supposed to.

The décor in Genie's Diner was true to its name. A diner through and through. Black-and-white-checkered tiling. Booths with red upholstery. Walls covered in shiny black records and outdated license plates from all fifty states.

"What can I get y'all," Genie said, sidling up to the table.

Genie was middle-aged, with hair bleached so blonde it almost looked white. It sat piled atop her head, big and flashy, true to her Texas roots.

"I'll have a coffee, black, and a cinnamon roll," Katie said.

Genie nodded and her gaze shifted to George. "Same. Except no cinnamon roll and lots of cream and sugar."

Katie rolled her eyes. George's humor had always annoyed her. It was so dad-like in its unfunniness. But Katie had endured it, even found it endearing at times. That sentiment had died with his promotion. Especially since he had taken to treating *her* like a child.

"I'll get those for y'all. Back in a flash," Genie said.

The diner was nearly empty. The lull between the lunch and dinner crowd. True to her word, Genie had their orders in front of them within a few minutes.

"Just holler if you need anythin'," Genie said with a wink before disappearing into the kitchen.

"So, Rachel Smithson's case," George said as he dumped an enormous amount of creamer into his coffee.

Katie nodded. "We've interviewed everyone. Evidence was dropped off at the county attorney's office this morning."

"Do you have any concerns?"

Katie chewed on her bottom lip. She did, she just wasn't sure she was ready to share.

"I think we have everything tied up at this point," George said. He took a sip of his coffee. It was so heavy with cream that it looked more like milk. "The case is solid. There isn't much for the jury to think about."

"I don't know," Katie said. "What about the officer that Isaac mentioned in his interview?"

"What about him?"

"He could be the father."

George grunted noncommittally.

"Then there are all the rumors about the school counselor."

"Listen, Katie," George said, leaning forward. "I don't mean to sound insensitive, but why does it matter? So what if a cop is the child's father? Who cares if the school counselor paid Rachel a little too much attention? Neither of those people forced Rachel to drown her baby. They are completely irrelevant to our case."

Katie scowled. She cared, that's who. Yes, Rachel killed her baby and she deserved to spend the rest of her life in prison, but that didn't mean her potential abusers should get off scot free. Because that's what these men were, if the rumors proved true. Abusers. They were adults, men with power over Rachel. If they had taken advantage of that power, they should suffer the consequences.

"Okay, I can see that you don't like my answer. But the truth is that it isn't our problem. If those things happened—and that's a big *if*—they happened in Waukee. Let the Waukee Police Department sort it out."

He had a point there. "Okay. Fine. I'm still a little worried that Ashley's going to surprise us with it at Rachel's trial."

George shrugged. "That's not our problem either. The prosecutor will take care of it. You worry too much, you know that?"

For a moment, Katie thought she saw the glint of her old friend behind George's tired eyes.

"Is there something else?" George asked. "Any other loose ends to tie up with Rachel's case?"

Katie had concerns about Isaac, but she had nothing concrete to point to. He was controlling and odd during his interview, but that wasn't a crime.

"All right." George made a beckoning motion. "I know something is bouncing around in that brain of yours. Out with it." A demand rather than a request.

Katie narrowed her eyes. "It's Isaac Smithson."

"Rachel's father?"

Katie nodded. "There's something about him that doesn't sit right with me."

"I don't see any issues with Isaac. He seemed just fine to me."

Katie's inner temperature ticked up a couple degrees, her fury rising with each passing second. George was being dismissive again.

"I still think we should take a deeper look at his life," Katie insisted.

George shrugged. "I don't think it's anything, but you are free to look into it if you want."

Katie scoffed. She didn't need his permission to do her job.

"I can see that you are getting angry again. You need to calm down, Katie."

George's tone was patronizing, stoking her anger. It didn't help that her blood was already boiling from her run-in with Forest. If she sat there much longer, she was going to lose her temper.

"Whatever," she said as she threw a five-dollar bill on the table. "This should cover my coffee and cinnamon roll."

George's eyes darted to the untouched pastry. "But you haven't eaten any of it."

"You eat it, then. You don't seem to have a problem taking things that should be mine anyway."

"Katie...wait."

She met his gaze. For a moment, it felt as though they were once again on equal footing. The way they had been a year earlier, back when they were friends. But that sentiment died the moment he opened his mouth again.

"Come on, Katie. Don't storm off like that. I was trying to let you follow your gut."

A snort burst from Katie's nose. "Yeah. See, there's the problem. The fact that you think you are *letting* me do anything. Chief Carmichael is my boss, not you. So stop acting like it."

"Okay, okay," George said, raising his hands in surrender. His words were gentle, but they weren't an apology. He was treating her like a lion that needed taming.

Katie rolled her eyes, spun on her heel, and marched out of the restaurant. She had better things to do than waste her time arguing with George. He might be too dumb to realize that Ashley had something up her sleeve, but Katie wasn't. She needed to find out the identity of Rachel's baby and unearth what Isaac Smithson had hidden in his past. Intuition told her that his secret would spell trouble for Rachel's prosecution.

Because Isaac's arrogance had left a tingling in Katie's gut. A sense of wrongness like a loose thread on a favorite sweater. Tug just right and it would start unraveling. Keep pulling and the sweater would begin to come apart. The only way to keep the sweater intact was to take a pair of scissors and snip the thread off at its base. That was what Katie needed to do with Isaac Smithson. Find the thread and snip it off before Ashley could start pulling.

8

ASHLEY

72 days before trial

"Do we have discovery for the Smithson case yet?" Ashley said as she stepped out of the hallway and into the receptionist area of the public defender's office.

Discovery was the name for evidence the prosecutor intended to use at trial, usually consisting of police reports, medical examiner reports, and video recordings. Ashley needed it to assess the strength of the State's case against Rachel. Four days had passed since Ashley's initial visit with Rachel, and all she had were a few flimsy police reports, the Trial Information, and the Minutes of Testimony.

Elena clicked a couple buttons on her computer, leaning close to the monitor. "Nope. My notes say I requested it all on Monday." She shrugged. "But we still have nothing."

"Damn it," Ashley said, running a hand over her face. Her eyelid twitched and her cheeks felt like they were sagging. Her body was so exhausted that even her skin was affected. It wasn't a good look for her. She'd been working too hard.

"Also." Elena held up an envelope. It was the same deep red color reserved for Valentine's Day. "You have more mail from your admirer."

"Just throw it away." Ashley had tired of her fan club after that man had grabbed her arm outside the courthouse.

"One other thing..."

Ashley groaned. "What?"

"A reporter from *The New York Times* called this morning. She wanted to talk to you. Should I call her back?"

"No."

"What do I say if she calls again?"

"Tell them that I decline to comment. Not now, not ever," Ashley said through gritted teeth.

She had no intention of speaking with any newspaper, no matter how prestigious, about Rachel's case. But the call did remind her of Carley, the reporter from the *Des Moines Register*, who wanted to talk about something other than Rachel. She'd also helped Ashley with her stalker problem. Carley had given Ashley her card and asked her to call. Ashley decided that she would. To thank her. It was the least she could do.

Elena furrowed her brow, misunderstanding Ashley's frustration. "Is there something I should be doing differently?"

Ashley shook her head. "No. Sorry. You're great." She needed to be more careful with her words. Elena was a worrier, and she took everything to heart. "I just have a lot on my mind."

Ashley's life felt like such a mess these days. There was the issue with Tom—who still wasn't answering Ashley's calls—and then there was the lack of discovery in Rachel's case. She needed the evidence to start forming a defense. Without it, she was left twiddling her thumbs.

"Okay," Elena said uncertainly.

"I just don't know what to do." Ashley began pacing, shoes sliding along the heavily worn carpet. "I can't move forward with Rachel's case until I have discovery. But nothing is happening. Charles, that stupid prosecutor, is sitting on the file. Wasting time. I just know it. All the while Rachel is stuck in jail."

Ashley had made the request for the instillation of equipment so that Rachel could work toward her GED while incarcerated, but that wish was promptly denied. Budget cuts. Or so the sheriff's office claimed.

"What about those thingies you sometimes have?"

"Thingies?" Ashley repeated.

Elena spoke both English and Spanish fluently. Ashley could understand some Spanish so long as it was spoken slowly, but it was Elena's teenage-girl language that had Ashley confused. Teenagers, including nineteen-year-olds like Elena, seemed to invent words, and they expected proper adults—people over thirty—to understand. Ashley didn't even have the energy to try.

"You know." Elena's eyes drifted toward the ceiling. "Where you ask the questions, and they have to answer."

"Depositions?"

"Yeah. Those."

Ashley chewed on her lip. It was early in the case to take depositions. She usually waited until she had the evidence and a chance to review it. But, then again, a speedy trial didn't leave a lot of time. Depositions would allow her to subpoena the witnesses' duces tecum, requiring them to appear for questioning and bring all their police reports, photographs, and recorded documents. It wasn't conventional, but Ashley could use it as a way to get her hands on the evidence.

"Good idea," Ashley said. "Draft a notice of depositions. I'll need several hours for each witness, so squeeze them in wherever my calendar is free."

"Do you want me to check with the prosecutor to see what dates work for him?"

Ashley shook her head. It was professional courtesy to find mutually agreed upon dates, but Charles wasn't affording Ashley any courtesies. He had the evidence, she felt sure of it, and he wasn't giving it to her. It wasn't a problem for him. It was his right, at least as long as he didn't hold evidence past a reasonable amount of time. But it was her right to notice depositions whenever she damn well pleased. Was it petty? Yeah, it was. But Ashley didn't care.

"Consider it done," Elena said with a nod. "I'll send you the list of dates and times for approval once I've cross-checked them with your calendar. Then I'll get the notice on file."

"Thank you," Ashley said with a smile.

She headed back toward her office. It was Friday afternoon and she had visited Rachel at the jail every day that week. The girl was slowly starting to open up, but the trust was still not where Ashley had hoped it would be at this juncture in the case. Trial would be here before they knew it. There were things that Rachel wasn't telling her. Facts likely beneficial to Rachel's defense. Ashley could see it in the way she fidgeted when asked questions about her baby or her life before the baby's birth.

Ashley's phone began to ring, startling her out of her thoughts. She reached into her bag, fumbling around. She never could find anything when she needed it. After searching several pockets, her hand closed around the phone.

"Hello?"

"Hey," Tom said. His voice sounded strained. Far away.

"It doesn't sound like you are in your car. Are you on your way?"

Tom always came to Brine on the weekends. He arrived Friday afternoons, usually sometime before two. But it was 1:30 already and the drive was over an hour.

"Umm, no. I'm actually not going to be there until tomorrow."

"What, why?"

Tom was silent for a long moment. Ashley allowed the silence to drag on. She was not going to make the situation more comfortable for him. A burst of girlish laughter in the background cut through the tense quiet.

"Oh," Ashley said, her tone darkening. "And who is that?"

Tom made a shushing noise, but the laughter continued, growing louder and more obnoxious until the person snorted. A pig-like sound that put an abrupt stop to the background noise, but only for a moment, before the girl started laughing even louder.

Ashley's mind whirred, shifting back to her youth. When she was ten, she had known a girl who had snorted like that while laughing. The girl had lived with Ashley, her mother, and her older sister for a time. A foster child. Her name was Lydia. She was the same age as Ashley. A beautiful girl with big, doe-like eyes and a perfect little nose.

Ashley had been excited to have a sister her age. She and her older sister, Karen, had never quite got on. They were only half-sisters, as Karen loved to point out, especially since Karen's father had every-other-weekend visitation and Ashley's father was absent. The five-year age gap didn't help either.

When the social worker brought Lydia, Ashley had been overjoyed. She'd met Lydia at the door and thrown her arms around her, hugging her tightly. But Lydia didn't reciprocate. Her arms hung limply at her sides. But when Ashley stepped aside, Lydia ran to Ashley's mother, wrapping her arms around her. As she did, she met Ashley's gaze, and there was a glint in Lydia's eyes that said *she's mine now*. It had gone downhill from there.

Ashley shook her head, dispelling the unpleasant thoughts. A past that had been buried and forgotten long ago. "I asked you a question, Tom." She placed her free hand on her hip. "Who is that?"

Tom didn't answer. He was stalling. A flash of rage shot up Ashley's spine. Whether that was due to the girl's laughter, the unwelcome memories, or Tom's unwillingness to answer, she didn't know. The three things came together, clashing like cold and warm fronts just before they started rotating, twisting into a tornado.

"I said," Ashley growled through gritted teeth. "Who. Is. That?"

"Umm." Tom made another shushing noise. The girl was still laughing. It had gone on for an insane amount of time.

"Ummm?" Ashley tapped her foot impatiently.

"Harper."

"Harper, huh?" Ashley's face grew hot. "You've been spending an awful lot of time with this Harper, haven't you? Is that why you aren't coming today? You're busy playing house with her?"

Ashley wasn't quite sure why she'd said it. She had never been the jealous type. Jealousy was a sign of insecurity. Something that didn't plague Ashley. At least not until now.

"Don't do that."

"Do what?"

"That. You're being clingy."

Clingy? Did he know the definition of that word?

"You know what," Ashley said, her nostrils flaring. "Don't bother coming this weekend. I don't want to see your face."

Then she hung up and jammed her phone into her bag to keep herself from throwing it. The last thing she needed was a shattered phone. Not because she wanted to talk to Tom, but because her clients needed a way to reach her. She didn't want anything to do with Tom anymore. Or, perhaps she did, but she knew that she shouldn't. Her hands still twitched, finger-tips filled with fury. She needed to smash something.

The box of homemade candies still sat on Ashley's desk. Her eyes landed on them. There had been a couple dozen. She'd eaten only a few throughout the week. There were still plenty left. She picked up the box and squeezed it between her hands. The cardboard collapsed. Then she twisted it and slammed it into her trash can.

Good riddance, she thought. But she didn't mean it. She loved Tom. Or at least she thought she did. Sure, they hadn't said those exact words to one another, but she thought he felt the same way. Apparently not.

She began to pace from one end of her tiny office to the other. Only three steps in each direction. Step, step, step, turn. Step, step, step, turn. She needed to talk to someone, but that was the problem with her guarded nature. It meant she only had a few people within her inner circle. To Ashley, those people consisted of her mother, Tom, and Katie. She couldn't complain to Tom about Tom, obviously, and her mother had died close to two years earlier. That left Katie. She couldn't call. They'd fight. But maybe she could text.

Yeah, she thought with a nod. *Texting is safe. Probably.* But probably was better than the alternative. They may be on opposite sides of the law, but Katie was still Ashley's best friend.

Ashley grabbed her phone and began typing. *I'm about to commit rela-tionship suicide. Or is it homicide?*

It took a few moments, but three familiar bubbles appeared beside Katie's name, dancing and waving as she typed. *I believe the term you are looking for is murder-suicide.*

A smile quirked into the corner of Ashley's mouth. The bubbles appeared again.

Why? What did you do?

Ashley typed with both thumbs. *He was with a girl when he called.*

And...

And he said he wasn't coming until tomorrow.

And...

Damn it, Ashley thought.

Katie had a point. It sounded so silly when it was broken down to its simplest terms. When it was all laid out in black and white, all emotion removed, Tom hadn't done anything wrong. He had called. Told her what he was up to. Then she'd freaked out because Harper was there. It wasn't like her to overreact like that.

Ashley turned back to her phone. She didn't know how to respond. She tried, *It made me mad,* but quickly deleted it. That sounded childish. *I didn't like it.* Also immature. Finally, she settled on, *It just bothered me. I don't know why.*

The bubbles appeared by Katie's name again. It went on so long that Ashley thought Katie had been interrupted and stopped mid-text. But finally, after what seemed like forever, the text came through.

Listen, Ashley, normally I'd suggest we get drinks. I won't do that for obvious reasons. What I would tell you if we were out is this: get some sleep. You are working too hard. I don't say that as a police officer, tired of your shenanigans (even though I am).

Ashley smiled again.

I am saying it as your friend, the message continued. *Your car is parked in front of your office every time I drive by day or night. It isn't healthy. Go home. Pet your dogs. Have a glass of wine. Relax.*

Ashley nodded as she read. It was solid advice.

Then, tomorrow, once everyone has cooled off, you can call Tom and apologize. Not because you think you are wrong. Because you and I both know you cannot, for the life of you, admit that you are wrong. But because you love him, and you don't want to murder-suicide your relationship. Nothing is dead yet, but it will end up that way if you let it fester.

Ashley sighed and began to type back. *You're right.* She paused, then sent another message. *Don't tell anyone I said that, though. And if you use that against me during your deposition, I'm going to be super pissed.*

Deposition?

Great, Ashley typed. *Thanks for your help. See you Monday!*

Monday?

Ashley didn't respond.

Several moments later, Ashley received another text from Katie. *When will you see me Monday?*

Ashley still didn't respond. Katie would receive her subpoena soon enough.

A flurry of texts followed. All from Katie.

Ashley.

Answer me. What deposition?

Seriously?

What.

Did.

You.

Do!

Katie wasn't going to like giving a deposition on such short notice, but at least Ashley had warned her. It would soften the blow. What would have turned into an argument would now be more of a mild hiccup. Katie would forgive her. She always did.

The more complicated issue would be Tom. She'd told him not to come. Katie was right that Ashley needed to apologize. Tom's feelings were easily hurt. They had argued in the past, but nothing like this. She wondered if they would ever recover from it.

Ashley set her phone aside just in time to avoid the splash of blood that spilled from her nose. *Shit,* Ashley thought as she grabbed several tissues and held them over her nose. As she leaned over, she noticed that Carley's card was still on her desk. She hadn't called the reporter yet. Perhaps she would tomorrow.

The potential of raising more funds for her office was growing more and more appealing. She was exhausted, stressed beyond all reasonable bounds. If her nose kept bleeding like this, she'd be anemic by the end of next week. What Ashley needed was an investigator. At least for Rachel's case. Doing everything herself was not working.

As she held the Kleenex to her nose, she grabbed Carley's card with her free hand. She flipped it over several times, then tucked it into a pocket of her laptop bag. *Tomorrow,* she thought. *I'll make the call tomorrow.*

9

KATIE

71 days before trial

It was Saturday, but Katie didn't have the day off. There was no 9-5 shift for police officers, especially when the department had only six. Correction, five officers and one detective. Chief Carmichael had yet to replace John Jackie after his arrest and subsequent conviction. The chief claimed that he was waiting for a worthy applicant, but Katie doubted that was the case. It was the newly imposed fiscal constraints courtesy of Forest Parker and his merry band of budget slashers. If the budget cuts continued, Chief Carmichael would have to start laying off employees.

Katie shook her head, dispelling all thoughts of Forest. She could spend an enjoyable afternoon pondering all the ways she'd like to get even with him, but she had better things to do. She needed to focus on the Smithson investigation. It was almost done, just a few tiny issues to shore up. Three to be exact. The cop, the school counselor, and Rachel's father. Katie would start with Isaac Smithson. He was closest to Rachel and the victim. Father and grandfather, respectively. He'd been evasive during his interview, and she was determined to figure out why. She would not let Ashley surprise them at trial.

Katie sat at her desk in what passed as her office at the police station. It was one of five cubicles, all small and lined up in a row. Each contained three flimsy walls, no windows or doors. Just a missing final wall, which meant that anyone who walked by could clearly see her computer screen. It wasn't usually all that annoying, except those occasions when King George decided to leave the confines of his solid-walled office to mingle with the commoners.

"Facebook? You women are such social creatures," he had said one time, feigning shock.

She had been on Facebook, but not to socialize. She'd heard her victim in a case was recanting and she wanted to see if there were any public statements about it. She hadn't told George that, though, because it was really none of his business. If Chief Carmichael had a problem with how she spent her time—which he didn't—then he was perfectly capable of discussing it with Katie.

"Online shopping, eh? Girls will be girls," was another of George's gems.

She hadn't been shopping. She was checking the value of a stolen set of drill bits to determine the degree of theft appropriate for a charging document.

"MapQuest, huh? I didn't even know that existed anymore. Directionally challenged, are we?"

No. She was not directionally challenged. She was researching the mileage in a motor vehicle theft case. The car had been driven from Brine to Des Moines, where it was discovered. Lost gas was part of restitution for the victim.

She blinked hard, forcing thoughts of George from her mind. She had to focus on the task at hand. The men in her life were frustrating, to say the least, but there was another man who needed her attention. *Isaac Smithson*, Katie thought, shaking her computer mouse. The screen popped to life. The desktop image was a picture of Katie, Tom, and Ashley apple picking at the nearby orchard.

She smiled. Tom and Ashley had become Katie's only true friends. She'd known them since before they were a couple, but Katie always thought they belonged together. She hoped they could work through their argument. Katie hadn't thought much of what a breakup would do to the three of them. It would force her to choose. Naturally, she'd pick Ashley, but it wouldn't be an easy choice. She hoped that Ashley had called Tom like she had suggested. Maybe they had been able to patch things up.

She pulled up her browser and started with a simple search of the father's name. Nothing came up. No social media accounts. No news articles. Apparently, Mr. Smithson had lived a very unremarkable life. That, or he had chosen to stay off the radar. Which wasn't a crime by any stretch of the imagination, but it was abnormal. Even if Mr. Smithson was not a social person, she had expected him to have a LinkedIn account for business connections. Although, she really had no clue what Mr. Smithson did for work.

That was a dead end. Katie then tried searching his wife's name. The screen populated with multiple articles, mostly from Des Moines society pages. Katie clicked on the first one. An article about the construction of a meat packing plant just outside Brine. That plant had to be twenty years old now. It was owned and operated by the Arkman family. A photo of the family accompanied the article. It showed two parents and four smiling children, one of whom was Lyndsay Smithson.

Lyndsay Smithson is Lyndsay Arkman, Katie thought.

The family was well known throughout Iowa. Katie's family had once been in the Arkmans' social circle. Back before Katie's dad embezzled millions of dollars and went to prison. The Arkmans had disowned one of their daughters because she had eloped, marrying someone they considered far beneath her. It was a big deal at the time. Katie remembered overhearing her father telling Mr. Arkman that he should yank the girl's trust fund.

Katie had thought that was a little harsh, but it didn't matter. Mr. Arkman had apparently already tried and couldn't do it. His daughter had waited until she was over the age of twenty-one, when she gained control of the trust. There was nothing he could do.

That explains where the Smithsons' money comes from, Katie thought. A trust fund.

Katie searched the public records to find the marriage certificate for Lyndsay Arkman and Isaac Smithson. Wedding date September eleventh. An unfortunate date. But that wasn't the only thing that caught Katie's attention. It was the year. Exactly eighteen years earlier. A month before Rachel Smithson's birth. Katie easily remembered Rachel's birthday. It was seared into her memory because Rachel was barely eighteen when she killed her baby, which allowed Katie to charge her as an adult and completely bypass any potential juvenile court involvement.

But why marry a month before Rachel's birth? The obvious reason was to legitimize the baby, but Katie doubted that was the case. Lyndsay had given up her entire family and her place in society so she could marry Isaac. There was no reason to legitimize the birth at that point. Nobody to appease unless it was Isaac's family.

That left one other less obvious potential. Besides true love, of course. Judging by Isaac's treatment of Lyndsay, Katie seriously doubted their union had anything to do with love. It was a bit of a stretch, this idea of Katie's. A possibility that stuck in the back of her mind all the same. A hunch that required her to take a trip to the county recorder's office and look at Rachel's birth certificate.

Unfortunately, it was Saturday. The county recorder wouldn't be open until Monday. Katie stood and stretched, lifting her arms above her head and arching her back. It felt so good that she issued a groan of satisfaction. A throat cleared behind her. It wasn't loud, but the silence of the small police station amplified the sound.

Katie whirled, her heart racing. "Oh," she said in surprise.

It was only a sheriff's deputy, fresh-faced and young in his brown uniform with a gold star placed just above the heart. "Umm," he said, grinding the toe of his heavy black boot into the carpet. "I didn't mean to scare you, but I have something."

"For me?" Katie asked, placing a hand on her chest.

He took a step toward her and held out a document. "Yes, ma'am."

Katie accepted it and reviewed its contents. A subpoena duces tecum. Commanding Katie's presence for a deposition at nine on Monday morning. The signed attorney line said *Ashley Montgomery*.

So, this was what Ashley meant.

"Thank you," Katie said to the deputy before turning and grabbing her phone.

Seriously, Ashley? she typed. *A subpoena duces tecum? You have a copy of Rachel's interview. I gave it to the county attorney weeks ago.*

A subpoena duces tecum demanded her presence as well as the production of evidence. In this case, the evidence was the video recording of Rachel Smithson's interview. George had been the point person for the questioning, as always when it came to His Highness, but Katie had been present the entire time. She'd turned the camera on before the interview started, but that was all. That recording was the video Ashley wanted.

No, I don't, Ashley said. *Chuckie hasn't handed it over yet.*

Katie had to snicker at the nickname for the prosecutor. Charles Hanson did not tolerate nicknames. He made that abundantly clear during his first week on the job when Ashley had called him Chuck. He freaked out, demanding that she use his "full Christian name," insisting that he would not respond to Charlie or Chuck, and certainly not Chuckie.

Well, Katie typed to Ashley. *I gave Charles my only copy.*

It was all fine and well for Ashley to push the prosecutor's buttons, but Katie had to work with Charles rather than against him. With budget cuts, she wasn't in a position to start burning bridges lest she find her name first on the chopping block when the inevitable downsizes came to fruition.

Then get a copy from him.

"Damn it," Katie said aloud. It was the weekend. Charles wouldn't be back at the office until Monday.

Friend or not, Ashley wasn't going to let her off the hook. She'd have to waste her time tracking the video down. Charles should have given it to her by now, but Ashley also didn't have to use a subpoena duces tecum. Both attorneys were playing games, and Katie was caught in the middle of their shenanigans. She tossed her phone aside and headed down the hall, looking for George. She found him in his office.

George was leaning back in his chair, hands behind his head and feet propped up on his desk. His eyes were closed, and she could see his chest rising and falling in the easy, rhythmic fashion of someone in deep sleep.

"You've got to be fucking kidding me," Katie grumbled before banging her knuckles against the open door.

"What, what?" George said, jumping up. "Where's the fire?"

"Whoa there, sleeping beauty," Katie said, striding into his office. It was something he would say to her. It was nice to twist his words and use them against him.

"I wasn't sleeping."

"And I'm a millionaire."

"In that case," George said, settling back into his seat, "I need to borrow some money, but I don't plan to return it."

"That's not borrowing, then. It's a gift. And I think there's a tax for that."

"You should know," George said.

It was a reference to Katie's past. Back when her parents, and Katie by extension, had millions of dollars. Back when they had been friends, George was one of the few Katie had entrusted with that knowledge. Now she wondered if he would someday use her father's incarceration against her. Or perhaps he already had.

Katie blinked several times, reining in her temper, then handed George the subpoena. "Did you get one of these?"

"Nope."

"Well, then, here's your heads-up. Ashley is going to depose you."

There was no way that Ashley would stop with Katie's deposition alone. Usually, she would depose all officers on the same day so that later deponents wouldn't have a chance to discuss her questions with those who testified first.

"I'm not surprised," George said. "She always deposes everyone in serious cases like Rachel's. Have you seen this?"

George held up a copy of that morning's *Brine Daily News*. Katie recognized the photo above the fold. A portrait-style picture of Forest Parker, smiling, smug and proud. His teeth were so white they practically sparkled, and his wavy hair was just unruly enough to be considered rugged yet professional. He was handsome, Katie couldn't deny that, but he was a jerk. A characteristic that leeched all the attractiveness straight out of him.

"Yeah. What of it?"

The article was about Forest's recent attempts to cut the police department's budget, yet again. Normally, the general public would ignore him, but the arrest of a former Brine police officer had drummed up plenty of support for Forest's cause. It wasn't fair, but it also wasn't surprising.

George snapped the paper and huffed a sigh. "He won't rest until we are all out of a job."

"I'm not sure what we can do about it."

"Stop him," George said, leaning forward. He stared at Katie with an oddly intense gaze, saying nothing for a long moment.

At first, she didn't understand what he meant. Then it clicked. "Me? You expect me to do something about it?" She shook her head. "There's no way I'm getting through to him. He hates me."

"Maybe," George said with a chuckle, "but he wants to hate-fuck you."

"What?" Katie said, shocked. It was a ridiculous suggestion, one that George, as a coworker, should not have voiced. It was borderline sexual harassment. "He does not."

"Take him out, get him drunk. Take some pictures of him drooling or something."

"No," Katie said emphatically. George was suggesting that she blackmail Forest. Blackmail was part of the reason that John Jackie ended up in prison. She would not take that route, no matter what the stakes. "I'll talk to him, but that's it."

Tension had been brewing between Katie and George for nearly a year, but she'd never been quite so furious with him as she was in that moment. His suggestion—that she should essentially commit a crime to save his job —was completely out of line. She wanted to punch him in the face, and he didn't even notice. It was like his promotion had come with a pair of rose-colored glasses that he'd chosen to put on and never take off.

He motioned with his hand. "By all means. But my plan is better. You aren't going to get anywhere talking."

Maybe not, Katie thought, but she wasn't going to stoop anywhere near John Jackie's level. "Whatever," she said, turning on her heel.

She marched back to her office and picked up her phone. Forest had been a witness in a case a while back, but it was long enough ago that she couldn't remember the facts anymore. At the time, she had saved his cell phone number in case she needed more information.

She scrolled through her contacts, took a deep breath, and clicked on his name.

10

ASHLEY

70 days before trial

Steam rose from Ashley's coffee. She watched the tendrils of heat twist and turn before vanishing. She was in a back corner booth of Genie's Diner. It was quiet for a Sunday morning. The calm before the post-church storm of people. She lifted the coffee to her lips and took a sip, thinking of the conversation she had with Carley yesterday.

She had called the reporter Saturday morning and Carley answered on the second ring. It was nice to finally get through to someone. To hear a voice actually say "hello" rather than Tom's voicemail telling her that she should leave a message. She had left messages, but he hadn't responded.

Ashley had started the interview unsure. She didn't trust the reporter to avoid Rachel-related questions. But Ashley began to relax as the questioning moved forward and Carley kept true to her word. All her questions were centered around office finances. Apparently, she was writing a piece on the disparities between money allocated to prosecutors' offices, which were funded by the counties, and public defender's offices, whose funding came from the state.

Near the end of the conversation, Carley had even expressed an interest in helping to raise funds to level the playing field between prosecution and public defense. Ashley was trying not to get overly excited—people often had good intentions. The follow-through was the problem. But Ashley couldn't help getting her hopes up. She needed an on-staff investigator. And soon.

Ashley's phone was on the table next to her coffee cup. It buzzed and the face lit up. Her heart lifted, but it wasn't Tom. Just a breaking news notification. She used facial recognition to open the phone and clicked on her text message thread with Tom.

All the messages were in blue and on the right side of the screen. There were twenty of them dating back to Saturday morning when she'd tried to reach Tom and the call had gone straight to voicemail.

I'm sorry I was so upset with you yesterday. I'm under a lot of stress with Rachel's case.

No answer.

Your phone keeps going straight to voicemail. Will you call me?

Nothing.

Are you there?

I know you are upset, but I'm starting to worry about you.

Please, Tom. I just need to know that you aren't on the side of the road somewhere.

And the messages continued like that. Ashley was growing more and more concerned about him. Had one of her crazy stalkers attacked him?

"Ms. Montgomery," a man said, pulling her out of her thoughts.

"Mr. Frank." Ashley rose to her feet and shook the Waukee High School therapist's hand.

"Call me Michael," he said, sliding into the booth across from her.

"Mr. Frank is fine." Ashley couldn't keep the suspicion from creeping into her voice. They were not friends and would never be on a first-name basis. "What is this all about?"

The Waukee High School counselor had contacted her yesterday to arrange a meeting. She'd been inclined to refuse, but he had insisted that he knew information important to Rachel's defense. When Ashley remained hesitant, he told her that he'd come to meet her in Brine. Reluctantly, she had agreed.

"Thank you for meeting me."

Ashley nodded. She wasn't going to placate him by saying *anytime* or *you're welcome*. Because the interview was not welcome, and it wouldn't be happening any other time. This was his one chance.

Mr. Frank cleared his throat. "How is Rachel?"

"It's the same answer as yesterday. I'm not telling you."

"Right." Mr. Frank pulled at his tie. "Sorry. I remember."

Why was he wearing a tie anyway? Was he trying to make a point? It was the weekend. She was in yoga pants and a long-sleeve jogging shirt.

Ashley took a sip of coffee, studying the school counselor. He squirmed under her scrutiny, but he didn't seem to need to fill the silence.

"Again," Ashley said, trying not to sound too impatient, "what is it that you want to tell me?"

"Yes, well, it's about Rachel?"

"You said that yesterday." She wanted to add *so get the fuck on with it already*, but she didn't.

"I was working with Rachel at school."

"How so?" Ashley blew on her coffee.

"In my professional capacity. As a school counselor."

"What kind of *counseling* were you providing?"

Ashley was suspicious of this man who claimed to be "emotionally bonded" with his students. She'd seen him on the various news stations describing Rachel as a *beautiful young woman, inside and out,* and as someone who would *light up the room*. Naturally, there was speculation about the closeness of their relationship. His public appearances had come to an abrupt halt after that. Ashley wondered if he'd been fired or placed on administrative leave. She made a mental note to look into it.

"Just regular talk therapy. One-on-one sessions."

Ashley quirked an eyebrow.

Mr. Frank fidgeted with the rolled silverware sitting next to him. "I can't tell you the things she told me during our sessions, but I do believe she has a borderline personality disorder."

If there was one thing Ashley understood, it was privilege. Attorney-client privilege wasn't all that different from doctor-patient privilege. He was right that he couldn't give her details from their sessions, but that should also mean that his diagnosis of her was privileged. Unless Rachel had signed a release of information. Which she hadn't.

"That's a serious condition," Ashley said.

She thought she understood where he was going with it. Borderline personalities were often promiscuous. Was he trying to get out in front of an accusation? Blame the victim before she outed him?

"What kind of credentials do you have? I mean, you are a high school counselor. Are you really in a position to make such a diagnosis?"

Mr. Frank sat up straighter, folding his wiry hands in his lap. "I have my PhD in clinical psychology."

The more time Ashley spent with this man, the more questions he raised. "Why work at a high school? Shouldn't you be teaching at the college level? Or perhaps providing clinical care to the community?"

Mr. Frank shrugged. "I like the kids."

Ashley considered the man in front of her. He was not attractive. He looked to be in his early fifties. A thin man in every part of his body except his belly, which protruded like a woman seven months into pregnancy. His glasses were so thick they shrank the size of his eyes.

"Do the kids like you?"

"Rachel does."

Was it just her, or did he answer a little too quickly? Ashley made a mental note to discuss the school counselor with her client.

"Is that all you came to tell me? That you believe Rachel is borderline and that she likes you?" Ashley paused to take a sip of her coffee. "Because none of that is very helpful for Rachel's defense."

"Right, yes." Mr. Frank nodded and pressed his napkin against his brow. "I met with Rachel a lot of times. She was a loner with the other girls, but the boys all kept an eye on her. I mean, you know boys. How could they not?" He chuckled in a boys will be boys kind of way. It didn't sit well with Ashley.

"Okay. And your point is..."

"In all our sessions, Rachel never really opened up to me."

I don't blame her, Ashley thought. His personality was a weird mixture of forced positivity and judgment. Ashley couldn't imagine any kid feeling comfortable around him.

"And..." Ashley motioned for him to go on.

"But she missed a lot of school. She was sick at least once every few weeks. When she returned, she'd have bruising on her arms."

Now this was important information. "So you think there was trouble at home? Someone was abusing her?"

"I wouldn't go that far. I confronted the parents a few months ago. They said they didn't realize Rachel was missing so much school."

Ashley narrowed her eyes. She didn't trust this man, and she didn't trust either of Rachel's parents. "So, Rachel's parents had *no idea* that she was skipping four times a month? And how did they explain the bruising? Track marks?"

Mr. Frank shrugged. "They said they didn't know about the bruising."

"But you did. What did you do about it?"

"Nothing. Rachel said it was nothing. An iron deficiency or something like that. Like I said, she never really opened up to me. She's a good girl. You have to know that. If she was skipping school and doing drugs, it was because one of the boys at school had convinced her to do it."

"Did you know she was pregnant?"

Mr. Frank sighed deeply. "I suspected, but I didn't know for sure."

"Is the baby yours?"

"Mi...mi...mine?" Mr. Frank stammered. Sweat poured down his face. He pulled at his collar. "Is it hot in here?" he asked, looking around.

"No." Ashley leaned closer. "Answer the question, Mr. Frank. Is Rachel's baby yours?"

He swallowed hard, his Adam's apple bobbing. "No."

His denial was not convincing. Hatred welled from somewhere deep within her. She felt certain that he either had an inappropriate relationship with Rachel or wanted to. Either option sickened her. She wanted him out of her sight. And now.

"Thanks for the information, Mr. Frank. I think we are done here," Ashley said, motioning to the door.

Mr. Frank stood and trudged toward the door, moving quickly as though running from something. But it was too late for him. If he had done something to Rachel, Ashley would find out. And she would make him pay.

11

ASHLEY

69 days before trial

Ashley spent the remainder of the day Sunday trying to get through to Tom, but his phone went straight to voicemail. Every. Single. Time. Which meant one of three things. Tom's phone was off, it was dead, or Tom had broken it somehow. He charged his phone regularly, so the second option was likely out.

That left either off or broken. Both of which were less than ideal. If it broke, Tom must have thrown it or smashed it out of anger. He wasn't the type to lose his temper. Ashley and Katie were the hotheads, not Tom. He took everything in stride. If he'd thrown something, Ashley's behavior on Friday had really gotten under his skin. Something she hadn't seen before, not even while Tom was jail administrator and dealing with unruly inmates.

If she'd made him that mad, then she must have a unique ability to coax a violent response out of a nonviolent person. It didn't bode well for the future of their relationship. But that was still better than the last option, that he had intentionally shut off his phone. If he had, it was a willful choice to shut her out of his life. And he'd been able to keep it up all week-end. It signified the beginning of the end.

She had gone to bed Sunday with a heavy heart, knowing that even in the best-case scenario, if they worked it out, she still wouldn't see Tom until the following Friday. In the worst-case scenario.... Well, she didn't want to think about that. After several hours of tossing and turning, she'd fallen into a restless sleep.

All too soon, Ashley's alarm starting blaring from the bedside nightstand. She turned the phone off and rolled over, casting her arm out toward the other side of the bed. An automatic reaction to the days before Tom left for school, searching for his familiar warmth. Her hand landed on a large ball of fur and a wet tongue.

"Princess," Ashley groaned, pulling her arm back and tucking it under the covers.

A second dog nuzzled under her arm, snuggling closely.

"Finn," Ashley said.

Finn was a black-and-white border collie, Princess a red merle Australian Shepherd. At one time, these two dogs were all she had. Back when her mother had died of cancer and Ashley was friendless. The events that led to her friendship with Tom and Katie occurred shortly thereafter, but these two dogs had helped her through that initial rough patch. Ashley was thankful to have them here for her through the current rough patch with Tom.

Princess jumped on Ashley's chest and stuck out her pink tongue, trying to lick Ashley's face. She caught the dog's head between her hands, scratching her behind the ears as she kept her just outside of licking distance.

"No licking," Ashley said, leaning forward and kissing her dog's head.

Ashley rolled over and dropped her feet to the floor, grabbing her phone and checking the call log. Maybe Tom had called or texted. Still nothing. It stung, but his silence had already cut her far too deeply. She would not let it go any further. Yesterday, she'd been depressed. Now she was angry. Who did he think he was, anyway? They were in a committed relationship. Or so she'd thought. And he was running around with this Harper woman, disappearing for a full weekend. It was intolerable.

Standing, she moved to her closet and carefully selected an outfit. It was Monday, which meant deposition number one in Rachel Smithson's case.

Ashley would be questioning Katie. Deposing a friend was a delicate job. Rachel needed Ashley to ask difficult questions. Her freedom depended on it. But Ashley also didn't want to hurt Katie's feelings. At least not so much that it would damage their friendship. The whole process required some careful balancing that would take every ounce of Ashley's concentration.

Not for the first time, Ashley wished that Katie didn't work for the police department. They didn't appreciate her anyway. Ashley respected Chief Carmichael, but all the rest of those chauvinistic cops could go to hell. Especially George Thomanson. She'd heard some rumors about possible marital problems, but that didn't give him the right to treat everyone around him like shit. Relationship issues plagued everyone, including Ashley.

Ashley dispelled all thoughts of relationship woes, forcing herself to focus on the issue at hand. She stared into her closet, shifting hangers around, trying to find the right suit. Unfortunately, her clothing wasn't organized in any fashion, just tossed on any open hanger. She shuffled past a pair of pants that had been out of style long enough that they were almost back in style, settling on a pair of black pants, a black jacket, and a white sweater. As she pulled on the sweater, she caught sight of a smattering of heavy bruising along her arm. They were an angry reddish-purple color, almost like she was bleeding under her skin. But that couldn't be right. Could it?

She shook her head, dismissing it as stress. Or perhaps she'd struck her arm on something? She couldn't remember doing it, but when she had a lot going on, her mind didn't register everything accurately. One time, during a stressful trial, she spent thirty minutes looking for her sunglasses just to glance in the mirror and see them sitting on her head. Another time, she pulled her car into a parking stall and tried to turn it off, but the key wouldn't turn. Then she realized that the vehicle wasn't in park. It had to be something like that, right? She was under a lot of stress. The alternative was illness. Maybe even a serious one that would require lots of tests and poten tially chemotherapy.

Nope, Ashley thought, *don't think about that.*

She pulled her jacket over her arms and stepped into her pants, using her armoire for balance. This room had been Ashley's bedroom since birth.

This house, the only home she had ever lived in. Yet she couldn't bring herself to move into the master. That room still felt like her mother's room. Sometimes she liked to go into the master bedroom and sit at the edge of her mother's bed. It almost felt as though her mother were still there.

Living in her childhood home was a blessing and a curse. It held so many memories, good and bad. A roof once shared by many now only sheltered Ashley and her dogs. What was once a home full of joy and laughter was now silent. Although, to be honest, Ashley's home wasn't always joyful, nor was it always shared with those she loved. This house was the very same home she'd once shared with Lydia, her foster sister. Luckily, that placement had ended within a year.

Lydia had been a nightmare. She was the same age as Ashley. Removed from her parents' care at the age of ten for reasons Ashley's mother had never revealed to her daughters. Not that it mattered. Lydia was pure evil. That's what Ashley and her older sister kept telling their mother, but their mother kept brushing it off, saying, "Oh, girls. Be kind. Lydia has been through a lot."

Which may have been true. Hell, considering the things Ashley saw in her current job, it probably was true. But that still didn't give Lydia the right to shove Ashley down the basement stairs. Ashley could remember it like it was yesterday.

A firm strike to the shoulder. Teetering on the edge, arms pinwheeling. Rolling down all twenty-three steps, blinding pain with every strike of a shoulder or knee, before smashing into the cement floor. The fall had resulted in a concussion and a broken arm. That had opened her mother's eyes enough to find a new foster placement for Lydia. Thankfully, that was the last foster child their mother had taken in.

Ashley didn't know why the sudden memory of Lydia had popped into her head. Maybe it had been because of the girl giggling in the background of her and Tom's call on Friday, or maybe it was something else. Perhaps her subconscious was telling her that it was time to forgive Lydia. Not that she would listen. That girl—well, woman now—could go to hell. And she probably would if she'd kept up the same kind of behaviors over the years.

Ashley shook her head, reminding herself that it was all in the past. Lydia was gone. A relic of a lost world. A past life. Then she descended the stairs to the main level of her home where it smelled of fresh coffee. Auto-brew set to a timer last night. Ashley inhaled deeply. The aroma was happy, warm. She wished she could suck the feeling inside her, bottle it up, and keep it in that empty space usually occupied by thoughts of Tom.

She selected a coffee cup that had lines like a legal notebook and the word "no" inscribed on it. One simple word, but it held such power, such strength. That's what she should tell Tom next time he called, if he ever called. Then she'd hang up.

The payback would feel good for a moment. Much in the same way she'd felt after telling Tom not to come that weekend. It felt wonderful to say at the time, to dole out punishment for all the bottled-up anger he'd caused, but later it had twisted into the heavy acid that now ate away at her stomach. It was a lesson that she'd had to learn the hard way. Momentary triumph wasn't worth it.

"Are you dogs ready to eat?" Ashley said, turning toward her two loyal friends.

Finn wagged his tail and Princess yipped, spinning two times before sitting back on her haunches. Ashley filled both bowls with kibble, then sipped her coffee as she watched them eat. Finn ate daintily, one kernel at a time. Princess scarfed her food down, swallowing many of the pieces whole.

"I hear you, sister," Ashley said as she patted Princess on the head. "I could stress eat an elephant right now."

It took Finn a full ten minutes to finish his breakfast. When he was done, Ashley opened the front door to let the dogs out. They dashed outside, leaping and soaring over something sitting on the front porch. Ashley moved closer to get a better look. It was a package. A white box tied with a red ribbon. Not something USPS or UPS would bring. Someone had dropped it off at her doorstep.

Ashley took a step back, her insides twisting with fear. Her first thought was of that psycho who had grabbed her arm after Rachel's sentencing. Had he figured out where she lived? She looked to her left, then to her right, but nobody seemed to be around.

Calm down, she told herself. *You're jumpy today.*

After all, she couldn't leave it sitting on the front porch forever. Sooner or later, she'd have to deal with it. She picked up the package and shook it. Multiple small items bounced around inside.

At least it isn't a bomb, she thought. Although her training in bomb detection was nil, so it wasn't exactly an expert's opinion.

She shrugged and brought it inside. Sliding the ribbon off, she closed one eye and held the box as far from her body as she could. Slowly, ever so gingerly, she lifted the lid. She held her breath for a long, tense moment. No boom.

After a moment, she opened both eyes and stared at the contents. A white letter sat on top of red tissue paper. She grabbed the letter, flipping it over. No words on the outside. She opened it cautiously, half expecting anthrax to fall out but finding none. It was just a simple letter in familiar handwriting. It read, *Sorry.* And was signed with Tom's signature.

Ashley dug into the tissue paper, finding another box of homemade candies. They looked to be assorted, some with caramel, some with nuts, like Tom had put a good deal of effort into them.

"What?" Ashley said aloud, turning back to the letter. She looked from one side to the other, flipping it back and forth as though the movement would unlock a secret message. But no, no secrets. Just one lousy word that didn't mean much without more context.

"Sorry for what?" she said. There were so many things that required apologies. Was this for all of them? One of them? If so, which one?

She dug in the box, hoping to find a second letter. There was none.

"What. The. Literal. Fuck," Ashley growled.

Was Tom messing with her? Why would he drive all the way to Brine to leave a box on her doorstep? Why hadn't he knocked on the door and hand-delivered it? It was completely asinine. If it was a grand gesture, it had fallen flat. Nothing grand about this one at all.

She could spend all morning wondering at his meaning, but luckily, she didn't have time for that. If she was going to make it to Rachel's deposition by nine, she needed to get on the road. She tossed the box in the passenger seat of her SUV and backed out of the driveway. She'd eat it later. Or perhaps never. Maybe she'd toss all the candies in the trash. That would show him. Except he wouldn't see her do it, so that would make it less satisfying.

Ashley drove the first several miles ignoring the box of chocolates. Then her eyes slowly drifted toward it. Her stomach growled. She'd fed the dogs, but she hadn't eaten anything herself. It wasn't ideal, but she decided she'd eat a couple pieces, just enough to tide her over until lunch.

The breakfast of champions, she thought as she tossed the first one in her mouth.

12

KATIE

"You've done this before, right?" Ashley's voice was as cold as the cement walls of the jail surrounding them.

It was always that way when Katie came face to face with the defense attorney while in their professional capacities. It was Monday morning, nine o'clock sharp, the time slated for Katie's deposition. Ashley and her client sat across a long, heavy table from Katie and the prosecutor, Charles Hanson. The court reporter, a middle-aged woman named Nancy, occupied the seat at the head of the table. Nancy typically had a jolly personality and an easy smile, but even her mood was affected by the tension in the room.

"A deposition?" Katie quirked an eyebrow. "Yeah. I've given plenty. I believe my last one was by you. Charlotte Spark's case."

Charlotte, too, was a killer. Although she'd chosen poison instead of drowning. Katie's eyes darted toward Ashley's client. Rachel's hands and feet were bound in chains, tucked under the table. The girl was slumped forward so far that her dark, stick-straight hair blanketed her face, obscuring her expression.

"That was..." Ashley tapped the end of her pen against her lips. "Six months or so ago, right?"

"Yeah. A black widow case. The defendant poisoned her husband with arsenic." Katie didn't have to say *allegedly* anymore. That jury had rendered a quick guilty verdict. Charlotte was rotting away in Mitchellville, the only women's prison in Iowa. A life sentence. Her only opportunity for release was in a body bag.

"You are employed by the Brine Police Department?"

"Yes. I've been working for the Brine PD for six years."

"What is your current position?"

Katie narrowed her eyes. "Patrol officer." Ashley knew Chief Carmichael had passed Katie up for the detective promotion. She also knew it was a sore subject.

"Are there any detectives?"

"Yes," Katie said through gritted teeth. She didn't know where Ashley was going with her questioning unless her purpose was to get under Katie's skin. If that was the case, her efforts were working. "George."

"George Thomanson?"

"Yes."

"He was involved in your interview with my client, Rachel Smithson?"

"Yes."

"Did you bring a copy of that recording with you?"

"Yes." Katie slid a disk across the table.

Ashley caught it with nimble fingers and flashed a smile. Not her mocking, lawyer smile, but the one she reserved for Katie when they were off duty. When they were able to be friends.

That small display of gratefulness eased some of the tension building in Katie's shoulders. She had been annoyed that she had to track the disk down at all. Getting her hands on it over the weekend hadn't been easy. She'd already turned it over to Charles. One might think it was as simple as calling him and requesting a copy, but it wasn't.

Katie's eyes darted toward the prosecutor sitting next to her, checking to see if he had a reaction to the disk, an apology for wasting her time, perhaps, but he wasn't even paying attention. He only cared about the disk when he thought he could keep it from Ashley. Now that it was inevitable that she'd get it, he wasn't interested. He'd brought a newspaper with him to the deposition and was reading it now.

"Since George Thomanson was the senior officer, the detective, would you agree that he was in charge of the interview?" Ashley asked.

"I suppose."

"When did this interview take place?"

"As soon as we could track Rachel down."

"How did you know that you were looking for Rachel?"

It was a good question. Katie hadn't known who Rachel was prior to the investigation.

"I spoke with the hotel manager. They provided a copy of the video recordings as well as a record of the hotel reservation. The reservation was in Rachel's name and the person on the recording matched Rachel's driver's license photograph."

"Is the recording from the hotel on this disk?" Ashley tapped it lightly with her index finger.

"No."

"Can I get a copy of that?"

Katie's eyes cut to the prosecutor. She'd given him *everything*. Apparently, he'd provided nothing to Ashley. "Yes."

Charles cleared his throat. "I'll get you the remainder of discovery by the end of the week." He didn't lower his newspaper.

"Okay," Ashley said in an annoyed tone. "Was Rachel's current address on her driver's license?"

Katie's eyes cut to Rachel. The girl hadn't moved. She sat there, unnaturally still, with her hair covering her face. It was creepy.

"Yes. We were able to use the address on her driver's license to track her to her Waukee address."

"Did you go straight to Rachel's home?"

"Yes."

"Who answered the door?"

Katie thought back. It wasn't a detail that she'd committed to memory. To her, it wasn't important. "Perhaps Isaac Smithson?" Although the memory was hazy.

"Rachel's father?"

"Yes. I believe Isaac is Rachel's father."

Ashley quirked an eyebrow. Nothing got past her. "You believe?"

"Well, yes. I haven't seen Rachel's birth certificate, so I can't say with one hundred percent certainty. But all individuals identified Isaac as Rachel's father."

"All individuals, meaning who?"

"Rachel, Isaac, and Lyndsay."

"Lyndsay is..."

"Rachel's mom."

"Okay." Ashley sat back and scribbled a few notes onto the second page of her notepad, careful to keep it out of Katie's line of sight. "So, how would you describe Isaac Smithson's demeanor at that time?"

Katie chewed on her lip, trying to remember. His face was beet red. She remembered that clearly. Like he was angry or upset. "He seemed flustered, like I had caught him off guard. Or in the middle of something." She paused for a long moment. "That's not unusual, though. The Smithsons are not the type of people who have law enforcement knocking on their door regularly."

"Oh," Ashley said, leaning forward, "and what type of people have law enforcement at their door regularly?"

It was a challenge. A barely veiled reference to racism and classism in law enforcement. It was also bullshit. Ashley knew Katie was fair to everyone. Or at least she thought Ashley knew that. "You know what I meant. I'm not a Waukee police officer so I don't know for sure, but I doubt there are any calls to service at that residence."

A call to service meant the number of times local law enforcement had to respond to a residence, no matter the reason. It could be 911 calls, welfare checks, child abuse complaints, or reports made to the tip line.

"You doubt? Does that mean you haven't checked?"

"I don't know why I would check. This is a case about a baby discarded in a hotel room by your client. It doesn't matter how many times the Waukee PD has been to the Smithson residence."

"It doesn't?" Ashley wrote another note, slowly this time, dragging it out for dramatic reasons. "Why not?"

"Rachel's baby wasn't ever there."

Ashley nodded. "Because you agree that a fetus is not a baby. Meaning that a fetus is not a living person under the law."

"Under the law, no. At least not the current law."

There was talk that the Iowa legislature was going to try to redefine the definition of life, but that hadn't happened yet.

"Do you know why Rachel came to Brine to have her baby?"

"I know why she said she came to Brine. I don't know that it's the truth."

"Why did she say she came to Brine?"

Katie looked at the girl again. Rachel was as still as a statue. "She said it was the first town she'd come to. She didn't know where she was. She knew she was in labor and wanted to have the baby somewhere private."

Ashley cocked her head. "Private from whom?"

"I don't know."

It was a good question. Katie wondered if it had something to do with the police officer Isaac claimed had been hanging around the house. Or perhaps Rachel had always intended to kill her baby and throw him in the garbage. After all, she had hidden the pregnancy for nine months.

These were the most obvious conclusions to Rachel's actions. Katie wished that George would have thought to ask during her interview. That was the problem when men headed investigations that involved issues like childbirth. The birthing process and reasons behind birth choices were issues that only women seemed capable of fully understanding.

"Could it be," Ashley said, smiling widely, "that the answer could have something to do with the number of calls to service at the Smithsons' Waukee residence?"

"I don't know." Katie made a mental note to look into it.

"You. Don't. Know," Ashley repeated, emphasizing each word.

"No. Like I said, I was there to record, not to intervene. George asked the questions. You should ask him. If I had to guess, I would say that Rachel chose to come to Brine because she didn't want her parents to know about the baby."

"Why would you say that?"

"Because she'd gone through all that trouble to hide her pregnancy from everyone, including her parents."

A wry smile spread across Ashley's face as she leaned forward. "Now, who told you that? It wasn't Rachel, was it?"

Katie thought back, trying to remember the details of Rachel's interview. After a moment, she shook her head. "No. Rachel didn't say she hid the pregnancy. Isaac did."

"Ohh," Ashley said, raising her eyebrows.

Ashley had a reason for her questions. She was too far down the rabbit hole for it to be anything other than intentional. Ashley thought there was a defense hidden somewhere inside those calls to service, and she believed it had to do with Isaac or the responding officer. Katie would be a fool to ignore it.

"Let's talk about the baby," Ashley said, switching subjects.

"Okay."

"Have you read through the medical examiner's report?"

"No," Katie answered truthfully. She hadn't received it yet, and doubted Ashley had either. "I didn't know it was available."

"If you haven't seen it, then you don't know the baby's cause of death, right?"

Rachel had admitted how she'd killed her baby in her interview. The cause of death was clear. "That's not true."

"Are you a medical doctor?"

Katie narrowed her eyes. "No. I'm not. But it doesn't take an MD to put the pieces together. A newborn baby placed face down in a bathtub while the water is running would die by drowning. Nobody, not even newborns, can breathe under water."

"So," Ashley said, a wry smile spreading across her lips, "if the medical examiner's report comes back stating the cause of death is anything other than drowning, it must be wrong?"

"I didn't say that."

Ashley was building up to something. It felt like a carefully laid trap. "How do you know that the baby was born alive?"

"I know," Katie said through clenched teeth, "because your client said she gave birth to a live baby." She nodded toward Rachel, who flinched at the word *baby*. "Rachel told George that the baby cried. That means he was alive." Ashley was on a fishing expedition and Katie didn't appreciate the attempt to hook her.

"I didn't ask what Rachel said. I asked if there is any indication that the child was ever alive."

"Yes," Katie said, her face growing hot. "I don't have the medical examiner's report, but I suspect it will confirm that the baby was born alive. To say anything other than that would be pure speculation. All I know is what I have told you."

"And that is..."

"That Rachel said the baby was alive. Which is a pretty good indication that it was a live birth."

"Are you certain?" Ashley waggled her eyebrows.

"I don't know," Katie said, crossing her arms. "I am not a doctor, and I haven't read the report."

"So, you'd agree that water must be in the baby's lungs to indicate a live birth?"

Katie's insides boiled. "I said nothing of the sort."

Her irritation was growing with each passing second. She was well past annoyed and dangerously close to pissed off. Something in her expression must have gotten through to Ashley, because she then suggested that they take a break.

"We can keep going today," Ashley said, glancing at her watch. It was already 11:00 a.m. They'd been at it for two full hours. "I can stretch this out until lunch so that I have time to watch this video, or we can adjourn this deposition with the idea that we will continue at a later date and time."

Charles Hanson sighed and lowered his paper, carefully folding it along the proper crease lines. "We can adjourn this time, but I'm not going to do this with every deposition. You should have come prepared. It's a waste of everyone's time to recess in the middle of a deposition."

"Me?" Ashley said, her nostrils flaring. "I should have been prepared? You should have given me the recording. You obviously had it, yet you sat on it. So if you want me to 'be prepared'"—she used air quotes—"then you'll stop playing games with the evidence."

"I'm not playing games," Charles said, crossing his arms.

Katie's eyes darted from the defense attorney to the prosecutor. Despite her anger with Ashley's line of questioning, she couldn't help rooting for her. Ashley could get under her skin, but to see that same intensity directed at Charles Hanson, Mr. Politics himself, was hilarious. Charles did not react well, and he looked very much like a petulant child.

"Then where is the medical examiner's report?" Ashley rose and shoved her laptop into her bag.

"Apparently you have it," Charles said.

"I never said I had it," Ashley growled.

"Then why ask those questions?" His gaze shifted toward Katie.

"Don't look at me," she said, scowling. "I don't have the report."

"It doesn't matter," Ashley said. "The point is that I'm still waiting on supplemental police reports. Where are those? We have sixty-nine days until trial. It's go-time. You know it, I know it. You're trying to force me to waive speedy trial. And I won't. You can't make me. Got that?"

"We'll see about that," Charles said, rising and storming out of the room.

Yup, Katie thought, *a child*.

All the bluster left Ashley the moment Charles was gone. She suddenly looked exhausted, pale, and a little sick. Something was wrong. Katie should have noticed earlier, but she had been too irritated with Ashley's questioning. She wanted to ask Ashley if she was getting enough sleep, but she kept the thought to herself. She wouldn't ask in front of Ashley's client. That would cause problems for both Ashley and Katie. Her appearance probably had something to do with Tom. Katie hoped they weren't still arguing. Ashley had enough on her plate without the added stress.

13

KATIE

67 days before trial

The bureaucratic red tape surrounding the Waukee Police Department was exceptionally thick. Katie had been trying to get a copy of the calls to service at the Smithson residence since her deposition on Monday. It was now Wednesday afternoon and her patience was well past worn and approaching dangerously low.

She picked up her phone and dialed the now familiar number to the Waukee Police Department. It rang several times, like always, before a bored-sounding woman picked up.

"Waukee Police Department, criminal division."

"Hi, yes. My name is Katie Mickey. I am a police officer in Brine, Iowa. I've called several times requesting some records."

"Oh, yes," the woman said in a monotone. "You want to talk to Dan."

"No," Katie said quickly. "Do not transfer me to Dan. Dan will not call me back and this is important. Is there someone else I can talk to?"

Katie had already left countless voicemails for Captain Dan Marino to no avail. With a name like that, she was starting to wonder if he even existed. Maybe the Waukee PD set up a fake account for calls they didn't want to deal with. She understood that they were busy, with better things to do—or so they thought—than dealing with a small-town officer.

"Dan's your man," the woman said. Katie could virtually hear her shrug through the phone.

"No," Katie said through gritted teeth. "Dan is not the man. Not my man or anybody else's man. Dan doesn't pick up and he doesn't return calls. Give me someone else. Anyone else."

"Can't."

"Listen to me," Katie growled. Her well of tolerance, which quite honestly was never all that full to begin with, had run dry. Bone dry. Old bones that had withered to dust kind of dry. "You will put someone on the line, anyone other than Dan, or I will drive down to your station and park my ass in your waiting room, harassing every police officer who comes within shouting distance until someone, I don't care who, gets me the things I need. And until someone does help me, I'll be sure to glare at you and make loud, annoying, throat-clearing noises during each of your phone calls. Got it?"

The woman was silent for a long moment, then finally said, "You can talk to Josh."

"Yes. I would love to talk to Josh."

There was a click and elevator music began playing. Katie sighed with relief. She was on hold. Hopefully in the midst of a transfer to Josh, who she hoped was a real person with half a brain.

"Hello?"

"Yes, hello? Josh?"

"Umm, yeah?"

Katie ran a hand down her face. She wanted to scream. "Yeah? With a question mark? Do you not know who you are? Because I need to talk to Josh. Are you, in fact, Josh?"

"Yes. I'm Josh. No need to get snippy. Who are you?"

"Well, Josh, you'd be snippy, too, if you'd spent the past two days trying to get a simple list of calls to service to one address."

"And you are..." His voice sounded almost playful now. Like he was flirting.

Katie was not in the mood. "Katie Mickey. Officer Mickey. I'm with the Brine Police Department."

"Yeah, sure, Katie. I can get you whatever you need."

He said the words in a low, husky tone. Was he trying to seduce her? If so, he was wasting his time. She didn't fall for the frat boy type. Dating a heavy partier was more of a babysitting job than a relationship. Not that Katie had the time or desire for either.

"Great. I need a list of calls to service to the Smithson residence. Isaac and Lyndsay Smithson."

He whistled a high-pitched note that dipped into something lower, like she was asking for something ridiculous. All he needed to do was run the report. A quick click of a few buttons on a computer, then send it to her. It wasn't rocket science.

"What? Is that going to be a problem?" Katie said.

"Like how long are we talking?"

"What do you mean how long?"

"How long back?"

Katie frowned. He'd only be asking that question if there were years of disturbances at the Smithson residence. "I don't know. As far back as you can go."

"I can take you back ten years. We don't save records past that." She could hear the clack of his keyboard. "How do you want me to send it to you?"

"What do you mean? Just mail it."

"It's not going to fit in a manila envelope, and we don't ship boxes without prepayment. Not even for other law enforcement agencies. You know, because of the cost."

A box? That meant a lot of records. Which would be heavy. And expensive. Chief Carmichael wouldn't—no, couldn't—approve an expense like that. Not with Forest Parker throwing his weight around City Hall. But that wasn't the only problem. Mailing would also take several days, which Katie didn't have. Something was going on at the Smithson residence, and it wasn't good. She'd have to find a way to get the records some other way.

"Can you email them to me? As a PDF?"

"Sure," Josh said, a smile returning to his voice. "Give me your email address and I'll send them your way."

Katie recited her email address. As she listened to him clicking buttons on his computer, she began regretting her initial assessment of him. He'd done far more for her over the span of a few minutes than Captain Dan Marino had in two days.

"Can you tell me why there are so many calls out to that residence?"

Josh clicked a few more buttons. "I just sent the email. Let me know if you don't get it. As for the Smithsons, they're a strange bunch. You're probably working on that child killer's case out there in the boonies, aren't you?"

Boonies? Katie tried not to roll her eyes. She'd lived in Des Moines in the past, and she remembered how she thought of some of the smaller towns in Iowa. She understood where he was coming from, but it was still irritating. Not all small towns were the same. They each had their own unique character.

"Yeah. I'm working on Rachel Smithson's case."

Josh whistled again.

"What?" Katie said through gritted teeth, unable to keep her irritation at bay. None of this sounded good for her case.

"I wouldn't want to touch that case to save my life."

"Well, I don't have a choice."

"Too bad for you."

"Why?" Katie said, throwing up her hands in exasperation. "Why is it 'too bad' for me? I don't understand."

"Like I said, the Smithsons are a weird bunch."

Katie sighed. "You're going to have to give me more detail than that."

"Isaac. People say he's the father."

"Whose father?" Katie sat up straighter in her chair. "Rachel's?"

"This is all rumor and speculation, but I wouldn't be surprised if it was true. Like I said, Isaac is a strange man."

"You wouldn't be surprised if what was true?" He'd intentionally skirted around answering her question.

"I probably shouldn't be spreading rumors."

"You can't say something cryptic like that without elaborating."

"I said it was rumor."

"Listen, Josh," Katie said, using her most *I'm completely reasonable and compassionate* voice. "You are a law enforcement officer, right?"

"Yes."

"You know that rumors often have at least a grain of truth in them."

"Sometimes."

"So, spill what you know."

A radio crackled to life in the background. Katie recognized it as a service call.

"I'm sorry, Katie. I don't have time to get into it right now."

"Come on. Just five minutes." But then she heard the codes as they came through Josh's radio. It was an emergency call. "Never mind," she said. She couldn't justify holding him on the line while someone in Waukee needed his help.

"Did you get my email with the attachment?"

Katie shook her mouse, and her computer sprang to life. The top email was from JMartin@WaukeePD.gov. "Yes. I've got it."

"I gave you my cell. Meet me for dinner and I'll tell you more."

Ugh, Katie thought. "Why do you want to meet me for dinner? You don't know what I look like. I could be hideous. Or gay. Or I could be married."

"Jesus, Katie," Josh said, chuckling. "So forward. I wasn't asking you out. I just wanted to talk shop."

Blood rushed to Katie's face, flushing it a deep crimson. She was in her cubicle, but she still ducked her head in case George happened to walk by.

"Just kidding. You sound hot. Let's make it a date."

"Meeting," Katie said through clenched teeth.

"Date." Josh paused for a moment to say something into his radio. "But really, I need to go. Email me a day and time. I'll make it work."

"Fine," Katie said.

Frat boy was right. Her initial assessment had been accurate all along. She knew better than to second-guess her gut. And with all the calls to service, she wondered if he was the police officer Isaac had referred to. The one who had been "hanging around," watching for Rachel. Either way, Katie was not impressed with this Josh, but he had information she needed. She would meet him, and it would not be a date. It would be an interview.

"See you soon," Josh said.

Katie hung up without responding.

She sighed and turned back to the email, clicking on the attachment. A PDF document populated her screen. Katie's eyes traveled to the top of the document where the pages were enumerated. She was on page 1 of 152. *One hundred and fifty-two calls to service*, Katie thought. That meant police officers—and maybe one officer in particular—had responded to the Smithson residence more than once per month for ten years.

No wonder Ashley brought it up during Katie's deposition. Finding this file was like striking gold for a defense attorney. Katie wondered if Ashley already had a copy or if she was going off a hunch. Regardless, it didn't bode well for the prosecution. Ashley was going to get a copy of these calls either from the Waukee PD or from Charles Hanson. Information like this could be used as a weapon in court. A weapon that Ashley knew how to wield quite deftly.

It added more to Katie's growing list of follow-ups for Rachel's case. She needed to go through the calls to service with a fine-tooth comb, then interview Josh and find out if there was any connection between him and Rachel. And she still had to get a hold of Rachel's birth certificate to find out if Isaac was listed as Rachel's father.

But the case grew murkier the more Katie dug into Rachel's life, into her background. It was probably why George had stopped investigating. Katie felt like she had jumped through a rabbit hole that never seemed to end. Yet she couldn't stop looking. She didn't even know if any of it would tie back to Rachel's case, but she had a gut sense that each missing element meant something. And her gut was rarely wrong.

14

ASHLEY

66 days before trial

It was Thursday and Ashley still hadn't heard anything from Tom. Almost a full week had passed since their argument. They had never gone so long without talking, even before they started dating. Ashley couldn't stop thinking about him. Her mind kept rewinding and replaying the fight. Yes, she had overreacted. She shouldn't have told him not to come to Brine last weekend. She might have deserved him ignoring her over the weekend, but he had kept it up throughout the week. It was overkill. Especially for Tom.

Earlier that week, Ashley had been concerned about his safety. Worried he'd been hit by a bus or the victim of a late-night mugging. But Tom wasn't the typical college student. He never missed a class and often stayed late to speak with his professors. Someone would have noticed his absence and reported it. If not a professor, then Harper. He seemed to spend plenty of time with her. So he wasn't dead or seriously injured. Which were perhaps the only two excuses Ashley would accept for his current behavior.

Her emotions were so twisted. She was equal parts furious and devastated. She wanted to wring his neck while hugging him tightly and telling him never to leave again. She wondered if this was what love was always like. The push and pull of a power struggle. If it was, she didn't have the energy for it. Maybe that was why she'd never fallen in love before. It was too much work.

But mostly, what she wanted more than anything in the world was to talk to her friend Tom. The person she knew before their relationship turned romantic. She needed to understand why he was ignoring her. It wasn't like him. Tom wasn't vindictive. Or at least he hadn't been in the past. If she knew where he was coming from, then perhaps they could get past this. Maybe not as lovers, but possibly as friends.

I'll go see him, she thought.

The idea just popped into her head and she wondered why she hadn't thought of it earlier. It was so obvious, so simple. She had hearings throughout the day Thursday and Friday, but she could make a trip to Des Moines on Saturday. She had to go to the Waukee Police Department anyway to pick up the calls to service at the Smithsons' Waukee address.

Requesting the calls had been a hunch based on Rachel's odd behavior, but Ashley suspected that it would pay off. The Waukee Police Department was requiring her to appear in person. They claimed it was for identification purposes—they couldn't release sensitive documents to just anyone—but Ashley suspected it was a stalling technique. Which meant there was likely good information hidden in those calls.

So that's what she would do. She'd see Tom on Saturday, then they'd hash it all out. Between now and then, she was going to have to keep her mind busy. It would not be difficult, despite her anxiety about the future. Since taking on Rachel's case, she was busier than ever. She'd always had more to do than there was time to do it in, but Rachel's case had taken over her life.

Thoughts of Rachel reminded her of the video of Rachel's interview. The disk had been sitting in her office since Katie's deposition, gathering dust. Ashley had been so eager to get her hands on it, but once she did, she hadn't made time to watch it. Every day that week, she'd told herself she'd review it. Then the end of the day would sneak up on her and she hadn't touched it. But what was she doing now? Nothing but stewing over boyfriend troubles. She might as well do something useful.

It was only six in the morning, but Ashley had already been at her office for close to thirty minutes. She liked coming in early when the halls were dark and everything was silent. No phones ringing or emails pinging. It was the ideal work environment to catch up. Besides, sleep didn't come easily for her these days.

She grabbed the disk and inserted it into her computer. When the file folder popped up, she double-clicked on the video.

The screen populated with the back of George Thomanson's head. It was a handheld camera. The Brine Police Department didn't have the cash to buy body cameras for every officer, so they made do with older technology. The recording jostled and bobbed as Katie made her way down the hallway. George paused outside the interview room, his fingers lingering on the doorknob. He took several breaths, then turned to address Katie.

"I'll take the lead," George said.

"Are you sure you don't want me to? I mean, she's more likely to talk to a woman."

Katie had a point, but Ashley quietly rooted for George to shut her down.

"I'm the detective," George said in a gruff tone.

Ashley's brows rose in surprise. She'd known George and Katie for several years and never heard him talk to her like that. Apparently, his promotion was going to his head. Which was ridiculous, because it was a promotion only in name. He hadn't received much of a pay raise. Ashley knew because all public employee salaries were printed in the paper, and George's had not risen all that far past a cost-of-living bump. Although, she supposed, that was more than any of the other officers had received.

"Fine," Katie said. "Whatever."

George opened the door and stepped into the room. Rachel was seated at the end of the large conference table. Alone. She wore a sweater with the image of a gray cat in a Santa hat popping out of a stocking. Rachel's head was down, her hair covering her face. The posture was typical for her, but something was off about the way Rachel was seated.

Ashley paused the video and studied her client, from her head down to the seat of her chair, which was all Ashley could see of her. Rachel's facial features were normal considering the situation. Eyes closed, lips pursed. But the arms. They were all wrong. Rachel had them wrapped around herself, crossed and clutching at either side of her hips. Ashley had never seen her client sitting like that. Not once.

Was she? Ashley thought. *No. It couldn't be.*

Ashley looked at the video's date and time stamp. It was recorded within an hour and a half of Rachel giving birth. The drive from Brine to Waukee was a good forty minutes. That meant there hadn't been time for Rachel to receive proper medical treatment. Ashley knew from the medical records that Rachel had some fairly severe vaginal tearing. It took twenty-five stitches to close the wound properly. If this interview occurred before Rachel saw a doctor, then she was literally holding herself together.

"You've got to be fucking kidding me," Ashley said aloud.

What the hell was Katie doing? How had she allowed such a thing? But if George's behavior at the beginning of the interview was any indication, Katie hadn't had much of a choice in the matter. What were his words? Oh, yes. "I'm the detective."

He may not be detective after I'm done with him, Ashley thought as she pressed play again.

"Rachel," George said, his voice honey-smooth. "How are you?"

"I...ummm..." Rachel stammered.

"Wonderful," George interrupted. "You're here willingly, right?" He sank into the chair closest to Rachel.

Rachel started to lean back, grimaced, then stilled. Movement was obviously painful for her.

"You, umm, picked me up."

"Yes. But I didn't arrest you and you said you would come."

"Yeah." Rachel's voice was small, resigned. "I mean I didn't refuse to come."

"So you are here willingly?"

"I mean, I guess."

"You know why you are here, right?"

Rachel closed her eyes for a long moment, took three deep, steadying breaths, then reopened them. "I think so."

"You killed your baby."

Rachel fell silent, her eyes darting toward the table. A few minutes passed before she looked up. "I didn't mean to hurt him."

"Him? You knew your baby was going to be a boy?"

Rachel shivered. "I didn't *know* until I had him, but I thought he would be a boy."

"Why? Are you psychic or something?" Here, George chuckled like a total dick. Ashley wanted to slap him in the face.

"I'm not psychic." Rachel swallowed hard. "I'd never want to know the future. There's no changing it, so what's the use?"

"Then why did you think you were having a boy? You didn't receive prenatal care, did you?"

Rachel shook her head. "I just had a feeling. A boy would be the worst."

George chewed on the end of his pen as though mulling over Rachel's statement. Then he spoke, louder than earlier. "You said that you didn't mean to hurt your son. Do you consider murder something other than harm?"

"I didn't murder anyone."

"Let's go over the facts here," George said, pulling out a pad of paper and a pen. He leaned back, flipping the pen around his finger. "You checked into a hotel room, right?"

"Yes."

"You brought a bottle of vodka and some towels with you, didn't you?"

"Yes."

"You intended to have that baby in the hotel room, right?"

"Yes."

"You drank vodka while pregnant." George paused. When Rachel didn't answer right away, he said, "Isn't that true?"

"The vodka was for the pain."

"You birthed your baby there in the hotel bathroom, right?"

"Yes."

"You were alone." A statement, not a question.

Ashley made a note of the time stamp on the video. Judges often gave law enforcement a lot of leeway in their interviews, but George was really overstepping.

"And then you killed him."

Rachel shook her head. "I didn't."

"Okay. Then you let him die."

"No." Tears were streaming down Rachel's face, but she didn't release her grip on her hips to wipe them away.

George spent the next hour asking the same question over and over again, but in different ways. He took at least two breaks, getting coffee and using the restroom but offering nothing to Rachel. Katie suggested water once, but George shut her down with, "I'm the detective. I know what I'm doing."

It was obvious, at least to Ashley, that he did not. His behavior was borderline torturous. Coercive at best. Ashley didn't have any children of her own, but women didn't complain about childbirth for nothing. It was no walk in the park, even with medications and medical assistance. But without either for hours on end, Ashley couldn't imagine the excruciating pain Rachel had endured.

It took George one hour and thirty-seven minutes of repeated questioning to finally break Rachel.

"Can I go?" Rachel asked.

Her body had begun to quiver. Ashley could see it in her lips and shoulders, a heavy shuddering that rocked her entire body. She looked at the time stamp on the recording again and made a note to reach out to the local hospital, see if she could get a doctor to testify that the girl was in shock or something else that would potentially invalidate Rachel's eventual confession. Because it was clear that her resolve was breaking. She would soon say anything George wanted so she could get out of that interview room.

"You could, Rachel, but you aren't answering my questions truthfully. You can leave as soon as you are honest."

Translation, Ashley thought, *you won't get medical treatment until you tell me what I want to hear.*

"Okay." Rachel's voice was small. "What do you want me to say?"

"Oh no, Rachel. Not what I want you to say. All I want is the truth. And the truth is that you killed your newborn son, didn't you?"

Ashley rolled her eyes. It was a law enforcement trick used by many older officers to say, *all I want is the truth*, and then follow it with the "truth" they wanted to hear. Asking for the "truth" was only for the benefit of the recording. He didn't want that. Rachel had already tried to give it to him.

What he wanted was a confession. It was bullshit. If it wasn't overstepping the line, it was certainly toeing up to it.

"Umm hmmm."

"Is that a yes?" George's tone was laced with an excitement that was unusual for him. His expression was full of anticipation. He turned and looked back at Katie with a wink, a way of saying, *I've got her. Are you taking notes?*

Ashley hated everything about the interview, but she would love to see Katie's expression in that moment. Her eyes were probably alight with fury, lips dipped into a firm *who the fuck do you think you are* scowl.

"You washed your baby off, right? There in the hotel bathtub?"

Tears leaked from Rachel's eyes, falling onto the table. "Yes. He was covered in blood."

"He cried, didn't he?"

A long pause.

"Didn't he?"

"Yes."

"And then you placed him face down in the bathtub, didn't you?"

Rachel didn't answer aloud at first, but she did shake her head. A small, nearly imperceptible gesture. Something George, who didn't want to hear anything other than what he had expected to hear, wouldn't ever notice. But Ashley did. She noted the time stamp. It would be something she'd point out to the jury if she was unsuccessful in suppressing the video.

George slammed his hands down on the table. "Didn't you!"

Rachel pressed her lips together so firmly they turned white.

"Didn't you!" George shot out of his seat, surging toward her. "Answer my question or so help me..."

"Yes," Rachel said, flinching back, then crying out in pain from the movement.

"George!" Katie hissed.

The video footage jostled around as Katie stood and moved between George and Rachel. Ashley couldn't see Rachel anymore, only George's face twisted with fury. His expression was wild, mean.

"Stop this now..."

The recording went black, cutting Katie off mid-sentence. She had turned off the camera. Ashley wondered what had happened next. She would need to ask Rachel, and then address it in Katie's follow-up deposition. But that would come later. It was tertiary to the other information clearly contained in the video. The coerciveness of it.

Ashley popped the video out and put it back in its sleeve. She'd have Elena make a copy of it when she came in. It would be evidence for the suppression hearing. But first, she needed to draft the motion. She opened a word document and started doing just that.

Rachel's video "confession" would not come into evidence. Ashley felt sure of it. It was coerced. All of it. She hoped Judge Ahrenson would feel the same. If he didn't, and the jury heard that confession, Rachel was likely sunk. They'd launch an appeal, but only after Rachel spent several years in prison would they have an opportunity for a second bite at the apple. If they ever did get a second chance.

15

KATIE

65 days before trial

The wind whipped at Katie's cheeks as she made her way to City Hall, a few blocks north of the police station. It was early November, usually pretty mild in Iowa, but this year winter was well on its way.

Kate pulled up her coat collar, trying to cover the lower part of her face. She picked up her pace and headed for the side entrance of City Hall off Main Street. Few people knew about the entrance because it required a keycard. Katie, as a law enforcement officer, had one of the few keycards, handed out just in case someone in the east part of the building needed emergency assistance. She'd never used it for that purpose. There hadn't been cause to. Which she supposed was a good thing.

She waved her keycard in front of the reader. It beeped from red to green and she quickly opened the door, ducking out of the cold.

"Katie," a familiar voice said. "A little early for our meeting, aren't you?"

Katie looked up to connect with the penetrating blue-eyed gaze of none other than Forest Parker. As George had suggested, she'd scheduled a 12:30 meeting with him to discuss, and hopefully smooth over, his hatred of law enforcement. She didn't know how, exactly, she was going to achieve her goal, but she knew it wouldn't be by flirting her way into Forest's good graces, as George had suggested. Her job may be on the line, but she wasn't going to barter her dignity for it.

"I, umm..." Katie had planned to go to the county recorder's office for a copy of Rachel's birth certificate before meeting with Forest.

"Eager to see me, I suppose." Forest looked pointedly at his wristwatch. "I guess I have time for you now."

A retort formed in Katie's mind, but she didn't lend it voice. She was there for diplomatic reasons, not to add fuel to the fire.

"And using the employee entrance. How very..." He hesitated for a dramatically pregnant pause, tapping his index finger against his chin. "Entitled of you."

Katie narrowed her eyes. She didn't trust herself to speak. If she did, she'd say something like, "Entitled? Maybe you should check the Burberry tag on your coat before you start throwing around accusations." Because Forest was the son of an Iowa senator. A corporate farm family. Money and politics came as a silver spoon placed directly into his mouth.

"Anyway," Forest said, motioning for her to follow, "we might as well get this dreaded meeting done and over with."

She followed Forest into a small, tastefully furnished office. A mahogany executive desk sat across from two matching chairs. All looked handmade and expensive.

"Have a seat," Forest said.

Katie chose the chair closest to the door.

Forest started to close his office door, but Katie stopped him. "Leave it open a crack," she said. She knew better than to be alone with a male politician in his office. The rumors would surely lead to her termination. She vaguely wondered if that was George's true intention in sending her on this foolhardy errand.

"Right," Forest said, shooting Katie an appraising but not altogether nasty look.

Katie was silent as he sat down and positioned himself behind his desk. Her father—back in his business days—used to tell her that he never spoke first during a negotiation. It showed weakness. But Forest returned the silence. Apparently, his father had taught him the same.

Katie cleared her throat, reminding herself that her father's "business tactics" had landed him in a prison cell, so she would serve herself better by following her instincts. "Thank you for meeting with me."

"What, exactly, are we meeting for?"

Over the past few days, Katie had considered the things she would say to Forest. Even practiced some of them in the mirror. But none of them had quite come out right. She had no idea how to reach this man, let alone convince him to stop his full-on assault on the police department.

"I, umm..."

Katie cast her gaze around the room, searching for anything that was remotely relatable. Anything that was even close to common ground for the two of them. An enlarged photo of Forest standing shoulder to shoulder with Bill and Hillary Clinton hung next to a framed and unused law degree. Nothing there.

"You, umm, what?" He was growing impatient.

Then Katie saw it. A small photograph perched at the corner of Forest's desk. Katie leaned forward to get a better look. It was Forest, ten or so years younger, and an older man who looked very much the same. He had darker skin than Forest, but they both had the same blue eyes and sharp nose.

"Is this you?" Katie asked, nodding to the photograph.

Forest's eyes widened and his mouth dropped open. It was the classic deer-in-headlights look.

"I know this guy," Katie said, trying to remember where she had seen the man before. Then it clicked. "This is one of Officer Jackie's victims."

Last year, around Christmas, a former Brine police officer named John Jackie was blackmailing potential defendants instead of arresting them. He'd tell them that they wouldn't be charged if they paid him up front. It was these victims speaking out that led to Officer Jackie's arrest.

"Yeah. And he went to prison." Forest's voice held a bitter note.

Katie suddenly understood why Forest was hellbent on punishing the police department. Few of John Jackie's victims were later charged, because many of them were crimes like operating while intoxicated. Crimes that hinged on the officer's trustworthiness. But the man standing next to Forest in the photograph had embezzled from the local church. The witnesses were church members. This person, whoever he was to Forest, had been one of the few who was punished. It did seem unfair.

"I'm sorry," Katie said. "I remember him well. He was polite, remorseful." She looked up and met Forest's stony gaze. "I hope you know that I didn't want him incarcerated. I didn't think he deserved it. But the church elders felt otherwise."

The edge eased a bit from Forest's eyes.

"Who was he to you?"

Forest didn't answer. Judging by his reaction thus far, it was a well-kept secret. Maybe he would open up—forge the beginnings of a bond—if she entrusted him with one of her own secrets.

"My father is in Anamosa Prison." Katie had to force the words out of her mouth. It was a secret she told only a few people, and nothing felt natural about revealing it to an enemy. But it felt like the only way to take a step toward friendship.

One of Forest's heavy eyebrows lifted in intrigue. Encouragement for her to go on. She didn't know if she was saving the police department or making the biggest mistake of her life. Forest could end up politicizing it, using it against her. Against Chief Carmichael.

"Why?" It was the first thing Forest had said in a while. His voice had grown heavy, like he had been carrying a heavy burden. One he longed to release.

"Embezzlement. I was sixteen when it happened. I lost everything, including my mother. She ran off with some guy she met down at the country club. He had no interest in a teenage daughter, so..." She shrugged.

"You finished high school on your own?"

Katie nodded. "Then I took the first job I could. One that was the complete opposite of anything my father would ever want me to do. That's how I ended up as a small-town police officer."

A lightbulb ignited behind Forest's eyes. He leaned forward and said, "You're Kathleen Machello, aren't you?"

Katie nodded. "I changed my name as soon as I turned eighteen. Katie Mickey is close enough to my real name but not too close."

A silence descended upon the room. Forest's expression was unidentifiable. If he had an inclination toward poker, he was probably very good at it.

Finally, after what felt like forever, Forest leaned forward, casting his voice low, secretive. "Maybe we have more in common than I thought."

It was Katie's turn to quirk an eyebrow.

"That's my biological father." He nodded to the photograph. "I reconnected with him ten years ago."

"Biological? You're adopted?"

"Yes," Forest said. "As a baby. My mother died in childbirth and my father was too grief-stricken to raise a baby. So he put me up for adoption."

"That's where the Parker family comes in," Katie finished for him.

"Yes. My parents paid a good deal of hush money to keep the adoption quiet, but these things have a way of coming out."

Katie nodded. Skeletons had a hard time staying buried.

"And while I still love my adoptive family," Forest continued, "I have grown very close to my father, Peter Jennings."

That was his name. It had been nagging at Katie for the entire meeting, tugging at the tip of her tongue.

"He lost everything," Forest said. "Peter, that is. My parents could have helped him out, but he didn't want their assistance. He said they'd done enough for him by taking such good care of me." Forest swallowed hard, possibly fighting back tears. "That's what kind of guy he is. Always thinking of others."

Katie's view of the city councilman was changing. His life wasn't all perfection and politics. He'd lost someone he had only just begun to know. He was lonely in the same way she was.

"All the other victims got off with a slap on the wrist, if that. But not him. Not Peter. He went to prison." Forest sighed, picking up the picture and gazing down at the two smiling faces. "I blamed you for it. I thought that you should have cut him a break. Given him another chance, considering the circumstances." He looked up, his eyes meeting Katie's. They were wide, sparkling, pleading with her to understand.

"I didn't have a choice," Katie said, sighing. "I remember him well. I did feel bad for him—I still do—but the case was out of my hands at that point. Elizabeth had been arrested, too, so everything had gone to the attorney general, who chose to pursue charges since his victim was a church. I think it was more for political reasons than anything. To show that law enforcement wasn't broken."

Elizabeth Clement was the former Brine county attorney. She'd been involved in the blackmailing scheme and murder plots, all of which were carried out by others including John Jackie. Katie had thought all that was behind them. Obviously not. Forest Parker still believed law enforcement was broken and so did many others within the Brine community. The sentiment had driven Forest to punish the police department.

"He's not a bad person, he just made a mistake."

Katie quirked a small smile. "You sound like Ashley Montgomery."

"Ashley tried to help," Forest said, "but she couldn't get him completely out of it. She did cut his sentence in half, though."

"That's something." They were both silent for a long while, lost in their own thoughts. Finally, Katie spoke. "So, that's what has been driving your 'shortchange the cops' movement."

Forest shrugged. "If a thing's broken, throw it out and start fresh."

"But I solved those crimes. Remember? Both John Jackie and Elizabeth Clement were tried and convicted. At least your father wasn't the only one to go to prison."

"I know," Forest said, shaking his head. "It just didn't feel fair to me. Jackie and Clement's crimes were so much worse than my father's. They used a position of power to victimize people. My dad always intended to pay the church back."

"I didn't make any promises. Not to any of the witnesses," Katie said in her most reassuring tone. For now, she understood the root of Forest's anger. It was based on what he perceived to be the unfairness in the eventual outcome. That was something she could sympathize with. "I told them all, including your biological father, that I couldn't promise immunity. That the prosecutor could do what he wanted with the evidence provided by John Jackie's victims. Secretly, I did hope that the attorney general would go easy on them. Which he did, for the most part..."

Forest nodded, but he didn't make any concessions. Katie could only hope that at least some of what she had said had gotten through to him. The silence stretched out, filling the room.

"So..." Forest said. "We both know each other's secrets, don't we?" He leaned forward and his eyes twinkled in a mischievous, almost flirtatious way.

"I guess we do."

"Not to change subjects, but I assume you wanted to meet with me to discuss something other than our family histories."

Katie opened her mouth and then closed it again. If she ended the conversation now, they'd leave on good terms and there would be a foundation to build on the next time they spoke. The problem with such a diplomatic approach was that she was under a severe time crunch. She also wasn't all that good with diplomacy.

Katie took a deep breath, releasing it through her nose. *Here goes nothing*, she thought. "I wanted to talk to you about the budget for the police department too."

"I thought so," Forest said, leaning back in his chair and placing his hands behind his head. "I can't divulge much information now, but I can virtually promise that things will work out for *you* in the end."

Virtually promise? That was an optimistic way of saying *hope*, and hoping was for dreamers. She was a realist. "Does that mean the money will be reallocated to the police department?"

Forest shook his head. "No. It doesn't. But it does mean that you'll be fine. I can practically guarantee it."

Heat prickled at the back of Katie's neck. She was growing irritated with his non-answers—his politician responses. He was saying words that sounded like something but were packaged in a way that allowed an exit route if he chose not to keep to his word.

"I don't understand what you are saying."

"You will, Katie," Forest said, flashing a smile. "You will."

"You know what," Katie said, rising to her feet. "I've got something to follow up on in the recorder's office." She could not risk sitting there any longer. She would lose her patience with the politician and likely say something that would upset the delicate balance of their truce.

"It was nice talking to you," Forest said, his eyes sparkling.

"Likewise," Katie said as she moved toward the door.

"Katie," Forest called after her.

She paused and looked back at him.

"Don't get too worked up about what's happening at the police department. It will work out in the end. To both of our advantages. You'll see."

Katie had no idea what he meant. There was absolutely no way it could *work out* for both sides. They were completely at odds. Instead of arguing the point, which would get her nowhere fast, she continued toward the door and called, "Have a good day," over her shoulder. She'd have to figure out how to deal with him later. For now, she needed to get to the recorder's office.

Katie headed down the long hallway toward the staircase, passing the two other city councilmembers' offices. Both were men, but they were very different than Forest Parker. One of them was a staunch Republican and in full support of the police department, the other a swing vote that had been swinging in Forest's direction more often than not as of late.

The door to the Republican's office was closed and a large sign hung on it that read *Support Our Boys in Blue*. One word stood out. *Boys*. Katie looked down at her uniform. It, too, was blue. Yet she didn't fit in the good ol' boys club that controlled much of Brine's upper echelon. She sighed and kept walking. Sometimes she didn't feel as though she fit anywhere.

The county recorder's office was on the second floor. Katie took the steps two at a time. A clerk greeted her warmly as she stepped inside.

"Hello, Katie. How can I help you?"

"Yes. Keisha. Wonderful to see you. This job suits you."

Keisha had graduated a year early from Brine Senior High School, taking night classes in order to do it. All so she could get a "real job" with medical insurance instead of working at the animal shelter. Katie and Ashley had helped her get the job with the county recorder the moment a position had opened.

"Thanks." Keisha wasn't one to be influenced by flattery.

"I'm here to get a copy of a birth certificate. Not an official one. Just a copy."

"Okay," Keisha said, her eyes narrowing. "I'm not sure I'm supposed to do that."

"True. But then I'll just get a county attorney subpoena and come back for the same thing. It'll save us all a lot of time if you do it now."

"All right," Keisha said warily. "Whose is it?"

"Rachel Smithson."

Keisha blinked several times. "I know you don't mean that girl they have locked up for baby killing."

"I do."

"I thought she was from Waukee or something."

A wry smile spread across Katie's lips. She'd been surprised to discover the news herself. "Rachel Smithson grew up in Waukee, but her mother gave birth in Brine." What nobody understood was why Mrs. Smithson had driven an hour away to give birth when there were plenty of excellent hospitals in the Des Moines metro area. That was something Katie intended to figure out.

"I'll look," Keisha said, stepping away from the counter and disappearing into the back.

She was gone for a good five minutes but returned with a document, holding it away from her body as though it were radioactive. She slid it across the counter to Katie.

"Thank you," Katie said, looking down at the document.

Then her breath caught. Next to "mother," the document read, *Lyndsay Smithson*. The "father" line was blank. So, there it was. A possible reason for Lyndsay to drive to a small-town hospital to birth a baby. An attempt to avoid her husband. To keep his name off Rachel's birth certificate. But why? And had Rachel followed the same reasoning when she checked into that hotel in Brine?

It was time for Katie to have a chat with Lyndsay Smithson. Outside the presence of her husband. The only problem was that Isaac Smithson was always around. He would never allow his wife to speak for herself, especially if it had the potential to incriminate him. She'd need to come up with something creative. At the moment, no ideas came to mind.

16

ASHLEY

64 days before trial

Ashley gripped the wheel of her SUV tightly as she drove toward Des Moines. The radio was set to low, just enough to cut through the silence. A distraction rather than entertainment. Thoughts of Tom consumed her concentration. Still, she hadn't heard a word from him. Not by text, message, or mail, aside from the baffling package left on her front porch. She was at her wits' end.

"I'm going to give him a piece of my mind," Ashley said to herself. "Then I'm out."

Unless Tom had a really good reason for his behavior, their relationship was over. Their friendship, too. Over the past several days, she'd cycled through every emotion, switching from fear, to sadness, to helplessness, to fury, then back to fear.

A stray piece of hair fell into her eyes, tickling her nose. Ashley brushed it aside, and as she did, the sleeve of her sweater inched up, exposing the bruising that spread all the way from her hand, down her wrist, and toward her elbow. She hadn't paid much attention to the bruising because she had thought it was starting to heal. But it was back again in full force. Dark purple blotches, like tiny pools of blood just below her skin.

It had to be stress, right? The same cause as the nosebleeds and chronic fatigue. Nothing else had changed, at least as far as she knew. And she'd read online that stress can cause nosebleeds. Granted, she'd read it on a webpage written by a man who called himself Dr. Awesome. It wasn't exactly a scholarly journal, but it served its purpose. It explained her problems in a way that wasn't *dying of a serious disease*, which was good enough for her.

If it was stress related—and she hoped it was—then she might as well get used to the symptoms. Rachel's case was still in the discovery phase and there was a lot of work left to do. All murder cases were difficult, but Rachel's was exceptionally soul sucking. Partially due to its nature, but also because Ashley was growing fond of her client. Even though the allegations, if true, were difficult to stomach, she still felt drawn to the girl.

But Rachel's case was not Ashley's only source of stress. She was also dealing with Tom. He had created unnecessary anxiety. Tension that she could address. Or at least try to. Ashley had overreacted when she heard Harper laughing in the background, but his response was ridiculous. He was avoiding her, but he couldn't keep it up forever. If he wanted to end the relationship, then fine. It would hurt, but she'd survive. This weird limbo where he ignored her calls while sending her homemade chocolates had to end.

Tom lived in an apartment building not far from Drake University. It was once a large, grand house with gleaming white pillars and sprawling gardens, but it had long ago been broken down into four separate apartments, a shell of its former self. Like a once beautiful girl, grown wrinkled and bent with age. Yes, the old pillars still existed, but large splotches of paint had peeled away, leaving the yellow, rotting wood below on full display.

Ashley parked in the circular drive out front. Hers was one of seven other vehicles. Tom's truck was among them, but she didn't recognize the others. Not that she'd expected to.

"You can do this," Ashley said to herself as she sat in her vehicle, taking deep breaths and gathering her strength.

She spent her time leading up to today's trip to Des Moines thinking of ways she would confront Tom. Things she would say, insults she would fling. She'd developed a script of sorts. A list of words strung together to express the full extent of her hurt and anger, all of which had disappeared from her mind. But she couldn't keep putting off the confrontation.

"Now or never," Ashley said to herself.

She issued one last sigh and unbuckled her seatbelt. If she didn't force herself out of the car, she never would. She'd lose her nerve. *That would solve nothing*, she reminded herself. *I'm here to put an end to this relationship limbo for good or for bad*. Her purpose was to resolve one source of stress. Nothing more. Besides, procrastination always made things worse.

The car door closed with a bang, and gravel crunched beneath Ashley's feet as she approached the front door. Everything was still, silent. It was still early, only 8:30 a.m. While Des Moines was no college town, this area was occupied by mostly college students. Few would be awake. Three steps led up to the front porch. They groaned a heavy, ominous protest as Ashley ascended.

Four mailboxes hung by the main entrance. Ashley scanned them all, looking for Tom's last name. She had never been to his apartment. He had always driven to Brine on the weekends. It had started out as him offering, then it just became almost an unspoken rule. Now that she thought about it, Tom hadn't even invited her to see his place. Not once. It was odd, but she had been too busy to notice before now. Which, she supposed, had probably contributed to their relationship woes.

The third mailbox had two names posted just below the number 3. *Archie*, Tom's last name, and *Langston*, a name Ashley did not recognize. A heavy sense of foreboding settled in her stomach. Tom had never mentioned a roommate, a fact she should have known if not as his girlfriend, then as a friend. It wasn't an overlooked trivial matter that could easily be explained away. This Langston person lived with him, yet Tom had failed to mention him even once. He had intentionally kept her in the dark about this person. But why?

Ashley's stomach roiled, her insides twisting. Part of her needed to know who this person was, discover the reason for Tom's lies of omission, while the other part of her screamed for her to *leave now*. To never ask, never learn the truth. *Running won't solve anything*, she reminded herself. She was there to solve a problem. Her stress. To end an unbearable romantic purgatory. She gathered her wits and stepped up to his door, knocking two times.

All was silent for a long moment. Maybe nobody was home. But why was Tom's car there? Then she heard footsteps. Not Tom's heavy footfalls, but they weren't dainty either. An unfamiliar cadence that stoked Ashley's anxieties. It had to be the roommate. Ashley's heart raced at the thought. But her purpose for the visit was to confront the unknown. While this particular unknown was unanticipated, it was now part of the equation.

The footsteps stopped in front of the door. There was a long pause as the person inside studied Ashley through the peephole. A moment passed, then two, before a lock clicked, the door swung open, and a familiar face greeted Ashley. She sucked in a sharp intake of breath.

"Lydia," Ashley said, almost breathless.

"Harper," the woman said. It wasn't a denial but a correction.

Ashley shook her head, disbelieving. The woman standing before Ashley was the spitting image of her former foster sister, only older. She had the same large, doe-like eyes, each a deep mahogany brown. Long eyelashes that fluttered in the same way they had so many years earlier, back when they were both ten. While no longer cut in the childish style of Lydia's youth, the hair color was still a dark chocolate brown.

Ashley's eyes traveled up to the woman's hairline, searching for an oddly shaped mole. Two round ears and a head like Mickey Mouse. It was there, just peeking out from beneath a fringe of bangs. "No. It's you, Lydia."

The woman quirked a smile. "Harper. Lydia. Langston. My *parents* changed my name when they adopted me." She spat out the word *parents* like it was poisonous. A disgusting word that she loathed to use. She leaned against the doorframe, picking at her nails. "They let me keep my old name as a middle name. So gracious of them, right?" Her words were sarcastic, biting.

Ashley took a step back, shaking her head.

"Thought you'd never see me again, didn't you?" Lydia's eyes met Ashley's as a devilish grin spread across her perfectly proportioned face. "Surprise," she said while mocking Ashley with jazz hands.

Ashley's heart pounded so hard that she felt the sound was audible. She needed to get out of there. Away from this psychopath. But Lydia was not Ashley's reason for coming, Tom was. She was not leaving like this. It wouldn't solve anything. Running now would only make things worse, and she was tired of the nosebleeds. She didn't need an ulcer on top of it. She gathered her nerves and steeled her emotions.

"Where's Tom?"

"In *our* room," Lydia said, chuckling darkly.

Our room? What. The. Literal. Fuck.

"Tom!" Ashley shouted at the top of her lungs. "Get out here. Now!" Her voice rose several octaves to a near screech. This desperation was completely unlike her. Distraught to the point of unrecognizability.

A few moments later a door flew open and Tom came stumbling out, rubbing his eyes. "What is it..." His sleep-garbled words trailed off when he saw Ashley in the doorway. He sucked in a deep breath and his eyes popped open, an expression that would be comical if Ashley's world wasn't crashing down around her.

There was a long beat of silence as Ashley and Tom eyed one another. Lydia stepped aside. Not out of kindness or deference, but to watch. To place herself front and center to the show, the demise of Ashley and Tom's romance.

"You lied to me," Ashley finally said, breaking the uneasy silence.

"I..."

"You've been avoiding my calls and texts for a week. *A week!*" Ashley balled her hands into fists, her fingernails biting into her palms. "I came here to apologize. To work things out." That wasn't what Ashley had told herself on the drive up, but now that she'd uttered the words, she knew they were true.

"Missed calls?" Tom quirked his head to the side as though confused.

"Don't give me that bullshit. I've called and left about a thousand voice-mails. I've sent probably a hundred text messages. I even tried email. But nothing. Radio silence. I finally drove up here to make sure you weren't dead and what do I find?"

"Ashley," Tom said, taking a slow, tentative step forward. He kept his movements deliberate, hands raised in the air as though approaching an angry tiger. His beautiful face had contorted into something unrecognizable. He was no longer lovely. At least not to Ashley.

Ashley backed away, gesturing for him to stay away. "What do I find?" she repeated, taking another step closer to her vehicle. "I find you playing house with my former foster sister. The one who tortured me as a kid. You know all about her. I told you. Yet you didn't think it was important to inform me that you're living with her. You're unbelievable."

"Foster sister?" Tom shook his head. "I didn't know..."

"You didn't know," Ashley scoffed. "Maybe it might have come up if you bothered to mention that you had a roommate at all. But you kept that a secret as well."

"It wasn't like that. I couldn't afford a place, so I found a roommate. That's it, I swear. I didn't tell you because I didn't want to upset you."

"Well, congratulations, Tom. You've failed miserably. If that was, in fact, your goal. But here's another potential goal. You wanted your cake and to eat it too."

"Cake?"

"Good God." Ashley threw her hands up in exasperation. "It's a saying, you fucking moron. Meaning you wanted to try out something new with Lydia, but keep me on the backburner in case it didn't work out."

"Lydia?"

"Oh, my God." Ashley ran her hands through her hair, gripping it at its base and tugging. She took several deep, calming breaths, pulling herself together. Could he really be that dumb? "Save your bullshit for someone else," she said as she turned on her heel and marched toward her SUV. "And do me a favor," she called over her shoulder. "Stay the fuck away from me. We are through."

Ashley didn't look back as she ripped her SUV door open and jumped in the driver's seat. She couldn't. If she did, she'd see his face and she might lose her nerve. But this, Lydia living in his house, was unforgivable. Anger and adrenaline surged through her veins, guiding her actions. Soon, both of those emotions would melt away, leaving an impenetrable darkness in their wake. She would not let Lydia or Tom witness her break. She had to get out of there before they had the chance.

Tom approached Ashley's car, but she flipped it into gear and stepped on the gas. The vehicle took off, rounding the circular drive, skidding before turning onto the main road. Driving as fast as the speed limit would allow, Ashley tore out of the neighborhood and onto Highway 235, headed toward Waukee and Brine. Tears rolled down her cheeks. She didn't wipe them away or try to stifle them. She would indulge the sadness for a few moments before pulling herself together for long enough to pick up those calls to service from the Waukee Police Department.

Then she'd drive home and allow herself to fall completely apart. Her eyes flicked to the passenger seat. The box of homemade candies that Tom had left on her doorstep was still there. She'd eaten a few earlier that week, but the majority still remained. She grabbed the box and ripped it open, shoving a chocolate peanut butter ball into her mouth. It was delicious, melting in her mouth, but it was also terrible in an unhealthy binge self-loathing sort of way. She swallowed it and grabbed another.

In the fifteen minutes it took to drive from Des Moines to the Waukee Police Department, she'd finished the entire box. At least twenty chocolate pieces. She parked and got out of her vehicle. As she approached the front door, her stomach twisted, an apparent protest to the sugar rush. A moment later, her nose began to gush blood. She sank to her knees, searching in her bag for a tissue.

Once she found a Kleenex and pressed it to her nose, her stomach twisted again. She was going to vomit. Crawling toward the edge of the side-walk, she vomited. She stared, wide-eyed with shock. It was full of blood. She tried to push back up to her feet, but she didn't have the strength. Her heart raced, pounding so quickly that it felt as though it was skipping beats.

Her stomach twisted again, and she braced for her body to vomit up more blood. What was happening to her? She needed help, but the front door to the police station seemed so far away. She didn't think she had the energy to take a single step, let alone the fifty it would take just to get inside.

No, she decided, *it's quiet out here. Peaceful.*

For somewhere in her soul, a part of her knew that she was dying. Unlike common belief, her life did not flash before her eyes. She did not see visions of her mother laughing or her dogs snuggling up next to her on the couch. There was no fear or trepidation. Merely acceptance. Her life was over, and she'd done the best she could with it. She tried to do right by others. To help those who had nobody else. That was enough for her. Her stomach twisted again, and she rolled into the fetal position, pulling her knees up to her chest. The pain was unbearable. Death was a welcome release.

17

KATIE

Katie had arranged to meet Josh, the officer from the Waukee Police Department, for lunch. Since she hadn't lived in the Des Moines area for many years, she had agreed to meet him at the police department and follow him to the restaurant.

Josh had offered to meet her somewhere in Brine, but she was quick to refuse. There were few places to eat in such a small town, all of which would be packed with people Katie knew. The rumors of her "date" with an out-of-towner would last for months. Katie had successfully kept herself out of the Brine rumor mill for the past six years, and she intended to keep it that way. It was a necessary choice if she cared to keep her father's skeletons buried.

Katie pulled up outside the Waukee Police Department at eleven on the dot. She was in her off-duty vehicle even though this meeting was strictly business. Gas was expensive and Chief Carmichael didn't have the funds to pay for an officer to drive out of town.

The chief was shifting the expenses to his employees, just like school districts did with teachers, but that wasn't his fault. There was no other option. Yes, she and Forest Parker had come to a tentative truce, but that hadn't translated into monetary relief. At least not yet, but it was also possible that it never would. Forest's "shortchange the cops" movement had a lot of traction. That wasn't something easily changed, even with Forest's silver tongue.

Katie's meeting with Josh would be an early lunch. Eat, discuss Rachel Smithson, and back to Brine by one. She had work to do if she wanted to tie up all the potential loose ends before the trial. She had the calls to service, but she hadn't had time to read through them yet. With so few officers in town, she was almost always assisting with another call. Crime didn't stop just because she was busy. She was only able to make this meeting work because it was her day off.

As Katie made the turn into the parking lot, she noticed that it was large and recently resurfaced. Quite a few vehicles were parked there, most clustered near the door, but a few spaced further out throughout the lot. All were trucks except for one sports utility vehicle. A white Tahoe that looked just like Ashley's vehicle.

No, Katie thought, *it can't be Ashley. Why would she be all the way out here?*

Katie squinted, but she wasn't able to read the plate until she drove a little closer. It had Brine County tags. It was Ashley. She wondered if she would bump into her friend while inside. Part of her hoped that she would, but a larger part desired the opposite. They were both dealing with high levels of stress that could lead to short tempers and easy arguments. Some of it because of Rachel Smithson, but they each had outside anxieties as well. Ashley was dealing with Tom's shenanigans and Katie was worried about her job security.

Katie parked near Ashley's Tahoe and hopped out of her vehicle, heading toward the police station. It had recently snowed, but the parking lot had been cleared and salted heavily enough that the granules crunched beneath her boots. The lot was freshly paved, a sign that Waukee wasn't struggling for cash. At least not like the Brine PD.

If the parking lot upkeep hadn't given away Waukee's superior fiscal shape, the building itself would have. It was two floors high, built in a modern fashion that was virtually all gleaming windows. Katie wondered whose job it was to clean all those windows from the exterior. Someone had to do it regularly for they sparkled in the late-morning sunshine.

Katie had parked far away, like she always did. She liked to stretch her legs throughout the day. Parking at the edge of a lot was an easy way to get a little bit of exercise without feeling like she was, in fact, exercising. Every step counted. As she approached the building, it seemed to grow in size and grandeur, further putting Brine's little law enforcement center to shame.

She stepped onto the sidewalk, following the evergreen bushes that lined it. As she rounded the trees, the sidewalk approaching the front door came into view. Katie's gaze shifted to the ground and she froze. Someone was there. No, not just anyone.

"Ashley," Katie cried. Her voice was high-pitched, foreign to her own ears.

Ashley lay near the edge of the sidewalk, blood surrounding her. Katie dashed to her best friend's side.

"Ashley," she said, shaking her shoulder. "What happened?"

Ashley's eyes blinked open, shifting toward Katie. Blood covered her face, but Katie couldn't discern the cause of it. There was so much, but no obvious injuries.

"Did someone hurt you?"

Ashley's eyes fluttered closed again. Katie had taken some medical courses throughout her years in law enforcement. A Brine police officer's job was not solely crime and punishment. Often, she was expected to act as an ambulance as well. Not for the first time, she was grateful for all the extra training. It made her mind switch from petrified, grieving friend to the automatic movements of a professional.

She bent over Ashley, checking for a pulse. It was present, but weak.

"I'll be right back," Katie said in her most reassuring voice.

Katie needed help, but she did not want to move Ashley for fear of causing more damage. If the cause of Ashley's condition was physical, like an assault or a gunshot, movement in the wrong direction could make the difference between paralysis and full recovery.

Katie ran to the building, her hands balled into fists. The cold air stung her lungs, forcing a cough from her chest, but she didn't stop until she burst through the opulent glass front door. A reception desk sat a few feet away, just inside the high-ceilinged grand entrance. A man and two women sat behind the desk. They all looked up, but nobody greeted her.

"Call for an ambulance," Katie said. She sounded calm, cool, collected, although she was certain her appearance was wild.

"Ambulance?" one of the women asked. She was the oldest of the three with curly silver hair and thick eyeglasses.

"Yes. Someone is lying out front. She's alive, but I don't know for how long."

The man picked up the phone, speaking into an intercom. "Medical. Medical to the front entrance. Emergency. I repeat. Emergency." He lowered the intercom, his eyes locking on Katie's. "This better not be a joke."

"Joke?" Katie said, shaking her head. "Why would I..."

"Because all hell is about to break loose around here," the man said. "A call like that"—he pointed to a nearby intercom—"means all hands on deck. You'll be in real trouble, little missy, if this is some kind of prank."

Little Missy? Katie thought irritably. She straightened and glared at the man, ready to launch into him. Did he really think he could speak that way to her just because she looked young and was female? What was wrong with people? But before she could open her mouth to protest, all hell did break loose.

The sleepy station burst to life, like a vehicle jumpstarted. People came streaming out of offices and into the hallways. Most wore police-officer blue, but others donned white, indicating medical personnel. Waukee actually had an on-staff medical team. If Katie hadn't been so worried about Ashley, she would have spent some time pondering the type of budget that could afford such a luxury. Instead, she turned and ran back out the front doors, crouching down at Ashley's side.

"Help is on the way," Katie said, taking Ashley's nearly frozen hand into her own.

An ambulance pulled up out front and several people in Waukee EMT uniforms hopped out. An additional group of people in white also streamed out the front door, meeting the EMTs. Reluctantly, Katie stepped back to give them unfettered access to her friend. She couldn't do anything for Ashley anyway.

The medical team moved methodically, a choreographed dance of people working in tandem. Each person knew their job and executed it without the bark of orders first filling the air. There was no debate about who would drive and who would administer emergency care. In fact, it was eerily silent aside from the shuffle of feet and scratch of Velcro. Nothing like the chaos and scrambling that came with the mostly volunteer EMTs in Brine.

A woman broke away from the group, approaching Ashley. Her hair was slicked back into a tight ponytail, her expression stern. "What happened?"

"I'm a Brine police officer."

The woman eyed Katie's jeans and Stanford sweatshirt, one of the many gifts her father had given her for her sixteenth birthday. Back then, they'd both believed the sky was the limit. The ratty condition of the old sweatshirt told the truth of Katie's adult life.

Katie zipped up her jacket, suddenly self-conscious. "I'm off duty. I came here to meet with a Waukee officer about a case. And I found Ashley here."

"You know her?" the woman asked.

"She's a public defender in Brine. I'm a friend of hers."

"What's her name?"

"Ashley Montgomery."

"How well do you know her?"

"Pretty well."

"Does she have any known medical conditions?"

"No."

"Is she on blood thinners?"

"Not that I know of."

"Okay." The woman nodded. "Thank you." Then she turned on her heel and hopped in the back of the ambulance.

Although it seemed like forever, the medical team had Ashley on a stretcher and in the back of the ambulance in a few minutes. The doors slammed shut and the driver began walking toward the front of the ambulance.

"Wait," Katie yelled, running toward him. "Where are you taking her?"

"Methodist. Downtown Des Moines. She's in pretty bad shape," the man said as he jumped into the driver's seat.

Katie nodded and stepped back. She watched as the vehicle drove off, lights flashing and sirens blaring. Tears pricked at Katie's eyes and trickled down her face, forming trails. Katie's heart broke as the ambulance turned and disappeared out of sight. She didn't know if this would be the last time she ever saw her friend alive. They had been avoiding one another since Rachel Smithson's arrest, but Katie now regretted that decision. If Ashley didn't make it, she would never forgive herself for all those lost moments.

"Do you know her or do you have that big of a heart?" a voice said from beside Katie.

Katie jumped and spun. A man stood next to her. His hair was dark brown and buzzed nearly to the scalp. He was handsome in a boyish way with apple cheeks and full lips. She'd thought that she had been alone. But, of course, she wasn't. People swirled all around, trying to figure out how a half-dead woman found her way to the front entrance of a police station. It was a potential crime scene, and these were police officers. She would be doing the same thing had something like this occurred in Brine.

"Umm, yeah," Katie said, turning back to where she had last seen the ambulance. "She's my friend."

"Do you want to go check on her?"

Katie nodded. In that moment, she wanted nothing more in the world than to go to the hospital.

"I'll take you."

Katie turned, facing the man. As she looked at him straight on, she realized he was even more handsome than she had previously thought. Almond-shaped eyes. Skin the deep gold of fresh sand, barely kissed by the sun. Arm muscles bulging beneath his blue uniform. He looked like a model in a calendar titled "Police Hotties," not a true-life officer.

"I'm sorry," Katie said, shaking her head. "Who are you?" She didn't make a habit of accepting rides from strangers.

"Josh," he said, a wide grin splitting across his face, displaying a mouth full of perfectly straight teeth. "And you must be Katie."

"Umm, yes. How did you know?"

"I never forget a voice," Josh said with a wink.

"Right," Katie said warily. "I appreciate the offer, but I think I can find my way to the hospital."

"Nonsense," Josh said. He pulled a pair of keys out of his pocket and clicked a button. The front lights of a nearby fire-engine red Ford F150 flashed. "My truck is right here."

Katie's eyes darted toward the back of the lot, where her beat-up Impala was parked. She could run to her car, but that would waste precious seconds. Besides, she was a little self-conscious considering the obvious expense of his vehicle compared to hers.

"Fine," Katie said.

She headed for the passenger door, setting a quick pace. She wanted to get to Ashley as soon as possible, and she also wanted to prevent him from opening her door for her. He seemed like the type of man to find that kind of behavior chivalrous rather than degrading. But she was perfectly capable of opening a door. A man's assistance was not required.

Josh hopped into the driver's seat and buckled his seatbelt. He glanced at her to see that she was buckled in, then he took off, heading for the hospital. He had satellite radio, and it was set to a '90s alternative station called Lithium. Nirvana, "All Apologies," was playing. A song and station that Katie liked, but it didn't fit with Josh's frat boy persona. She wondered vaguely if there was more to him or if his choice in music was just a fluke, but then her mind turned sharply back to Ashley.

Katie's stomach twisted into knots as her mind whirred, shuffling through the potential scenarios. Was an angry victim of one of Ashley's clients hiding in the bushes? Had that person jumped out and stabbed her? Or maybe it had been a stalker. Or was it a drive-by shooting targeting the Waukee Police Department? Maybe Ashley was simply at the wrong place at the wrong time.

In truth, Katie had no idea what had happened. She didn't even know why Ashley was in Waukee. So many questions, all of which would have to wait. First, she had to make sure that Ashley recovered. That was most important. Then she would find the guilty party and make the person pay.

18

RACHEL

The toilet in Rachel's cell ran. A constant hissing sound that formed the background of her new life. To many, the sound would be grating. But to Rachel, it was the music of freedom. An untraditional use of the word, considering the bars surrounding her, but Rachel didn't think in the same way as others. For her freedom was from those things that were not controlled. In jail, everything had a control. Life was regimented, and there was a sort of liberty in that. Not a freedom of the body, but of the mind.

She settled into the corner of her cell she had dubbed her reading corner. It consisted of two blankets and a lumpy pillow. All gifts from Kylie once the jailer had determined that Rachel wouldn't use the blankets to hang herself. Rachel had finished her last book and moved on to a new one. *Tuesday Mooney Talks to Ghosts*. It involved an adventure. A great treasure hunt, and a main character who was an outcast, like Rachel.

The book was almost new. The spine was barely cracked before Rachel had gotten her hands on it. It had been thoroughly broken in now that Rachel had read and reread each and every chapter. She wanted to remember the adventure. To trap the feeling of weightlessness that came along with a good story. To bottle it up to use in the future in case the trial didn't go as she expected.

A few minutes into her book, Rachel heard the telltale sounds of boots against pavement. Normally, that sound would instill fear, for men were usually the wearers of heavy, steel-toed boots like that. But men weren't allowed in the women's side of the jail.

"Lunch," Kylie said as she rounded the corner.

Kylie was balancing a large tray in one hand while clutching something in the other. As she approached, Rachel realized Kylie had a stack of letters.

"I've got some mail for you, too," Kylie said, opening Rachel's cell door and handing her the tray.

Lunch wasn't anything to brag about, but it was food. Today was a turkey sandwich. Several slices of meat and processed cheese stacked on white bread. It came with green beans. They were bright green and slimy, indicating they came straight from the can. The peach slices were covered in heavy syrup. Also from a can.

"Thank you," Rachel said, and she meant it. Kylie had been so kind to her. Part of her wished that she could stay in this jail forever, although she knew that was impossible. The only two options were release or prison.

"And here are your letters."

Kylie handed Rachel three envelopes. All of them had been sliced open, a clean cut with a letter opener. The jailers read through all mail before delivering it to make sure that inmates weren't violating protective orders or trying to smuggle in contraband.

Rachel looked down at the letters, turning them over in her hands. She wasn't sure that she wanted to read them, but she would. She always did. Some of them were awful, full of threats and accusations, but Kylie had told her that was how Ashley's letters had been when she was in jail. Rachel had been shocked when Kylie told her the story about Ashley. That her attorney was jailed, wrongly accused of committing two murders. Ashley had occupied the very same cell as Rachel. It made her feel closer to the attorney. A shared bond that few others could understand.

"Kylie," Rachel said, looking up at the jailer. "Have you seen Ashley?"

Usually, her attorney came in the mornings. Rachel had grown accustomed to the routine of Ashley's visits. Trust had built, and Rachel was almost ready to open up to her. To tell her everything.

"No, but I'll see if I can track her down."

"Thank you," Rachel said gratefully.

"I'll be back for your tray in thirty minutes or so," Kylie said, nodding toward Rachel's lunch. "Hopefully I'll have an Ashley update by then."

Kylie turned and left. Rachel picked up her sandwich and turned to the letters. The first was from some religious leader. A Thomas something or other. She scanned the letter. It was nearly identical to the other letters from men in similar positions. Dire warnings that her soul was in danger of damnation. Advice to repent. Followed by an invitation to visit her in jail to help invite the Lord back into her heart.

Rachel tossed the letter aside. She knew other religious men. Men who claimed to have the Lord on their side. They weren't always good people. Rachel knew from experience. Her *father* was religious. And Rachel would not willingly invite his "Lord" into her heart. Never. She'd rather risk hell and damnation.

The second letter was from a man who called himself "Jack Daniels." Was it a pseudonym or did the man's parents actually hate him enough to name him after liquor? Or perhaps it was the opposite. Maybe they couldn't think of anything they loved more than liquor, so they named him after it. Either scenario was nearly as sad as Rachel's past. *Nearly*, but not quite.

Jack's letter was riddled with incorrect punctuation and misspellings to the point of distraction, but Rachel was able to understand the sentiment behind the misspelled words and garbled grammar. Jack thought Rachel was a baby killer and he wanted her to face the electric chair. His wish was not a possibility. Ashley had already told Rachel the potential punishments. The death penalty was not an option in Iowa.

Rachel tossed Jack's letter on top of the religious letter, turning to the last one. She opened it quickly, unfolding its contents. She gasped. The penmanship. She recognized it. Slanting cursive so perfect it could be a Microsoft Word font. It belonged to her father. The letter wasn't signed, but the writing was unmistakable. It said, *"A life for a life."* That was it.

She dropped it, fingers tingling as though the letter had been soaked in poison. That paper had only recently been in his hands. Touched by him. His hot breath bearing down on it as he scratched his words, his threats, into it. Fear encircled her heart, gripping hold and squeezing. But then it was gone as quickly as it had come. For she had realized that this was the worst he could do to her. Write letters. All his power was gone. She'd stolen it from him. The thought made her want to cackle like a movie villain.

Footsteps in the hallway tore Rachel's attention from her thoughts. It hadn't been thirty minutes already, had it? The steps came quicker than usual, as though Kylie was moving at a near run. The jailer rounded the corner, a stricken expression on her face.

"What's wrong?" Rachel said, rising to her feet and coming to the bars.

"It's Ashley," Kylie said, eyes wide and wild. "She's in the hospital."

19

KATIE

63 days before trial

It was a difficult night. Katie had stayed in the hospital waiting room, hoping for any news. Praying to every God from every conceivable religion, begging for Ashley's condition to turn out to be something minor. In her heart, she knew otherwise. Hospitals didn't admit patients overnight for minor issues. They didn't have the space or the staff.

She couldn't sleep and her mind continued whirring, her thoughts darkening with every passing moment. Hope seemed more and more fleeting with each click of the second hand. The doctors hadn't told her a thing, even though she identified herself as a police officer as well as a friend. The secrecy worried Katie more than anything. It meant that Ashley wasn't awake.

To keep her mind from spiraling, Katie decided to turn to the PDF document that Josh had emailed her a few days earlier. Josh and the volume of calls to the Smithson residence was the whole reason she had driven to Waukee, which was probably the same for Ashley. Maybe something was hidden in those pages that had motivated someone to harm Ashley.

Katie pulled out her phone and clicked on the email icon, scrolling back a few days. She clicked on the email from Josh and opened the file. Tiny words populated the miniature screen. She zoomed in and brought the device closer to her face. It was going to be difficult to read, but she had to make do. There was no other option.

It started with the most recent calls to service at the Smithson residence and went backward in time, with the oldest calls on the very last page. Katie began reading the most recent call, which occurred the day before Rachel checked into the hotel to have her baby.

1534 hours: A call came to the emergency line. An individual who identified herself as Ava Townsand stated that she was walking her dog past 1210 Destiny Drive, Waukee, Iowa, when she heard a woman screaming.

1535 hours: The first car on scene arrived, Badge Number 145, Joshua Martin. 145 notified dispatch that he could hear audible sobbing coming from inside the house. 145 was told to wait for backup before attempting to make contact.

1536 hours: Backup arrived, badge numbers 100 and 87. They accompanied 145 to the front door.

1537 hours: 145 knocked on the door. Crying could still be heard from outside the residence.

1539 hours: Isaac Smithson answered the door. The crying grew exponentially louder when the door opened. Isaac refused the officers entry and identified the crying as a hysterical teenager. The Smithsons have a daughter, Rachel, who is a senior at the local high school.

1540 hours: 145 requested to speak with Rachel or Lyndsay Smithson. Isaac refused to retrieve either. 145 shouted Rachel's and Lyndsay's names over Isaac's shoulder. Nobody answered and the crying stopped.

1541: All officers left the residence. They did not have enough information to obtain a warrant.

End of interaction

Katie lowered her phone, stunned at the contents of this first call. It said so much and so little all at once. She had spent plenty of time with both Rachel and Lyndsay during interviews. Their personalities could only be described as demure. They were not the type of women to draw attention to themselves. Certainly not by screaming loud enough to alert a passerby without cause.

Katie turned to the second call from a few weeks earlier.

1400 hours: Call from Waukee Public Schools to the non-emergency line. The school therapist, Michael Frank, reported that Rachel Smithson, a student at the school, had appeared for an appointment with visible bruising up and down her arms. She would not disclose the cause of the bruising, but based on his previous interactions with the family, he was concerned that it involved child abuse.

1430 hours: Car 145, Joshua Martin, responded to the school. Mr. Frank reported that Rachel had grown suspicious of his questioning and left school. He reported that she left on foot only a few moments earlier and was likely headed home.

1435 hours: 145 caught up to Rachel just outside her house, 1210 Destiny Drive, Waukee, Iowa. Rachel wore a large coat even though the weather was mild. 145 requested that she remove her coat and she complied. Rachel had on a long-sleeve, oversized sweater. 145 reported that she appeared to carry a significant amount of weight in her stomach and nowhere else.

1436 hours: Rachel displayed her arms, and they were covered in bruises, some yellow with age and some that looked fresh. 145 took photographs, which are included.

Katie scrolled to the next page to see the pictures. She gasped, placing a hand over her mouth. Deep, angry bruises ran all the way up Rachel's arms. They were a dark purplish-red, like blood pooling below the surface of her skin.

"What is it?" a familiar voice asked.

Katie turned and met Josh's gaze. Just the person she wanted to see. Judging by the first two calls to service, badge 145, or Josh Martin, had been heavily involved with the Smithson family, but not in the way she had previously suspected. The first call to service involved three officers. It was not Josh's word against Isaac's.

"I thought you had left," Katie said, setting her phone aside.

A pageant-ready grin spread across his face, reaching all the way up to crinkle the corners of his eyes. "Yeah. I changed my mind and picked up some coffee instead." He held a Venti-sized Starbucks cup toward her. "It's regular coffee. Black. I didn't know how you take it."

"That's perfect," Katie said, accepting it in grateful hands.

She removed the lid, watching the tendrils of heat dancing in the air before inhaling deeply. It smelled like heaven.

"How's it going?" Josh said, sinking into the chair next to hers.

He had changed out of his police uniform and into street clothes. A black Pink Floyd T-shirt and jeans. Notably, non-frat-boyish. But he smelled of Axe body spray, which was the opposite. A draw.

"The same," Katie said with a sigh.

The medical staff hadn't come out to the waiting room for hours. Katie wasn't sure if that was a good sign or a bad omen.

"What were you looking at?" Josh said, gesturing to her phone. "A message from your boyfriend?"

Katie narrowed her eyes. It was a brazen way to determine her relationship status.

His tone turned teasing. "Because you shouldn't agree to go on dates with hunky Waukee police officers when you have a boyfriend."

Katie rolled her eyes, but she couldn't keep from smiling. He was trying to lighten the mood. It was working, albeit only slightly.

"It wasn't a date, remember? It was a meeting. One we didn't even have."

Josh nodded toward her coffee and then at his. "We do have coffee, though. We could make it a coffee date. Rescheduled for right now."

"Coffee meeting."

"Tomato tomahto," he said, waving a hand. "You call it what you want, and I'll call it whatever I want."

"I don't think it works that way."

"You didn't answer my question."

"Is this an interrogation?" Katie asked. His questions were jumping in a way that seemed intentionally confusing. It was a common tactic to throw an interviewee off their planned narrative.

"Interview," Josh said, his smile broadening.

"What was the question?"

"Do you have a boyfriend?"

Katie narrowed her eyes. "You didn't ask me that. You asked me what I was looking at and then you made a statement claiming that I was reading a message from my boyfriend."

"So..." Josh gestured for her to continue. When she didn't respond, he looked pointedly at her left hand. "I see no ring, so marriage or engagement is out. I suppose you could be into girls, but perhaps you play for both teams?"

"I play for no teams."

An expression of exaggerated shock twisted Josh's handsome features. "We're going to have to change that, now aren't we? I mean, it's good to know, honestly, because at least it means you aren't tied up." He pursed his lips, making a show of thinking. "Can you at least tell me which team you are leaning toward?" He leaned forward, fluttering his long, dark eyelashes.

Katie tried to force her lips from betraying her by curving into a smile. They were not behaving, and the result was a sort of twitch at both corners of her mouth. She had to look away and clear her throat before she could refocus.

"The calls to service," she said.

"What? That's not the sort of team I was talking about."

"That's what I was looking at on my phone."

Josh's smile dropped and his expression grew serious. "How far did you get?"

"Only the first few." She paused, studying his expression. "You knew Rachel was pregnant, didn't you?"

Josh was silent for a long moment. Then he slowly nodded. "Yeah. I mean, I didn't *know*. I suspected. That second call pretty much spells it out. There just wasn't anything I could do about it. Child Services didn't want to get involved because Rachel was eighteen, an adult, and the baby wasn't born yet. Their involvement would only come after the child was born alive. Besides, there wasn't any indication that Rachel wouldn't take care of the baby." Josh sighed. "Honestly, Rachel wasn't my concern."

"Your concern was Isaac."

Josh nodded. "I feel like I let Rachel down."

"You can't say that," Katie said, placing her free hand on top of his.

Josh looked up, their eyes meeting. A flash of something passed between them, but Katie looked away before it built into something larger.

"Rachel was an adult. Old enough to make her own decisions."

Josh issued a deep sigh. "I wish I could agree with you, but sometimes it isn't that simple."

Katie wondered what he meant, but she didn't push him. She suspected the answer lurked in the remainder of the calls. She had only read through two. There were ten years of calls, many of which would likely point to physical abuse. It was shocking that not a single one of the reports turned into a criminal offense. Probably because neither Lyndsay nor Rachel told the truth of what was happening behind closed doors. It spoke volumes about the strength of Isaac's hold over them.

20

ASHLEY

The loud, incessant beeping of machinery pushed through Ashley's slumber, pulling her out of a deep, dreamless sleep. She was reluctant to open her eyes. She had been cocooned in a cloud of peaceful slumber and she did not want to leave it. It was tranquil. Quiet. At least up until the beeping started.

Beep. Beep. Beep. She could not identify the source of the sound. It was foreign to her ears. A metallic squall that rose in volume, like an alarm. Not a sound she would expect to find in her home. So, where was she?

Ashley's eyelids fluttered open. The lighting was set to dim, but it illuminated the room just enough to see. She was in a hospital room, clean and sterile. A machine tracking her vitals sat next to her, still beeping, but it had jumped up four octaves and increased in volume in a way that could only be described as screaming. It was an alarming noise, one that surely meant something was wrong.

"Stupid machine," a nurse said as she bustled into the room. Her accent sounded like it came from somewhere in Central America.

The nurse was a middle-aged, heavyset woman with silky black hair pulled back into a tight bun. Her scrubs had little turkeys trotting all over them, each holding a tiny sign that said *gobble gobble*. Ashley supposed that Thanksgiving was coming up. Not that she had anyone to celebrate with.

Her mother had passed of cancer and she had never known her father. Her only sister lived in New York. Ashley had expected to spend the holidays with Tom and Katie, but Tom had betrayed her, and Rachel Smithson's case would keep Katie and Ashley separated for at least another couple of months.

The nurse pressed several buttons on the machine. "Sure, go with the cheapest contract," the nurse muttered to herself. "The monitors are all the same. *Mierda.*" The machine stopped shrieking and the woman stepped back, satisfied.

"Hello," Ashley said. Her voice sounded scratchy, like she hadn't used it in days. Maybe she hadn't. She had no idea what day it was or even where she was. Yes, it was a hospital, but where?

The woman jumped back. "Oh," she said, pressing a hand to her heaving chest. "You frightened me. I didn't realize you were awake."

Ashley nodded toward the machine. "That thing woke me up."

The nurse nodded. "Of course it did." She cast a dark look at the machine. "They make sleeping difficult."

"What is it?"

"It's to monitor your vital signs."

"Is something wrong with me?"

"No." The nurse shook her head. "I mean, yes, but you are stable. These machines are junk. They just go off like that. You're fine. I'm Angelica, by the way." When she smiled, her entire face lit up.

"What happened?" Ashley asked. "And why am I here?" She lifted her arm to gesture to the room surrounding her. It felt unnaturally heavy, like her bones were filled with lead.

Angelica bit her bottom lip. "I'll let Doctor Malloy answer that. She should be here in a few moments. She's making her rounds now. In the meantime, what would you like for breakfast?"

Ashley wasn't satisfied with Angelica's answer, but she didn't press the nurse. Angelica was not the decision maker. Ashley had spent plenty of time inside hospitals while her mother went through cancer treatment. Back then, she had learned one very vital bit of information. Nurses followed a doctor's orders, but that didn't mean they were powerless. In fact, they wielded a great deal of power. Hospitals were never fun, and nurses were in a position to make life bearable. They were also able to do the exact opposite. Agitating the nursing staff was never a good idea.

"What are my breakfast options?"

Angelica handed Ashley a small pamphlet with a list of breakfast, lunch, and dinner options. "You are not under any dietary restrictions, but the doctor does want you eating full and regular meals. You lost a lot of blood. You need sustenance to regain your strength."

Ashley's mind shot back to her last memory, when she was outside the Waukee Police station. Her stomach had twisted into knots, then she'd started vomiting blood. She had no idea what had caused her body to react that way. She suspected it was somehow connected to the nosebleeds and fatigue. She had chalked up the early symptoms to stress, but that wasn't a likely option anymore. Hospitals did not treat patients for stress. At least not *this* kind of hospital.

"I'm in Des Moines?" Ashley asked. She hadn't driven herself to the hospital, so she must have arrived by ambulance. Waukee didn't have a large hospital of its own, so she guessed the ambulance would have taken her somewhere in the Des Moines area.

"Methodist. Downtown Des Moines." Angelica tapped the pamphlet in Ashley's hands with her finger. "Now, let's get breakfast started, shall we?"

Ashley scanned the options. "I'll just have some oatmeal."

"Do you like eggs?"

"Yes."

"We'll add some eggs to the order, too. You need protein. Turkey sausage?"

Ashley could tell by the stern set of Angelica's jaw that there was no point in arguing. "That's fine."

"I'll put that order in for you. Doctor Malloy should be in shortly," Angelia said before bustling out of the room.

The room felt empty and cold without Angelica. Everything was white and beige. Sterile and boring. She wished it was colorful like the children's hospital. Ashley used to volunteer every weekend at Blank Children's Hospital in Des Moines, but she'd had to put those visits on hold during the Smithson trial preparation. She missed the kids, but the days were too short and there was still so much to do.

A sudden and overwhelming sense of dread seeped through her skin and settled into her bones. How much time had she lost thanks to this hospitalization? A few hours? A day? More? Since Angelica had wanted Ashley to order breakfast, it definitely wasn't Saturday anymore. Her last memory on Saturday was from close to lunchtime. So Sunday, then. Hopefully.

Where's my phone? Ashley wondered, her eyes scanning the room. It would give her the date. It would also give her access to her voicemails. She suspected there would be one or two messages and texts from Tom, but those weren't the ones she cared to see. Her concern was for her clients. They needed her at all hours of the day.

She spotted her purse lying on the beige recliner in the corner next to the clothes she'd been wearing on Saturday. They were neatly folded, but Ashley could still see some of the blood stains from across the room. The clothing was ruined. Without a doubt. She started to shift her legs toward the edge of the bed, intent on retrieving her phone and inspecting her clothes, when someone interrupted her.

"Stay put, Ms. Montgomery," came a stern, chastising voice.

It reminded Ashley of her mother when she was young. A demand termed in a way that wasn't easy to ignore. Ashley froze and her head swung toward the short, stocky woman standing just outside the doorway.

"Thank you," the woman said as she stepped across the threshold and into Ashley's room. Her voice was less stern but still authoritative. "Good morning. I'm Doctor Malloy."

Doctor Malloy did not smile, but her eyes were kind. A bright sky blue that sparkled even in the depressing surroundings. Light blue scrubs peeked out from beneath her white coat, accentuating her eyes.

"Hello, Doctor. You're just the person I was hoping to see."

Doctor Malloy quirked an eyebrow. "Is that so?"

"Yes." Ashley propped herself up on her elbows. Her body was so heavy that moving was a struggle. "I need to get out of here. I've got to get back to work."

"You aren't ready for discharge."

A matter-of-fact statement that dashed Ashley's hopes. "When can I leave?"

"That depends."

"On what?"

"On how quickly you recover."

Ashley groaned. "Why? What's wrong with me?"

Doctor Malloy narrowed her eyes, assessing Ashley. "You don't know?"

"No," Ashley said, but the doctor did not look convinced.

"I've got a few questions for you." Doctor Malloy held up a finger as she stepped outside the door and grabbed a clipboard hanging on the wall. She scanned a series of documents as she returned to Ashley's side.

"I'll do anything to get out of here," Ashley grumbled.

"Good. I'm happy to hear you will be cooperative." Doctor Malloy said this without the hint of a smile. "Are you taking any blood thinners?"

"No."

"Not Warfarin or Coumadin?"

"No. Why?"

"Are you taking any medications at all?"

"No. Again, why?"

Doctor Malloy gave her a hard look. "Have you ever had thoughts of hopelessness?"

"Does now count?"

Doctor Malloy looked up, concern in the set of her downturned lips.

"I mean, it does seem hopeless that I'll get out of here today, doesn't it?"

"Very funny. But you're smarter than that. You know what I meant."

"Fine," Ashley said with a sigh. "No. Not really. I am stressed out a lot, but that's because I have hope, not the other way around."

"Hope for what?"

"That things will change."

"What kind of things?"

"Mainly the criminal justice system."

"How about your personal life?" Doctor Malloy said as she wrote something on the clipboard.

"How about it?"

Doctor Malloy looked up, giving Ashley a stern look.

"Okay," Ashley said with a sigh. She had a tendency toward sarcasm when she was nervous. "My personal life isn't ideal. I just caught my boyfriend with another woman. Someone I knew from childhood, and not in a good way."

"Have you ever considered harming yourself?"

"No," Ashley said, studying the doctor. What was she getting at? Did she think Ashley had tried to kill herself? "Why?"

Doctor Malloy flipped the page on her clipboard and silently read to herself. Then she looked up. "It doesn't look like you have a history of depression or suicidal ideation."

"Umm, no. I don't. Again, why?"

Doctor Malloy walked over to the other side of the room, where a large whiteboard occupied most of the wall. Both Doctor Malloy's and Angelica's names were already written there in red dry erase marker under "providers." Below their names was a section for "condition." It was empty. Doctor Malloy picked up the dry erase marker and popped the cap off. Turning her back to Ashley, she began writing. When she finished, she recapped the marker and stepped aside, allowing Ashley to read.

Anticoagulant Rodenticide Poisoning.

Ashley read the words, blinked several times, then read them again. "I'm sorry, what? Poisoning? That can't be right."

"But it is."

"Rodenticide? Is that what I think it is? Rodent? Like a rat? Are you saying I am here because I ate rat poison?"

Doctor Malloy nodded. "There are three options as to how this could have happened: homicidal, accidental, or suicidal. Judging by your history and your reaction to learning your condition, I think we can safely rule out suicidal. So, that leaves homicidal and accidental."

"You've got to be kidding."

"Do I look like I'm joking?"

The doctor's expression was grave. She did not look like she'd laughed a single time in all her life. "No."

"So, we need to talk about the other two options."

A wave of exhaustion washed over Ashley. She fell back against her pillow, staring up at the ceiling. There wasn't a chance that she'd accidentally eaten rat poison. She would never have something like that around the house. Not with her two curious dogs. That only left one option, and the very thought of it was overwhelming. Once again, someone was trying to kill her. It had only been a year since the last time this had happened, and the culprit back then was now in prison.

"I don't have rat poison. Not at my office or at my home."

"So that leaves homicidal." Doctor Malloy made another notation. "Which means you are in danger. Whoever did this isn't likely to give up because they failed. What do you remember from yesterday?"

"Yesterday?" Ashley said hopefully. "So today is only Sunday?"

"Yes." Doctor Malloy motioned with her hand for Ashley to go on.

Ashley sighed, looking up at the ceiling. It was white, unremarkable, a blank slate to try to piece the day together.

"I left Brine in the morning. I was going to see my boyfriend. Who I just broke up with, so I guess I should call him my ex-boyfriend."

"How did you feel at that time?"

"I mean, fine. Upset. Pissed, actually, but that had to do with my ex, not anything I'd eaten."

Doctor Malloy nodded, writing in her notepad. "Had you had any strange bruising or nosebleeds prior to that day?"

Ashley's eyes widened. "Yes. For a week or two. I just thought it was stress. Are they related?"

"Could be," Doctor Malloy said. "You ingested a massive dose yesterday. If you hadn't been outside the police station where there was a well-trained emergency response team, you would have died. Without a doubt. But the earlier bleeding indicates that you may have been exposed to smaller doses prior to yesterday. I'll have a nurse up here to collect some of your hair in a little while."

"My hair?" Ashley said, absentmindedly fingering the tips of her long, mousy-brown hair.

"They'll take some from the back of your head. You won't even notice. We need to test for earlier exposure. The poison will be in your hair."

"Like drug testing?"

Doctor Malloy gave her a curious look. "Yes. Should we be testing for controlled substances as well?"

"You could," Ashley said with a shrug. "But you won't find anything. I'm a defense attorney. It's my job to know how drug testing works."

"A defense attorney," Doctor Malloy said, writing another note on the clipboard. "Is it fair to say that you are exposed to a less than reputable section of society?"

A flair of indignation ignited in Ashley's chest. "Yes, but my clients didn't do this."

"You sound certain."

"I am."

"Then who do you think did?"

Ashley sucked in a deep breath and released it through her nose. "I don't know. Maybe one of those weirdos who sends me gifts in the mail. They are always sending me candies and letters claiming they are in love."

Doctor Malloy quirked an eyebrow. "You eat things that random people send you?"

"No. I'm not stupid. I don't eat anything unless the seal hasn't first been broken."

"What was the last thing you remember eating on Saturday?"

Ashley thought back. There was the argument with Tom. Then she'd stormed off. The box of chocolates he had sent her earlier that week was in her SUV. She'd eaten the entire box.

"Chocolates," Ashley said with a sigh. "My boyfriend had sent them to me."

"Your ex-boyfriend?"

Ashley nodded. "Yes."

"Was this the first package of food that he's sent to you?"

"No. There was one other."

"Did you have nosebleeds and bruising before or after you received the first box of chocolates?"

Ashley tried to remember, but the days and weeks flowed together. "I don't remember. But I don't think he did this."

"Why not?"

"I don't know," Ashley said with a sigh. "I just don't."

Doctor Malloy narrowed her eyes.

"I know it doesn't sound convincing. But Tom wouldn't hurt me."

"Tom." Doctor Malloy wrote the name on her clipboard. "What's his last name?"

"Archie. But like I said, he didn't do this."

Doctor Malloy ignored her. "So we've got potential poisoning in both Brine and Waukee. Is that right?"

Ashley nodded. She knew where this was going.

"Do you want me to notify the authorities?"

"Is that necessary? I mean, are you sure that it wasn't an accident."

Doctor Malloy's frown deepened. "That was the reasoning for my earlier questions. Would you like to revisit them? Maybe there is something more you would like to add?"

"No. Nothing more."

"Should I notify the authorities?" Doctor Malloy asked a second time.

Ashley sighed deeply. "Yes."

"I'll need you to fill out and sign a release of information." Doctor Malloy removed several documents from the front of her clipboard, then handed it to Ashley. "These top two pages are for the release of information. Make sure you include both the Brine and Waukee Police Departments."

"What's that?" Ashley nodded to the documents in Doctor Malloy's hands.

"These are for the eyes of medical staff only."

"All right," Ashley said, before looking down at the clipboard. She filled out the papers and signed with a flourish. "I would request that you speak to Officer Katie Mickey, if that's at all possible."

"She wouldn't be the woman who has been marching around the waiting room since you arrived, would she?" Doctor Malloy said, a sparkle lighting up her eyes.

"Does she have red hair, freckles, and a hot temper?"

"Yup."

"That's her."

"I'll notify both police departments and speak with Ms. Mickey when I finish my rounds. Are you two friends?"

Ashley nodded. "Most of the time."

"Most of the time?"

"Sorry," Ashley said. "Not like that. She wouldn't ever in a million years hurt me. We work on opposite sides of the law. Right now, we are in the middle of a contentious case. We keep our distance during cases like this one. To, you know, avoid arguments."

"Rachel Smithson's case," Doctor Malloy said. It was a statement, not a question.

"How'd you know about Rachel?"

"I watch the news. That's where I saw evidence of at least one of your previous nose bleeds."

Ashley remembered it all too well. It was right before Rachel's arraignment. Her nose had gushed blood right in front of all the cameras. Several of the more conservative news stations had claimed it was likely due to heavy cocaine use, which was an outright lie.

"I suppose it is safe to assume there are also potential culprits stemming from your representation of Rachel?"

Ashley nodded. Working with Rachel meant a seemingly endless field of potential perpetrators. Ashley wasn't well liked, thanks to her job. Death threats were a common occurrence, especially while cases like Rachel Smithson's were pending. Emotions ran high when cases had child victims. Her attacker could be anyone. The question then became, when and how would they strike again?

21

KATIE

It was early afternoon and Katie was alone in the hospital waiting room. The area had been bustling with others only a few hours earlier. She hadn't spoken with anyone other than Josh, but she took solace in the others' presence. It lent meaning to the phrase *misery loves company*. But then Josh was called back to the station and everyone else had left, one by one, trickling down the hall to see their loved ones.

But not Katie. She was left alone. Was it because Katie's loved one had died? She didn't know. She had no experience in the area. That was primarily because she had spent her entire adult life keeping everyone at a distance. She had no siblings, and her parents were horrible human beings. The only person who had been able to truly break through her exterior was Ashley. And now that one thread of friendship was possibly gone.

Katie's phone began buzzing in her pocket, pulling her out of her thoughts.

"Yes, George," she said, bringing the phone to her ear.

"Where are you?"

Katie blinked several times, confused. She was off duty until Monday. It was her first weekend off in as long as she could remember. She had planned to spend it holed up in her basement drinking red wine, ordering pizza, and watching a steady stream of vintage thriller movies, but that plan hadn't come to fruition for obvious reasons.

"What do you mean, where am I?" Katie growled in a sudden burst of fury. He had no right to talk to her like that. "It's my weekend off and I don't answer to you. You aren't my boss. Chief Carmichael is. And it's none of your damn business where I am."

"Okay, okay."

His placating tone did nothing to ease Katie's fury. He was acting like he was the ringmaster, trying to tame his beast. Her nostrils flared. "You called me, remember? You have two seconds to tell me what it is that you want or I'm hanging up. I've had a rough enough night without dealing with your bullshit."

Katie didn't habitually speak to her coworkers in such a gruff manner, but she was emotional and running on fumes. No sleep. Little food. Constant stress. Three conditions that added up to a disaster for even the tamest of individuals. And Katie, by nature, was anything but tame.

"I just..." He paused. "Something is happening around here."

"Really?" Katie said, now beginning to pace from one end of the waiting room to the other. "Well, something is happening here, too. I'm at the hospital. Waiting to hear if my friend Ashley is dead or alive. That's a pretty important something. Is your something more or less important?"

"Jesus, Katie. You don't have to rip my head off. I'm doing you a favor. I just wanted to tell you that Forest Parker got the other two city councilmen to agree to his proposed budget cuts. They voted last night." He lowered his voice to a near whisper. "Chief Carmichael is in an uproar, but there's nothing he can do. He's going to have to cut a position."

"Okay." Katie appreciated the heads-up, but she didn't quite understand the urgency behind it. She was far from the most recent hire.

"You should get back here." His voice dipped even lower, and it sounded like he was cupping his hand around the receiver.

"Why?"

"Because you don't want it to be you."

Katie was silent for a long moment, mulling over his statement. When she finally spoke, her words were dripping with sarcasm. "Oh, I see.

Seniority doesn't matter. My vagina is what places me on the chopping block."

"I didn't say…"

Katie cut him off. "It doesn't matter that I've been working tirelessly for six years. Or that I'm in the Des Moines area—on my day off, mind you—to tie up loose ends on the Smithson case. No. None of that matters when I'm the only vagina in a dick world."

"Katie…"

Katie hung up the phone before she could say anything more.

"That was quite the rant."

Katie looked up to see a female doctor a short distance away, looking at her approvingly. "Yeah, well, he deserved it."

The doctor had short blond hair, cut into a pixie style. Her expression was wary, but she had kind, gentle eyes. "I get it." She gestured to her white coat. "I know what it's like to be a woman making her way in a man's world. I'm constantly reminded when I am working with a male nurse and the patients refer to him as *doctor*. Every. Single. Time."

A reluctant smile twitched at the corner of Katie's mouth. "Thank you," she said, pocketing her phone. "It's been a long day. But I assume you aren't out here to discuss the issues I have with my colleagues."

"I am not." The doctor rocked from her heels to her toes. "I don't suppose you would happen to be Katie Mickey?"

Katie nodded. "Yes. How did you know?"

"Ashley told me to look for a redheaded cop with a quick temper." She shrugged as if to say *and you fit the bill*. "I'm Doctor Malloy, by the way. Doctor Ruby Malloy." She extended her hand. Katie took it. They shook hands, both with an equally firm grip.

"Nice to meet you, Doctor. I presume that Ashley must be all right if she's back there telling lies about me."

"Well, yes. To a degree."

"A degree," Katie repeated, trying to interpret what that meant.

"My conversation here with you is as an officer of the law, not as a friend to the patient. Do you understand?"

Katie's heart started pounding wildly. "What is it? Is she…" She swallowed hard, unable to finish the thought. Her mind had a way of jumping to the worst possible conclusion.

"No, she's alive. But I have determined that a crime has occurred."

"A crime? Like what?"

"We had a hard time pinpointing the cause of Ms. Montgomery's condition," Doctor Malloy said, shoving her hands into the pockets of her lab coat. "She was not responsive when she arrived, so we were not able to get a patient background from her. Do you know if anyone lives with Ms. Montgomery? Or potentially has access to her food?"

"Umm, no," Katie said, shaking her head. "Her boyfriend usually visits on the weekends, but I don't think he's been around for a couple of weeks."

The doctor's eyebrows knit together. "Do you know if Ms. Montgomery has eaten anything strange? A food given to her from an unknown person?"

"I doubt it," Katie said. "Ashley is a defense attorney in a small town. She has had death threats on more than a few occasions. I don't think she would eat anything if she didn't know where it had come from."

"Yes. That's what she said." Doctor Malloy shrugged. "But it's always best to double check."

"Why do you ask?"

"Well, like I said, we couldn't initially pinpoint the cause of Ms. Montgomery's distress. She was anemic. Her hemoglobin at a four. Yet her blood pressure was low. We gave her blood, which helped, but her international normalized ratio, or INR for short, was very high."

"I'm not sure what all that means," Katie said, shaking her head.

"When someone's INR is high, it usually means that they are taking a blood thinner of sorts, like Coumadin. Ms. Montgomery's regular physician is a doctor within our network, so I have access to her prescribed medications. She is not taking a blood thinner. Or, at least, she isn't supposed to be."

"Ashley wouldn't take medication unless it was prescribed. She hates medicine. She won't even take ibuprofen on a bad headache day."

The doctor nodded. "I assumed that. Blood thinners aren't usually something people take recreationally. So, we believe that it was given to her. Without her knowledge."

Katie quirked an eyebrow. "Come again?"

"She was poisoned. Most likely with rat poisoning."

"Wait, what?" Katie said, taking a step backward. "I don't think I am tracking what you are saying."

"We gave her vitamin K to reverse the effects of the poison. She is responding well. But I assume, Officer, that you will want to open an investigation."

Katie nodded, dumbfounded. Only one thought came to mind. *Here we go again.* It had only been a year since the last time someone had tried to kill Ashley.

"I've ordered a hair stat analysis as well. There is reason to believe that this isn't her only exposure to the poison."

Katie shook her head, unable to process the information dump. "So you think Ashley was poisoned multiple times."

"The most recent one seems as though it occurred in Waukee, Dallas County," Doctor Malloy said, nodding. "But I also suspect that she ingested the same poison several other times while in Brine."

If true, it meant that multiple counts of attempted murder would be brought in Brine County and one in Dallas County. That was if they could find the culprit.

"What's all this?" Josh said, coming to Katie's side.

"Oh." She whirled. "I didn't know you were back."

"Just got here. We got a call to talk to a doctor about a poisoning."

Doctor Malloy turned to Josh. "Are you from the Waukee Police Department?"

Josh gestured to his uniform. "The one and only."

"I get it that you're in uniform," Doctor Malloy said with a note of irritation, "but one can't ever be too careful these days." She was not amused.

"I understand."

"Do you happen to have a last name, Officer Josh?"

"Officer Joshua Martin," Josh said, holding up his badge.

Doctor Malloy glanced at the clock mounted above the nurses' desk. "I must get back to my patients. Ashley is resting for now, but you can speak with her when she wakes up. Will you be around?"

"Absolutely," Katie said without hesitation.

"I trust you will fill Officer Martin in on the details."

"Yes," Katie said with a nod.

Katie watched Doctor Malloy disappear back down the hallway, her head brimming with questions. Ashley had been poisoned. But by whom? She didn't know where to start. There were so many possibilities. Ashley had received at least thirty death threats and creepy love letters in the last year, and those were only the ones Katie knew about. The mail had likely ratcheted up with Ashley's representation of Rachel Smithson.

"What was that all about?" Josh asked, pulling Katie out of her thoughts.

"Ashley was poisoned."

"How? And where?"

"The doctor said it was something she ate. But where..." Katie shrugged. "Maybe Brine. Maybe here. Probably both." That was the thing about food. It could be consumed in one place, which would be the location of the crime, but the person might move around in the meantime. Even cross county lines. "Doctor Malloy has ordered a hair stat test to see how far back the exposure began, but I doubt we will know the results of that for another couple of days. She believes the most recent attack was in Waukee."

Josh quirked a smile. "Looks like we are going to be working together on this one, eh, Officer Mickey."

Katie tried to feign irritation, but this overly friendly officer was starting to grow on her. "So it seems."

22

KATIE

62 days before trial

"What is it, Katie?" Tom said. He was on the phone, but his voice sounded distant somehow, with an edge of frustration and potentially desperation.

"Where are you?" Katie must have called him one hundred times by now.

She'd been trying to reach him since she arrived at the hospital. It was strange that he wasn't there, and that she hadn't heard anything from him. It was possible that he didn't know about Ashley's hospitalization, but shouldn't he be trying to track Ashley down by now? And Katie would be the first person he would have called. But she'd heard nothing from him.

"You are a terrible boyfriend."

"Boyfriend?" Tom said with a snort. "Ashley broke up with me. And she won't answer my calls."

"Did she now?" Katie said, moving into investigation mode.

She had spoken to Chief Carmichael last night. Dispatch had received a call to the non-emergency line from Doctor Malloy, outlining her suspicions and requesting that Chief Carmichael assign an officer, specifically Katie, to the investigation. He had given her permission to remain in the Des Moines area as long as necessary to complete her investigation. Staying away from Brine didn't bode well for her if her job was truly on the line. Out of sight, out of mind. But she wouldn't worry about that now. Ashley was her priority.

"Yes." Was there a note of bitterness in his tone?

If Ashley hadn't contacted him, then Tom didn't know about her hospitalization. But Katie wasn't about to tell him. Doctor Malloy's notes had identified the "ex-boyfriend" as a potential suspect. At first, Katie hadn't wanted to believe that Tom had it in him. But his behavior now was outright hostile, like he was hiding something.

"Why did she break up with you?"

"She thinks I cheated on her. She wouldn't even let me explain. Some relationship, huh?"

In normal circumstances, Katie might be inclined to agree with him. Tom wouldn't cheat on Ashley. At least she hoped he wouldn't. But she didn't know what to believe anymore.

"I need to talk to you," Katie said.

"Okay. Then talk."

"In person."

Tom sighed, suddenly sounding exhausted. "This isn't high school, Katie. You can't fix my broken relationship with Ashley."

Katie couldn't believe he would even think she would insert herself in such a way. She had to fight the urge to scoff. She didn't want him to know that something was off. It was better that he believed her visit had to do with something else.

"I just want to talk to you. Can I stop by your place sometime this morning?"

There was a long pause. "You're going to drive all the way out here?"

"I'm in the area."

"All right," Tom said, "stop by in an hour. My roommate will be here, but she'll stay out of our way."

A roommate? Tom had led everyone in Brine to believe that he was living alone. If Ashley found out that Tom had been lying about a roommate *and* that the roommate was a girl, well, it wasn't surprising that she had ended things. Lies about other women never led anywhere good.

"Right," Katie said, looking down at her watch. "I'll be there at 9:30 on the dot." Then she hung up the phone.

"Where are you going at 9:30?" Josh said as he handed her a Venti-sized Starbucks cup.

Katie accepted it. "Thank you. I need something to keep me awake. I've slept like shit the last couple of nights."

"You could stay at my place," Josh suggested.

Katie narrowed her eyes.

"Whoa." Josh raised his hands in surrender. "I meant that you can have my bed and I'll sleep on the couch. I'm not going to jump your bones." He paused, chewing his bottom lip. "Unless you want me to."

"We'll cross that bridge when we get to it," Katie said.

"Which bridge? The hooking-up bridge or the me-on-the-couch bridge?"

"I'm going over to Ashley's ex-boyfriend's house in an hour," Katie said, changing the subject. Josh looked like he was on the verge of a mutiny, but he kept his cool. It was kinda hot.

"Okay. Do you want me to go with you?"

Katie shook her head. "No. I don't want to tip him off that he may be a potential suspect."

"Hmm," Josh said.

A noncommittal response. He would be coming with her whether she liked it or not. To be fair, he had his own investigation. Katie opened her mouth to insist that she go alone, but she was cut off by a familiar voice calling her name.

She swung around, coming face to face with Forest Parker. "Forest," she said, tucking her phone into her back pocket. "What are you doing here?"

"Ashley called me." He paused for a long moment, as though he was thinking. "And I knew you'd be here. You know, since you two are friends. I thought you would probably be alone." His eyes darted toward Josh, then back to her. "I thought I'd, um, check on her and offer you a little company."

She could tell by the way he continued looking at the Waukee police officer that Forest wanted Katie to explain Josh's presence, but she wasn't feeling kind toward the city councilman. Not after he'd convinced the other two councilmen to go along with his ploy to slash the police department's budget even after their conversation about their fathers. She'd thought they were working toward some kind of understanding. Hadn't he said something like *you're fine* or *everything will work out*? Apparently he hadn't meant it.

"Well," Katie said, crossing her arms. "I'm perfectly fine without *your* company."

Forest ran a hand through his wavy hair. "You heard about the vote, didn't you?"

"What vote?" Katie was going to make him say it.

"To reduce your budget."

Josh scoffed. "Brine is a small-town PD, right?" His words were directed to Katie, trying to cut Forest out of their conversation. "You probably weren't rolling in the dough to begin with."

"No," Katie said, her eyes locked on Forest, "we weren't. As a matter of fact, thanks to Forest here, I might be looking for a new job."

"Katie, you have to understand," Forest said, his tone imploring. "There wasn't anything I could do. The train had already left the station even before we had that chat at my office."

"I'm so glad I wasted my time, then," Katie said, turning her back to him.

Forest didn't try to speak to Katie again, but she could feel his presence behind her. Those round, puppy-dog eyes begging for forgiveness. Something she would not give him.

"Officer Mickey," Doctor Malloy called. "Officer Josh."

Katie looked up and saw the doctor approaching her at a fast walk, nearly a run.

"Ms. Montgomery is asking for you." Doctor Malloy paused. "Well, actually, she's just asking for you, Katie, but I assume Officer Josh will want to sit in on the meeting."

"It will expedite things if I come along," Josh said.

Katie had hoped for a few moments alone with her friend, but Josh was right. They were on a time crunch. Crimes were best solved quickly. That forty-eight-hour rule didn't only apply to murders.

Doctor Malloy's eyes darted toward Forest as she noticed him for the first time. "Another officer?"

Katie shook her head. "No. Just a friend of Ashley's."

Doctor Malloy nodded. "He can go back, too. Unless that's a problem from your end, Officer."

Forest's eyes darted from Doctor Malloy to Katie, then back to the doctor. Katie could practically hear the wheels turning in his head. He was trying to determine why Katie's status as an officer mattered. Then his eyes widened with shock.

"It's a problem," Josh said curtly. "He's a politician and I'd like to keep this interview private."

"Very well," Doctor Malloy said. "Follow me."

She turned on her heel and strutted back down the hallway. Josh and Katie scrambled to follow her. The doctor did not look back to see if they were following; she knew that they were. Katie also did not look back to see if Forest was watching. She knew that he was.

23

ASHLEY

After two full days of hospitalization, Ashley was starting to feel more like herself. Fatigue still weighed on her, but her mind was active and she had no access to her case files. She needed her computer. That's why she had contacted Forest Parker. He had become a friend over the past year after she represented his father, and she trusted him.

There was a knock on the door. A light rap of knuckles against hollow wood.

Ashley had a private room, but it was nothing fancy. A typical hospital bed with lots of buttons that Ashley had spent hours testing and still didn't understand how to operate. A TV near the ceiling, controlled by a remote connected to her bed. A rocking chair in one corner and an uncomfortable chair in another corner. That was it. It was almost as uninviting as a jail cell.

The door opened a crack.

"Ms. Montgomery," Doctor Malloy said through the small opening. "Can I come in?"

"Yes," Ashley said, adjusting her sheets so they covered her from the stomach down.

There was potentially less privacy in a hospital than a jail. And worse clothing. She wore a standard-issue hospital gown, which was like a knee-length nightgown that opened in the back. Only three measly ties held the entire thing together, not nearly enough to be considered decent. It hung, baggy, from her thin frame, and was white with some kind of moth or butterfly as a "design." She preferred the jail jumpsuits.

"How are you feeling today?" Doctor Malloy asked as she stepped through the door.

"Much better. Healed, actually."

She swung her legs over the side of the bed in a mock attempt to get up. It had turned into a sort of game she and Doctor Malloy played. Ashley would pretend to get up, saying that she was fine. Doctor Malloy would then say that she was *almost* fine, but not quite ready for discharge. Apparently, the good doctor was tired of the same old song and dance because she merely gave Ashley a stern look.

"Fine," Ashley said with a groan. "How much longer do you think I'll be here?"

"As long as it takes."

"In English, not doctor-ese."

Doctor Malloy stifled a smile. "I should think another couple of days. You should probably be safe for discharge by Wednesday. But that's only if you stay home for the remainder of the week and take it easy."

Ashley nodded enthusiastically. Relaxation was a promise she wasn't likely to keep, but she'd agree to anything so long as it meant she could go back to work. Rachel needed her, and so did all her other clients. They were probably wondering what had happened to her. Or they thought that Ashley had abandoned them.

"You have a couple of visitors," Doctor Malloy said.

"Oh, good," Ashley said, hoping Forest had come with her laptop. She'd texted him last night, begging for him to bring it to her. She couldn't just sit around all day. It was driving her crazy. Disuse was a plague rotting her brain.

But then her thoughts snagged on the word *couple*. Meaning more than one. So, not just Forest Parker.

"Wait a minute," Ashley said, narrowing her eyes, "I thought you weren't letting me have visitors."

It was a safety precaution. No visitors until the authorities could determine how rat poison had made its way into Ashley's system. She'd thought that Forest would have to drop off the computer and leave without seeing her, but maybe not.

Doctor Malloy threaded her fingers together. "Two police officers. A woman from Brine, and a man from the Waukee Police Department."

"Does the woman have red hair and freckles?"

Doctor Malloy nodded.

"Hot-tempered?"

A faint smile ghosted its way across her lips, but only for a moment before she regained her professional demeanor. "I had the benefit of over-hearing a phone conversation that led me to believe that yes, she may have a little of that in her."

"It's got to be Katie," Ashley said, hope surging in her chest. She hadn't seen anyone in the past few days other than hospital staff. While everyone had been extremely kind to her, it would be nice to see a familiar face. Especially Katie's.

"That's her. Katie Mickey. Shall I let them in?"

Ashley nodded. She wondered who Katie had been arguing with. Was it Tom? Had she been trying to get him to come to the hospital? Had he refused? She hoped this other officer, the one from Waukee, would ask a few cursory questions and clear out. Ashley needed to talk to her friend.

Doctor Malloy stepped outside and closed the door behind her before saying something. Ashley strained to hear, but Doctor Malloy must have been used to eavesdropping patients, because she kept her voice low, just above a whisper. Ashley couldn't make out a single word. A few moments later, someone knocked softly on the door.

"Come in," Ashley said, pushing herself up with her hands so she was sitting upright.

It was more laborious than she had expected. Moments earlier, she'd felt fine, but her body easily tired. Even that small movement, the simplest of tasks, had a taxing effect.

The door slowly creaked open and Katie poked her head through. "Ash-ley," she said, her voice tentative.

"Yes, yes," Ashley said, adjusting the blankets on her bed, "come in."

Katie stepped into the room. When the light from the window touched

Katie's features, Ashley could see that she looked tired. Heavy bags clung under her eyes, but her smile was genuine.

"Hey," Katie said almost breathlessly.

Katie's eyes traveled from one beeping machine to the next until they came to rest on the whiteboard. *Anticoagulant rodenticide poisoning.* Her expression hardened.

A male officer followed her inside, eyes cast downward, a bit sheepish. It was the hospital gown. Ashley was practically naked. She wished she'd have thought to cover herself with a robe first. But now it was too late.

"How are you feeling?" Katie asked.

She sat in the recliner directly across from Ashley's bed. The male officer closed the door behind him but stayed close to the exit, apparently trying to remain unseen. Like Ashley would forget that he was there.

"I'm fine," Ashley said, her eyes traveling toward the male officer. "Who is your boyfriend?"

Katie's face reddened. "Not my boyfriend. This is Josh. He's with the Waukee Police Department."

"I know that. I can read the words on his uniform. What I don't understand is *why* he's here."

Katie pursed her lips. "What do you remember about how you got here?"

"I was at the police department to pick up calls to service for the Smithson case." She paused, looking pointedly at Josh. "Which, by the way, if you're going to come around, you might as well do me a favor and bring those to me."

"I, um." Josh cleared his throat. "I'm not sure if I'm permitted to do that."

"Does she have them?" Ashley nodded toward Katie.

"Yes."

"Then I can have them. So, who is going to send them to me?" Ashley's gaze traveled from one officer to the next.

"I will," Katie said with a sigh. "I'm sorry, Josh. I should have warned you. Ashley can be a bit...prickly."

Ashley laughed. "A bit? I'm very prickly. Especially to police officers. I'm only decent to this one"—Ashley gestured to Katie—"because she saved my life once."

Katie rolled her eyes and pulled out a notepad. "Anyway. Let's get back to the official purpose of our visit. Shall we?"

"We shall," Ashley said, mimicking Katie's formal tone.

"You've been poisoned, and we all know it isn't a suicide attempt."

"How do we know that?" Ashley couldn't help it. It was in her nature to be sarcastic to police officers.

"Because you love yourself too much."

"Fair enough," Ashley admitted.

"So," Katie said, "what Josh and I need to know is who potentially poisoned you. I know this is probably a long list, but do you know of anyone who would want to hurt you?"

Ashley sighed. "Yes. And no. I mean, just like last year, the answer is everyone, which isn't much better than no one. You know how people feel about me."

"What about what you ate?" Josh asked, stepping closer to Ashley.

The moment he stepped out of the shadows and the light touched his face, Ashley could see just how handsome he was. She wondered if Katie had any interest in him. If she didn't, she should. Even if it didn't go anywhere. Katie needed a little release.

"I ate some chocolates on my way from Tom's place to the Waukee Police Department."

"Where does Tom live?" Katie asked. "And why were you coming from there?"

Ashley gave Katie the address. She wrote it down and motioned with her hand for Ashley to continue answering the second question. Ashley sighed, her eyes darting momentarily toward the male officer. It was embarrassing to divulge the crashing and burning of her romantic life in front of a stranger. An officer, no less.

"Tom has been avoiding my phone calls and text messages for the past week or so. I was fed up. So, I drove up here to find out what was going on. But when I got to his place, I found out that he had a roommate, and that roommate was my former foster sister. She goes by the name Harper now, but her name was Lydia when we were young."

Katie's jaw dropped. "You're kidding me. That son of a..."

Josh cut her off. "But did you eat anything?"

"Yes. Tom had sent me chocolates. Homemade ones. I ate nearly the whole box on my drive from there to the Waukee police station."

"Is that the only thing you ate?" Josh said, jotting a note on his pad.

"Yes."

"Have you received any other boxes of homemade chocolates from Tom?"

"Yes. One last week."

"Did you notice any illness or fatigue since eating candy from the first box?"

Ashley paused to think. "Actually, yes. I thought it was stress, but I was getting nose bleeds and I was tired. I also had some strange bruising on my arms."

"How many pieces of candy did you eat on your drive from Tom's house to the Waukee police station?"

Ashley shrugged. "Maybe fifteen or twenty." It was a little humiliating to admit that she'd eaten that many pieces of chocolate at one time, but she'd already told him her boyfriend was secretly living with her former foster sister. It couldn't get much worse than that anyway.

Josh wrote the number down. "How many pieces did you eat from the package before that?"

"Maybe three. All on different days, though."

Josh's eyes shot toward Katie, who issued a small shake of her head.

The wheels in Ashley's head began to churn, assessing that gesture, settling on his meaning. "Now wait a minute. Tom didn't do this. There's no way. He wouldn't. Not to anyone, but especially not me. You've got to look elsewhere."

"Like where? Usually, it is the person closest to the victim."

Ashley rolled her eyes. "Don't give me that *usually* bullshit. I'm a defense attorney. And a damn good one. I can read people and I'm telling you that it wasn't Tom."

"Then who? Who do you think it was?"

"I don't know. Maybe Harper. She hates me. Or maybe it was one of those psycho stalkers who sends me stuff in the mail. Perhaps it was someone who dislikes me because I'm representing Rachel Smithson. It could be any number of people. But I'm telling you right now that it isn't Tom. That's a dead end. You can stop going in that direction."

Katie placed a calming hand on Ashley's shoulder. "You're not supposed to get worked up."

Ashley settled back, but she didn't break eye contact with the Waukee police officer. She wasn't backing down. Not while she was in the hospital. Not ever. Tom was a shitty boyfriend, but he hadn't tried to kill her. No way.

"We will start by interviewing Tom and Harper," Katie said calmly. "I would also like to get a hold of that box of chocolates. Did you eat them all?"

"Yes," Ashley said with a nod. She laid her head back, a sudden burst of exhaustion overwhelming her. "But the box is still in my car. So is the note from Tom. You can get it."

"Okay."

"I mean *you*, Katie. Not him." Ashley nodded to Josh. "And don't go digging around. I have client files in there."

Katie smiled. "I won't. And what about the other box of chocolates? Was that one empty, too?"

Ashley shook her head, the room swimming with the movement. "I threw it away in my office. I was mad at Tom. There should be several pieces in the trash can. Ask Elena. She'll be able to get them for you. Tell her I told you that it is okay."

"Okay. I think I've got enough information to move forward." Katie patted Ashley's hand. "Tom is just the starting point. I'm sure that we will clear him quickly."

Ashley nodded. Her eyes were so heavy. She'd exerted too much energy during the conversation, thanks to Officer Josh. The arrogant prick. Ashley had thought he was handsome, but she changed her mind. She didn't want Katie to get involved with him. There were plenty of other fish in the sea. The thought reminded her of Forest.

"Katie," Ashley said, "is Forest Parker here?"

Katie snorted and crossed her arms. "Yes."

Apparently, Katie had heard about the board's vote. It made the front page of the *Brine Daily Newspaper*, so it wasn't surprising. Neither was her reaction to Forest.

"Give him a break, Katie. He's just doing his job."

"Well, his *job* might mean the end of mine."

"You'll be fine," Ashley said, laying her head back on her pillow. "Don't be so dramatic."

Katie's intense gaze bore into Ashley. "That's eerily close to what Forest told me during our meeting the other day. Do you two know something that I don't?"

Ashley waved a dismissive hand. "No. But could you send him in here when you are on your way out? He's got my laptop and I have work to do."

Katie nodded, but she didn't look happy about it. Then she left with Josh. That arrogant asshole. He wasn't the type to listen to Ashley. That was the problem with men as officers and men in general. They were unwilling to rely on a woman's gut, which was more often than not right on the money.

Ashley closed her eyes, only for a moment, attempting to gather her strength. But then she fell asleep. Quite by accident.

24

KATIE

Archie and *Langston.* Katie read the two names on the mailbox outside Tom's apartment. She and Josh drove straight there after interviewing Ashley. Katie had dreaded the meeting—the interview—the entire drive over. Coming face to face with her friend, analyzing his every move to determine whether he had attempted to kill her other friend.

And then there was the roommate issue. *Langston.* Tom had lied about her. Or at least hidden the truth. So what else was he hiding?

"What a prick," Katie muttered.

"What?" Josh said.

The front steps to the old home creaked under Josh's weight as he made his way to her side. He had tagged along to her meeting with Tom, despite Katie's continued protests that it would tip Tom off, put him immediately on edge, but the captain of the Waukee police had a different opinion on the matter.

"Nothing. Are you ready?"

Josh fiddled with something near his chest pocket and nodded. "Body camera is on."

Katie stared at the device, wondering what it would be like to have her very own body camera. Something that would verify that she was one of the good ones. But Brine didn't have the money and likely never would. Not after budget cuts. Katie would be lucky if she squeaked through without losing her job. Electronics were out of the question.

"Like what you see?" Josh's eyes traveled from Katie to his chest, then back to Katie.

"Shut up." Katie looked away. "I wasn't checking you out. I was looking at your camera."

"Yes, yes," Josh said with a chuckle. "Next time I'm behind you, I'll be looking at the pants pockets. Just so you know."

"You're impossible." Katie kept her face severe, but she was smiling inwardly. He was a clever one.

"Are you going to knock?" Josh asked.

"Yes." She rapped her knuckles against the door.

One. Two. She went to hit the door a third time, but it was already swinging open.

"I don't see the point..." Tom's voice trailed off when he saw Josh.

"Hello." Josh held up his hand and wiggled his fingertips.

"Hi." Tom looked from Katie to Josh. "Who are you?"

"Josh Martin. Waukee PD."

He held out his hand and Tom took it. "Tom Archie. Nice to meet you." He looked Josh up and down, then turned to Katie. "Ashley didn't do anything stupid, did she?"

"No. Ashley isn't in trouble."

"Then what's with the reinforcements?"

"Can we come in?" Josh looked over his shoulder. "This is a sensitive matter. Don't need the neighbors listening in."

Katie couldn't see any neighbors, but that didn't mean they weren't out there looking through peepholes and hovering next to open windows. People were nosy, especially when law enforcement was involved.

"Sure," Tom said, opening the door wide and moving aside.

Josh stepped across the threshold, head held high like he owned the place. His nose wrinkled as he looked around. A duke strutting into his subject's grubby hovel. Katie hadn't seen this side of Josh. The person he became when dealing with potential suspects. It wasn't uncommon for an officer to be one way in private and another while working, but it didn't impress Katie.

Tom gave Katie a questioning look. She shrugged and followed Josh inside. Bringing Josh along with her was a mistake. Not that she had any say in the matter, thanks to the captain of the Waukee police. She guessed that the decision had also been out of Josh's hands. The ultimate determination rested on a captain who probably didn't like taking advice from a female officer from a Podunk town.

"Have a seat." Tom motioned toward a round table and chairs in the kitchen area.

The makeshift apartment was long and narrow with a living area and kitchen at the front of the residence and a hallway that Katie guessed led back to a set of bedrooms and a shared bathroom. It was furnished, but the items were mismatched and outdated. A typical college home.

"I prefer to stand," Josh said, adjusting his belt.

Katie pulled out a chair and sat down. Tom wasn't merely a potential suspect. He was a friend. Yes, the evidence seemed to point at him, but deep down Katie didn't believe he would hurt Ashley. At least not intentionally. Besides, it wasn't her first time dealing with evidence that might have been planted. That was how Ashley had landed in a jail cell a year ago, despite her innocence. Back then, Tom had helped Katie solve the crime. She wasn't going to develop occupational amnesia and forget that fact.

"Katie," Tom said, turning his back to Josh, "what is going on?"

An array of potential answers floated through Katie's mind, some more truthful than others, but she was interrupted before she had a chance to speak.

A woman came whistling down the hallway, flipping a pair of keys around her finger. She was nothing short of a stunner. Long, wavy brown hair. Big, doe-like eyes. Legs for days. She wore a pair of ratty jeans and an oversized sweatshirt, but they looked couture on her thin frame.

"You must be Harper," Katie said, her tone darkening. This was the woman who had turned Ashley's world upside down, both as a child and as an adult. To hear Ashley tell it, this woman was a real sociopath. "Or should I call you Lydia?"

"Name's Harper now," she said, popping her gum. "Who's askin'?"

"Katie Mickey." Katie pulled out her badge. "Brine County Police Department."

"Ohhh." Harper widened her eyes and pressed her hands to her cheeks in an exaggerated gesture. "So, what? Do you want an award or somethin'?"

"Actually, we'd like to speak with you both." It was the first time Josh had said anything for a few minutes. All eyes swung toward him.

"Oh, hello there, Officer Hottie," Harper said, coming into the kitchen area. "I'll answer all the questions you've got." She reached past him and picked up an apple, then bit into it. Slowly, sensually. "You can even take me downtown. If you get my drift." Here she winked.

A hot burble of irritation flooded Katie's veins. It could have been the flippant attitude or her background with Ashley. Or maybe it was the fact that this beautiful woman was living with Tom behind Ashley's back. But certainly, at least in Katie's mind, it had nothing to do with her flirting with Josh.

"Let's cut to the chase," Katie said, slamming a flat palm on the table. "Someone has poisoned Ashley Montgomery and we need to know if either of you had something to do with it."

Josh gave her a *what the fuck* look, but Katie ignored him. No, she probably shouldn't have come right out and stated the reason for the visit, but it wasn't like they were fooling anyone. Tom's hackles were up, and Harper couldn't be bothered by anything. Not because she was laid back, but because she didn't seem to give a shit about anyone or anything other than herself.

"Poisoned?" Tom said, slowly lowering himself into a chair. "How?"

"That's what we want to know," Josh cut in. "You were her boyfriend. At least up until shortly before her hospitalization. She said you got into a fight. Is that true?"

"Umm, yeah." Tom was completely thrown, his demeanor suddenly timid. "Is she all right? She didn't..." He trailed off, unable to finish the thought.

"No, Tom," Katie said, her tone gentle. "Ashley didn't die. She's hospitalized right now, but she should make a full recovery."

"Oh, thank God."

"Yes," Harper said, taking another bite of her apple. "Let's do thank God for Ashley Montgomery. Everyone always has. She walks on water. Her shit doesn't stink and all that." Her tone was sarcastic, biting.

"*You* wouldn't have anything to do with Ashley's poisoning, would you?" Katie said, staring daggers at Harper.

"Me?" The tone was still sarcastic. "Why would I ever want to hurt little miss perfect?"

"Because you two used to be foster sisters," Katie said through gritted teeth. "And you pushed her down the basement stairs. She broke her arm."

"You did what to her?" Tom's eyes grew wide.

"I think Ashley remembers that little incident different than I do."

"How so?" Tom and Katie said in unison.

Harper rolled her eyes. "She fell. I didn't push her. That's how Ashley and her sister got rid of me, but I didn't do it. Ashley was a clumsy girl. She grew fast. All arms and gangly, lanky legs." Harper paused to make motions that mimicked a gorilla. "I was falsely accused."

"What about the other stuff?" Katie didn't believe Harper, but she wanted to know what she would say about the other things that Ashley had told her about the horrible year Lydia had lived in her home.

"What other stuff?"

"Cutting holes in the crotch of all her pants."

"Guilty," Harper said with a chuckle.

"Putting fresh dog poop in Ashley's bed." Katie paused. "Under the covers."

Harper laughed harder. "I forgot about that. Yeah. I did that, too."

"Letting Ashley's hamster out of its cage so the dogs would get it."

"Hamsters are mice without tails. They aren't pets. They are a menace."

"Do you deny it?"

"No."

"So why should I believe that you didn't poison Ashley."

"For one, I was honest with you about all the other stuff."

Harper had a point, but those were small crimes. All done by a child. Not something that could result in a long stint in prison, like attempted murder.

"Secondly, that was all kid stuff. Stupid little pranks."

"Okay." Katie wasn't even close to convinced.

"Finally, I have no reason to dislike Ashley. Yes, I was kicked out because of her lies, but that ultimately resulted in my adoption. Ashley's mom wasn't ever going to adopt me. Not with Ashley and her sister filling her head with lies. The next home, they did. So, really, I should be thanking Ashley. Besides, it's been like, how many years? I mean, nobody holds a grudge that long."

Harper sounded sincere, but that was the thing with psychopaths. They were good at lying. It was the whole lack of empathy thing. The tells most people had didn't exist for them. They lacked a subconscious sense of guilt. Judging by Harper's flippant reaction to the news of Ashley's poisoning, Katie doubted that she had a conscience.

"What about you," Josh said, focusing his attention on Tom. "I suppose you have all kinds of reasons why you couldn't have poisoned Ashley."

Tom shook his head slowly. "I would never. Katie." His desperate gaze shifted toward her. "When can I go see Ashley?"

"No way, pal," Josh said. "No visitors. Especially not you. Even if you aren't her attempted murderer, you are her ex-boyfriend. Considering your current living situation"—his eyes darted from Harper back to Tom—"I don't blame her."

Apparently Josh was as unimpressed by Harper as Katie was. A slight smile crept into the corner of Katie's lips, but she stifled it. It had nothing to do with any attraction she might have toward Josh. No way. It was his easy shut-down of Harper. A woman who probably rarely heard *no* from any man.

"We are just roommates," Tom said, directing his words to Katie. "You have to believe me. Please tell her."

Katie placed a gentle hand over Tom's. "I know. I believe you."

"You do?"

"But that's not the problem."

"What? Ashley seemed pretty upset about it when she left."

"Yes, well, think about it. The reason people react negatively to cheating is because it is a betrayal. Propped up by a series of lies. That's the true treachery, the lies. Otherwise, open relationships wouldn't exist. And why do open relationships work? They work because the cheating is agreed upon, without untruths. You. What you've done here." Katie gestured around her. "You didn't tell Ashley about any of it. Essentially, you've lived a lie since you left Brine." Katie shook her head. "I don't think that's something that will be easy to get past. Maybe Ashley can, but you're going to have to give her time."

Tom's head dropped into his hands, his elbows propped up on his knees. He looked devastated.

"I don't understand, Tom. If you care about her so much, then why were you ignoring her calls and texts? She was so upset about that. She even texted me, and you know that we don't talk during big cases."

"I wasn't. I didn't. The messages didn't come through. I don't know what happened."

"Is her number blocked?"

Tom grabbed his phone, unlocking it by pressing several obvious keys. *1-1-1-1.* Men could be so predictable sometimes. The screen sprang to life and he pressed several additional buttons before looking up.

"Yes. She was blocked. But I don't know how..." His voice trailed off as he turned to Harper.

She raised her hands in a gesture of surrender. "Don't look at me, buddy. I didn't touch your phone."

That, Katie felt sure, was bullshit. Harper had done it. To fuck with Ashley. But that didn't make Harper an attempted killer, even though she was looking like a pretty good suspect to Katie.

"Why didn't you try calling Ashley, though? I mean, her number was blocked, but that didn't mean you couldn't have called her."

"I didn't want to bother her during that big trial," Tom said, shaking his head. "You know how she can get. So sucked in. I didn't want to break her concentration."

"Hmmm," Katie said. It made sense, but she wasn't going to let him off the hook that easily. He should have tried harder.

"Well," Josh said, heading toward the door. "I think that's all the questions we have for today. We have some evidence to gather and send off for evaluation. We might be back to talk to you two later."

Katie stood as well. She cast Tom one last apologetic look over her shoulder before following Josh out the door. She and Josh had just waltzed into Tom's home and dropped a couple of heavily destructive bombs on him.

You know that woman who just broke your heart? The one you pined over for years before she'd give you the time of day? Well, that relationship is officially over. There will be no resurrecting it. It's done. And, oh yeah, that woman, she's in the hospital. You can't see her, but trust us, she's going to be fine. Also, if you thought that things couldn't get worse, yeah, yeah, they can. Because you're the primary suspect in that woman's attempted murder. You know, because it's always the ex who has the biggest axe to grind.

It was a lot for anyone. Even, or maybe especially, Tom.

25

KATIE

After interviewing Tom and Harper, Katie and Josh returned to the Waukee police station to search Ashley's vehicle. Ashley had given Katie the keys while at the hospital, but she held onto the key ring and wouldn't let go until Katie promised she would not let Josh anywhere near her car.

"So, where do we start?" Josh said, walking around Ashley's Tahoe, pressing his face to the windows while shielding the sun with his hands. All the windows were heavily tinted except the windshield and the front two.

"*We* don't start anywhere. Remember? Ashley's consent only extends to me. I'm going to search, and you are going to stand back and do the bagging and tagging."

"I thought we'd do it together," Josh said, winking suggestively. "You know, I bag, you tag."

"You can bag and tag on your own. I'm sure you're used to it." Katie was growing irritated with his innuendo. He was attractive, yes, but arrogance was starting to overshadow his good looks.

Katie snapped on a pair of gloves and opened the passenger door. The empty box of chocolates was right there on the seat. The container itself was unremarkable, white with a filmy finish and a lid that fit snugly on top. One of those found at The Container Store. There was a store right there in West Des Moines, smack dab between Waukee and Des Moines.

She found a letter written on white paper that read, "Sorry," on the seat next to it. Katie picked up the letter and flipped it over, looking for more writing. Other than Tom's signature, that was it. When Tom worked at the jail, Katie had seen his signature virtually every day. She could recognize it anywhere. Tom had signed this letter. Katie photographed both items using her cell phone, then picked them up and brought them to Josh, who sealed them in separate evidence bags.

"Well, that's it," Katie said, removing her gloves and tucking them in her back pocket.

"It is? You're not going to look for anything else?"

Katie placed her hands on her hips. "What, exactly, should I be looking for? Ashley gave us permission to take these items out of her car. That's it. Her consent didn't extend to the rest of the vehicle. She made that abundantly clear."

"Don't you wonder why, though?"

"No. I know why."

"Then what is it? What is she hiding?"

"Nothing. But she's a defense attorney, Josh. They take their constitutional rights seriously. Ashley would never consent to a search of her vehicle at a traffic stop even though she had nothing illegal in her car. She'd never consent to a preliminary breath test even if she hadn't had a single sip of alcohol. The fact that she granted us this limited access to her vehicle is a miracle. It shows me that she has absolutely *nothing* to hide."

"Or maybe you're too close to her to see clearly."

"What is that supposed to mean? What, exactly, do you think Ashley is hiding?"

Josh shrugged. "Maybe she poisoned herself. Made it all up so she could punish Tom for ignoring her. It wouldn't be the first time a woman scorned has decided to get even."

"Where did the note come from, then?" Katie said, pointing to the evidence bag still in Josh's hands.

"Maybe Tom did write it, but it was a long time ago and referring to something else. Ashley could have kept it for sentimental reasons, then decided to use it against him later."

"Wow," Katie said, shocked. "You are quick to blame the victim, aren't you? I mean, if true, that is one vindictive plan. Like super-villain level of malevolence."

"It's just a possibility to keep in mind."

"Noted." Katie was furious with Josh's suggestion because she believed Ashley would never stoop so low. But she also had believed that Tom would never lie about something so simple as a roommate. Maybe she didn't know her friends quite as well as she thought she did.

"Can you drop the evidence off at the lab in Ankeny?" Katie said, changing the subject. Ankeny was a half hour drive from Waukee, but ninety minutes from Brine. "I need to get back and check in with my chief."

Josh nodded. "And make sure you still have a job?" His tone was soft, sympathetic.

Katie winced. An automatic, involuntary reaction. She didn't want his pity. There was no need for it. She'd poured everything into her job for the past six years. It wasn't just a job to her. It was her identity. Who was she without a Brine police badge? She didn't want to find out.

"Let me know if you want me to put in a good word for you here," Josh said, motioning toward the massive Waukee police station.

"Thanks," Katie said. She stepped into her car and closed the door before she could also add, "But no thanks."

The more time she spent around such a large police department, the more she knew she didn't belong there. But she also wasn't in a position to burn any bridges. A few weeks from now, she could be begging Josh to help her get an interview. She hoped not, but it was a real possibility thanks to Forest Parker.

Katie waved to Josh as she backed out of her parking spot. Josh blew her a kiss. It was playful, not serious, but it was something that would have to stop if Katie was forced to work in Waukee. She groaned. She didn't want to start all over somewhere else. Police departments were a hierarchy. The new guy—or in her case, gal—was at the bottom of the totem pole. Pulling shit duty until proving themselves.

Focus on now, Katie told herself. There were still loose ends to tie up with Rachel Smithson's investigation, including reviewing the remaining calls to service at the Smithson home. She also had a new crime to solve: Ashley's attempted murder.

That reminded her. Before turning onto the highway, Katie picked up her phone and called the public defender's office. The phone rang once before a cheery voice answered.

"Public defender's office, this is Elena. How may I help you?"

"Hi, Elena. It's Katie."

Katie and Elena were friendly. Katie had spent a lot of her free time hanging around that office when no big cases were pending.

"Oh, hi, Katie." Elena suddenly sounded very tired. Her job load had quadrupled with Ashley's hospitalization. Hearings needed moving and clients placated until Ashley could return to work. "Have you seen Ashley?"

"Yes. She's fine. She'll be back out causing trouble in a couple of days."

"Thank God," Elena said with a heavy sigh. "I've only had a few texts from her. I was so worried."

"I don't think the hospital is letting her do much. She needs to rest."

There was a short pause, then Elena said, "Is there something I can do for you?"

"Yes, sorry. I know you are busy. This may seem like a strange question, but do you know if anyone sent any gifts to Ashley? Especially edible ones."

"We get gifts from a small list of Ashley's stalkers rather regularly. Usually it's love notes or a box of chocolates."

"What kind of chocolates?"

"The Russell Stover mixed chocolates. Ashley splits them with me."

"Have you ever gotten sick after eating them?"

"Umm, no. I don't know how I would get sick from chocolates." There was a long pause, then a quick intake of breath. "Is that why Ashley was hospitalized? The chocolates?"

"Probably not those chocolates if you both ate them and you are fine. Has she received gifts from anyone else?"

"Yes. About a week ago, Tom sent her a package of homemade chocolates."

"Did you eat any of those?"

"No. Ashley offered some to me, but I didn't want to accept something that her boyfriend made for *her*. It seemed wrong."

Elena's statement effectively ruled out any possibility that Ashley was using the poisoned chocolates to get back at Tom. If she had done something like that—and Katie seriously doubted that she would—she wouldn't have offered any to Elena. Not if she knew they were poisoned. But that meant Tom was starting to look more guilty.

Katie's heart began beating wildly. "Are you sure that Tom sent the chocolates?"

"The handwriting on the note looked like his. Ashley seemed to think he'd sent them."

Another note in Tom's hand, Katie thought. It was more damning. Framing someone once was one thing, but twice? It wasn't impossible, but it was improbable.

"Do you happen to have any of those chocolates at the office?"

"I don't know. I'll check." Katie heard the click as Elena set the phone on the counter. Silence followed until she returned a few minutes later. "Yeah. Ashley threw them away, but she hasn't taken out her trash yet."

"Good. Don't touch any of it. I'll be there in twenty minutes to pick it up."

Katie went straight there. Elena let her in, a deep worry line etched into her forehead. Katie headed straight toward Ashley's office, Elena hot on her heels.

"Is Ashley allergic to something in the candy?"

Katie didn't answer. Not because she didn't want to, but because it was an open investigation and Elena was not a police officer. Katie had brought some evidence bags inside with her, expecting to leave with at least one item fit for testing. She found a smashed box three-quarters full of chocolates and a note written in Tom's hand. She snapped on a pair of gloves and had everything bagged and tagged in a matter of minutes.

She said goodbye to Elena before heading back to her office.

George found Katie as she was locking the newly discovered evidence in the evidence locker. The officer assigned as evidence custodian would transport it to the Ankeny lab in a few days. It would delay the results, but one trip a week was all the small police department could handle.

"What do you need, George?" She could hear his shuffling footsteps behind her even before she swung around to see him.

"Chief Carmichael wants to talk to you." George wouldn't meet her eye.

"About what?" The question was automatic, but she didn't need an answer. She already knew.

George looked down at his shoes. "He's waiting for you in his office."

She tried to catch his gaze, to force him to look at her, to meet her accusation, but his eyes bounced around the room like pinballs.

Katie sighed and marched past him, bumping his shoulder with hers as she did. She found Chief Carmichael at his desk, studying a document. Katie knocked lightly. When he looked up, his eyes were puffy and red rimmed. A mixture of sleep deprivation and old age, Katie guessed.

"Come on in, Katie," he said. His voice held a false lightness. A forced cheeriness meant to soften the delivery of bad news. Chief Carmichael stood and gestured to the seat across from him. This, she knew, was a bad sign. He had bad knees and never got up for anyone, at least not unless he had to. "Please sit."

When she sat down, he did as well. He wasn't a coward, he did meet her gaze, but it didn't make Katie feel much better. Contained in those eyes was a heavy sense of sadness that could only accompany a *goodbye*. This man had been like a father to her. Which was saying a lot considering that her own father was no longer in the picture. She felt like she was losing her family all over again.

"This is extremely difficult for me," Chief Carmichael said, pressing a handmade handkerchief against his forehead. It had belonged to his late wife. He always kept it with him, but he never used it. The fact that he was now meant he was more distraught than she'd thought. "But I don't have a choice."

Katie didn't respond. There was always a choice.

"The budget cuts, well, I can't keep you. I have to let you go. I have the funds to pay you for another couple of weeks. Give you time to find a new job. But that's all we can afford."

The way he uttered the word *we* in "all *we* can afford" said it all. It no longer included her. She was already an outcast. Katie didn't want to find a new job. She'd worked her way up the ladder. Six years of dedication, and for what? To make it to third from the top before they cut her loose.

"You see, the others, the new hires, they all have far lower salaries than yours."

What about George, Katie thought, but she didn't say it. Because he made *more* than she did. Not by a lot, but still.

"I had to choose between all three of them or you." He lifted his hands in a *what could I do?* gesture. "Sometimes we just need bodies. Numbers to keep order. Even though you are an excellent officer, I couldn't justify choosing one over three."

"Quantity over quality, then. Is that it?"

"Something like that."

Everything about Chief Carmichael's tone and posture radiated apology, but Katie hated him in that moment. He chose George over her. Reading between the lines, that's what he was saying. Just like her father and her mother, choosing money over her. It was the story of her life.

"Is that all?" Katie set her jaw.

"Umm, yes." Chief Carmichael seemed perplexed. "Do you need anything from me? I will be happy to give you an excellent reference. I'm sure you can find a place anywhere you want to go. I really do mean that. You are an excellent officer. One of the best."

It was ironic that he was telling her she could find a job anywhere she wanted. She had the job that she wanted, and now it was gone. The rug literally ripped out from under her. Again.

"No." Her tone was cold. She was not going to make this easy for him. Yes, he seemed remorseful, but he'd still chosen George over her. "Can I go now?"

"Katie..."

She shot to her feet, her chair legs screeching across the floor like nails down a chalkboard.

"Don't do that."

"Don't do what?" Katie stared at her soon-to-be former boss, her head held high. "If I have to go in two weeks, I've got a lot of work to do. I can't trust *George* to do it."

Chief Carmichael nodded. A gesture of resignation. Of knowing that she was going to leave his office and never look at him the same way again.

Katie spun on her heel and marched out of the chief's office. It was bullshit, all of it. She was worth five extra officers. He knew it, she knew it, everyone knew it. As she made her way to her cubicle, she passed George's office. His genuine brick-and-mortar four-walled office. Chief Carmichael had always favored him. *Always*. But why? The chief was emotionally closer to Katie, often treating her more like a daughter than an employee. It made no sense. Unless George...

Katie halted, turned, and marched into George's office.

"Umm, knock much?" George said with his usual smugness.

"Why?" Katie pressed her hands against her hips to keep them from shaking with rage.

George took off his reading glasses, placing them on his desk before looking up at her. "Why what?"

"Why me instead of you?"

"You'll have to ask the chief."

"You used my dad against me, didn't you?"

An expression of wide-eyed shock passed through George's features. It was only there for a split second, but Katie recognized it for what it was. He wasn't surprised by the accusation, just shocked that she'd figured it out.

"You did, didn't you." It was a statement, not a question. "You told the chief that you'd tell everyone that my father is in prison if he let you go instead of me. It would be another reason for the public to hate us even more. Especially if you made some insinuations that I excused my father's behavior."

He didn't deny her allegation. It was as good as an admission.

"You're a fucking coward," Katie said.

George clenched his jaw. "I did what I had to do. You don't understand."

"Oh, I understand. You took advantage of something you learned in confidence. Used it against me to save your own ass. But mark my words, Chief Carmichael is going to be sorry. You've lost your touch. Your mind isn't in your work anymore. You screwed up with Rachel's interview and that's probably not the only time."

George opened his mouth to respond, but Katie cut him off.

"Don't bother with excuses. I don't give a damn what's going on with you. All I care about is that your work has been slipping and your arrogance is through the roof. You've become self-centered and a completely shitty friend. I'm done with you."

Then she stormed out of George's office and down the hallway, heading to the front doors. She needed some fresh air. Chief Carmichael would find out that he had made a huge mistake when the new hires were busy violating constitutional rights and losing evidence in suppression hearings. It was up to George to train them. Judging by his recent behavior, it was a recipe for disaster.

Ashley was going to destroy them in court. Brine could say goodbye to justice, at least for victims. Defendants were going to get away with murder. Literally.

26

ASHLEY

55 days before trial

After seven days in the hospital, Doctor Malloy finally discharged Ashley. Katie was there, her old Impala idling at the curb, when Angelica wheeled Ashley down the hall and out the front doors. Ashley was perfectly fine to walk, but Angelica claimed wheelchairs were standard protocol. Something liability-related, no doubt. Despite the foolishness, Ashley didn't protest. She was too busy basking in the glow of sweet, sweet freedom.

"How are you?" Katie asked as she opened the passenger door.

"I feel fine."

Ashley ignored the proffered hands and climbed into Katie's car. She waved to Angelica as Katie started the engine and took off. Sometime during Ashley's stay, Angelica had grown from caregiver to friend.

"So, what's been going on?" Ashley felt like she'd been in the hospital for an eternity. At a standstill. Stuck in place while the rest of the world kept moving.

Katie sighed heavily. Ashley turned to look at her friend. It was the first time she'd truly *looked* at her. The police officer had visibly lost weight and her red hair hung limply. Dull and disheveled.

"All right. Spill," Ashley said, turning from the window and focusing on Katie. "What's going on?"

"You know that Forest Parker won his bid to slash the police department's budget, right?"

"Yeah."

"Well, Chief Carmichael called me into his office last Monday. They have to let someone go. Apparently, I'm that someone."

Ashley's breath caught. It was terrible news for Katie. She loved that job. But not so horrible for Ashley or her clients. Katie had screwed up a few search warrants early in her career, but she was an excellent officer now. The type that didn't make mistakes. Officers like her were not good for the defense bar.

"I'm sorry."

"Are you, though?" Katie shot back.

Ashley shrugged. "I'm sorry that you are upset. But sometimes these things can be for the best. That job at the Brine PD was a dead-end job for you. You've learned what you need to know. It's probably time for you to move on to bigger and better things."

"Like what?"

Ashley had a few ideas, one that included Forest Parker, the other that depended on whether that reporter, Carley, had been able to raise the promised funds for the public defender's office.

"Give me a few days. But, honestly, it's going to be okay. It doesn't seem like it now, but it will."

"Thanks," Katie said, but she didn't sound optimistic.

A short pause, then Ashley asked, "When is your last day?"

"Friday."

"This Friday?"

Katie nodded.

"Wow. That's quick."

"Yeah."

"Why you? I mean, not to be critical, but George Thomanson is a fucking moron. He used to be fine, but he makes stupid mistakes that are going to cost the State some critical evidence."

Katie shrugged. "It's a good ol' boys club. You know that as well as I do."

"Touché."

It was one of the hard lessons that Ashley had learned through years of working in the criminal justice system. The men had each other's backs. She wished she could say the same for women, but that wasn't true. The former county attorney, Elizabeth Clement, had been a classic example. She could have helped Katie when she was a new officer, but she instead chose to sabotage her and tear her down.

"Were you referring to Rachel Smithson?"

"Hmm?" Ashley asked.

"When you said that George would 'cost the State evidence.' Were you referring to the motion to suppress you filed in Rachel Smithson's case?"

The hearing was scheduled the following Wednesday, two days away, at 10:00 a.m. Ashley would argue that George violated Rachel's constitutional rights and the entire videotaped confession should be suppressed. Meaning the State could not use it as evidence.

That left them with the medical examiner's report to prove cause of death. A document that Ashley had only just received a few days ago. It had been emailed to her directly from the medical examiner. Charles Hanson hadn't turned it over, so Ashley went directly to the source. She was happy that she had. The report was a goldmine.

"Yeah. I depose George this afternoon, by the way."

Ashley had lost too many days in the hospital. Both Doctor Malloy and Elena had urged her to take it easy for a couple days, but Ashley couldn't waste the time. She wanted to depose George before he testified at the motion to suppress hearing, and that left only Monday and Tuesday.

Katie pulled up beside Ashley's vehicle, parking at the Waukee police station. Katie handed Ashley her keys. She'd had them ever since searching Ashley's car for Tom's letter and the box with the poisoned chocolates. Ashley had tried not to think of Tom throughout her hospitalization. It hurt too much. She hadn't originally believed he would intentionally hurt her, but a nagging part deep inside of her was starting to doubt that conviction.

Because hadn't he betrayed her with his lies about Lydia? He had been living with her for months and hadn't said a single word to Ashley about it. Then there was his choice to ignore her phone calls, all while she was being poisoned. Was it coincidence? Possibly. But she'd be a fool to brush it off without giving it proper consideration.

"Don't tell him I said this," Katie said, pulling Ashley out of her thoughts, "but give George some hell in that deposition. He deserves it."

"Thanks," Ashley said.

Ashley turned Katie's words over in her mind as she got into her Tahoe and started the engine. A statement like that meant something coming from Katie. Was it possible that the officer was coming round to Ashley's way of thinking?

When Ashley arrived in Brine, she drove straight to the jail. Rachel looked better than ever. The teenager had put on some weight. She wasn't round by any stretch of the imagination, but she was no longer skeletal, and her cheeks finally had some color.

"You look great," Ashley said as they made their way down the hall and into the room designated for depositions.

"Took you long enough," George said as Rachel and Ashley were buzzed into the room. He and Charles Hanson were already seated at the table, both looking disgruntled.

"Yes," Charles said, tapping his watch. "You said ten."

"I came here straight from the hospital, you jackasses. And it's only 10:10." Ashley had no patience for their patronizing bullshit.

"Jackass?" Charles said, pushing his chair back with a screech and shooting to his feet.

"Oh, don't get your tighty-whities in a knot," Ashley said, waving a dismissive hand.

Charles did not sit back down. He glared at Ashley through intense gray eyes.

"Are we going to stand around arguing all day or are we going to do this? Come on, Charles, time is money, right?"

Charles grunted noncommittally, but he did lower himself back into his seat.

"All right," Ashley said, clapping her hands together. "Are we ready to go on the record?"

The court reporter nodded and swore George in. Ashley dove straight into the questioning.

"Good morning, George."

"I wouldn't call it *good*."

So that's how this is going to go, Ashley thought. George was already on edge. A positive sign. "It sounds like you want to skip the niceties."

"Yeah."

"We can do that." Ashley cracked her knuckles and leaned forward. "You interviewed my client, Rachel Smithson, correct?"

"Yes."

"And in that interview, Rachel told you several times that she did not murder her child, right?"

"She also said the opposite."

"No. She didn't. She agreed with the opposite."

"I don't remember it that way."

Ashley rifled in her bag and pulled out a stack of papers, shuffling through the documents until she found the one she was looking for. It was a transcription of Rachel's interview. Ashley skipped to a page she'd previously flagged near the end of the transcript.

Ashley cleared her throat dramatically, then began reading. "You asked Rachel, and I quote, 'you put your baby face down in the bathtub, didn't you?'" Ashley looked up, meeting George's furious gaze. "Did you say those words?"

"If that's what the transcript says."

"I'm not asking what the transcript says. I'm asking what *you* said. Did *you* say those words?"

"Yes."

"Okay." Ashley turned her attention to the next line on the transcript. "Then you asked Rachel if she turned the water on, right?"

"Yes."

"You asked her if she plugged the drain, correct?"

"I did."

Ashley set the transcript down and tapped it with her finger. "Do you see any problem with your line of questioning?"

"No."

"It doesn't bother you that Rachel didn't volunteer any of these alleged facts?"

"No. It doesn't matter if she volunteered them. She agreed with them."

"But her *agreement* was never more than the word 'yes,' was it?"

"That's right. But she did agree with me."

"But she never offered any details of her own, right?"

"Right."

"Okay." Ashley pulled another document from her bag and placed it on top of the transcript. "Have you had an opportunity to review the medical examiner's report in this case?"

"Objection," Charles Hanson interrupted.

Ashley looked up, cocking an eyebrow.

"Have *you* seen the medical examiner's report, Ashley?"

"Why, Mr. Hanson, I have it right here." She waved the copy of the report in the air. "Thank you for your concern, though. I'm sure you were planning on sending it to me right away." Her words dripped with sarcasm.

Charles's face reddened.

"Now, Detective Thomanson, please answer my question. Have you seen the medical examiner's report?"

"No."

"Do you know the cause of death?"

"Yes. The baby drowned."

Ashley slid the report across the table to George. "What I'm showing you has been marked as deposition exhibit 1. This is a copy of the medical examiner's report. Can you point out the cause of death listed on that document?"

George paused for a long moment, studying the report. Then he looked up and shook his head.

"Is that a no?" Ashley motioned to the court reporter at the end of the table. "This isn't your first rodeo, George. You have to answer out loud. You know the court reporter can't take down head movements."

"It's a no."

"The medical examiner's report says that no water was found in the lungs, right?"

"Yes."

"Which means that the child wasn't breathing when, or if, he was ever placed in the water, right?"

"It could mean that."

He was in denial. Ashley expected this. "Well, when someone drowns, they typically have water in their lungs, don't they?"

"Umm..."

"And you are claiming this baby drowned, aren't you? I mean, that's what you were getting at when you made my client admit to placing her baby face down in the bathtub, right?"

"I didn't *make* your client do anything."

"Debatable," Ashley said, but she wasn't going to hash out all the ways he'd screwed up the interview, including his failure to provide Rachel medical attention. She'd save that for the motion to suppress hearing.

"She could have killed him before placing him in the bathtub. He was completely dependent on her. She could have smothered him first."

"Now, George. You know as well as I do that 'could have' is not evidence. Any number of things 'could have' happened. But bathtub drowning is what you have alleged. You have no proof that Rachel killed the baby in any other way, do you?"

"Umm."

"The medical examiner's report actually lists cause of death as 'undetermined,' doesn't it?"

"Yes."

"So, it's very plausible that Rachel gave birth to a stillborn baby in that hotel room. Meaning the baby was never alive, right?"

"No."

"No?" George was digging in his heels. Full-fledged denial. "Well, there's as much evidence to support that conclusion as there is to support the opposite, right?"

"No."

This line of questioning wasn't going anywhere.

"So, your position is that my client killed her baby in some way, although nobody is quite sure how she did it?"

"No. My position is that Rachel drowned the baby like she said."

"Can you prove the baby was born alive?"

"Yes."

"How?"

"Rachel admitted that he cried. A stillborn baby doesn't cry."

"Ahh, yes, George. That was another thing Rachel *agreed* to, wasn't it?"

"Yes."

"But she didn't *agree* to it until after you started yelling at her, did she?"

"I never yelled at her."

"Okay, fine. Then after you raised your voice."

"I never raised my voice."

"Would you *agree* that the video recording is the best evidence as to the volume and tone of your voice during your questioning of Rachel?"

George gritted his teeth.

"Would you agree, Detective?"

"Yes."

Ashley nodded. She had gotten the information that she needed out of George. There was no need to drag the deposition out any longer. "That's all the questions I have for today. Thank you, George," Ashley said with a Cheshire-cat grin. "I'll see you on Wednesday."

27

RACHEL

53 days before trial

Aside from the time she spent in the hospital, Ashley had kept to her promise to visit Rachel every day. Jail didn't bother Rachel. Her incarceration was not the reason she cared about the number of times Ashley visited. She cared because Ashley had made a promise, and Rachel had never known adults to keep their promises.

You are in a safe place, the school counselor had said. That was a lie.

I will take care of you, her mother had claimed. Lie.

He will not touch you again, said the policeman. Lie.

I will help you. That was the worst kind of falsehood. It came from strangers Rachel thought, once upon a time, could orchestrate her escape. It, too, turned out to be a lie. Especially when it came from cops or child protective services.

"Good morning, Rachel," Ashley said, bringing Rachel out of her memories.

"Morning."

Rachel never said anything was *good*. Especially when it was, in fact, good. All good things could be taken. Labeling anything as such was like blowing out all your birthday candles and promptly telling everyone what you had wished for.

"How are you?"

Rachel shrugged. "I'm reading *To Kill a Mockingbird.*"

It was her way of telling Ashley she was just fine without jinxing it. Because, honestly, who could be unhappy while reading.

"I love that book," Ashley said. "I always saw a bit of Scout in myself. Or at least I try to be a bit like her."

Rachel nodded, but she couldn't quite understand the sentiment. She'd never had the luxury of wishing to be anything other than herself.

"Well," Ashley said, clapping her hands together, pulling Rachel out of her thoughts. "Shall we?"

Rachel cocked her head, confused.

"Your motion to suppress hearing is today."

"Right," Rachel said.

At that moment, Kylie came down the hallway, dragging Rachel's chains behind her. She unlocked Rachel's cell door, and Rachel spread her legs and stuck out her hands. A few moments later she was a whole lot heavier and they were on their way to the courthouse.

The moment the three women stepped outside, they were assaulted by cameras flashing and reporters shouting. Rachel could feel both Kylie and Ashley stiffen, but she didn't mind the reporters. It was just noise. They couldn't hurt her. Nobody could anymore.

The motion to suppress hearing started at ten o'clock sharp. The prosecutor, a slippery-looking man with a pinched face, barely made it on time. Ashley chuckled as he darted into the courtroom, frazzled and breathing heavily.

"Judge Ahrenson won't like his tardiness. He tends to run a tight ship," Ashley whispered to Rachel.

Rachel studied the judge from the corner of her eye. Ashley was right, he didn't look happy.

"Nice of you to join us, Mr. Hanson," Judge Ahrenson said, peering over the bench like a hawk eyeing his prey.

"Yes, sorry, Judge."

"Is the prosecution ready to proceed?"

"Umm, yes," Mr. Hanson said, dropping into his chair. His chest heaved as he mopped his forehead with a handkerchief.

"How about you, Ms. Montgomery? Are you ready to go on the record?"

"Yes, Your Honor." Ashley's voice rang out across the room, poised and clear as a bell.

Rachel was in awe of the attorney. How had she learned to speak like that—with no fear and absolute composure—to a man of such power? If Rachel had been given a different lot in life, she would have wanted to grow up to be like Ashley.

But God had seen fit to punish her. If there truly was a God. There was a time in her life when she had been a believer, but that was long ago. Back before her body changed and men started seeing her as a woman rather than a pretty little girl. No, she did not believe in a higher power. If one did exist, he had abandoned her. Yet another man letting her down.

"Call your first witness," Judge Ahrenson said, catching Rachel's attention. He was speaking to Mr. Hanson, but the chill in his tone sent a shiver up her spine.

The prosecutor stood. "The State calls Detective George Thomanson to the stand."

A man stood from somewhere near the back of the courtroom and approached the front. Rachel recognized him from her interrogation. He and another woman had conducted the interview. It felt like a good cop/bad cop routine, except the woman had stayed silent, leaving Rachel alone with the bad cop.

"Turn back around," Ashley whispered. "And don't make eye contact with anyone in the gallery."

Rachel obeyed. She didn't want to resist. Lots of people were there to watch the hearing. Every empty space was filled, but Rachel hadn't studied any of their faces. She was too fearful of what she'd see. The judgmental downturn of her mother's lips. The possessive control in her father's eyes. The school counselor's need for her attention. At one time, she'd had no other choice than to give them what they wanted. But not anymore. Her chains had freed her of their demands.

The detective passed between the prosecution and defense tables and stopped in front of the judge.

"Please raise your right hand."

George raised his left hand, then chuckled and switched to his right.

"Do you swear to tell the truth, the whole truth, so help you?"

"I swear."

"Have a seat," Judge Ahrenson said, motioning to the witness stand.

The detective sat down, and Mr. Hanson began his questioning. They eased in by talking about Detective Thomanson's training, then switched to his interview of Rachel. As the topic grew closer to Rachel's statements about what had occurred in that hotel room, her mind began to wander. Past the words she had said and back to her memories of that time.

She had planned it all out—what she would say to the cops—well before that interview had started. But she'd failed to account for the amount of pain that remained after giving birth. Nobody ever talked about that. People described the pain as sudden, urgent, and then gone. That hadn't happened with Rachel. She remembered searing agony. So much that she couldn't think. There was this fogginess in her head. Later she learned from the doctor that it was due to blood loss, but she hadn't known that at the time.

All she remembered were the endless rounds of questions. The same things asked in different ways over and over again. Hours of questions, all while she was in pain. She didn't complain, though. She knew better. Men did not like complaints. It would only result in something worse happening to her. The only way out of her pain was to wait for the man to leave and to ask the silent woman for help.

After an eternity, Rachel finally had decided that she would simply agree with the man. Her mind could not conjure up her original story, no matter how hard she tried. It simply would not work, and she needed this thing to end. For the life of her, she couldn't remember how she claimed to have "killed" the baby. Not that it mattered. Ultimately, she ended up where she had intended.

Movement around Rachel pulled her out of her thoughts. People were all standing, and Ashley was tugging on her arm so she would do the same. Judge Ahrenson stood and exited the courtroom through a door behind his bench. The hearing was over and Rachel hadn't paid attention to any of it.

"That went well," Ashley said, smiling broadly. Despite her palpable excitement, Ashley looked tired.

"Do you feel okay?" Rachel asked.

She didn't care about the hearing. Both Kylie and Ashley had warned her that the suppression of the video was a longshot. Not because it was a weak motion, but because of the seriousness of the allegations. No judge wanted to be responsible for releasing a baby murderer. Rachel fully expected the judge to deny the motion, and she was perfectly fine with that.

"Just tired," Ashley said. "I guess I should have listened to the doctor when she told me to take it easy."

A tiny nagging thought dug at the back of Rachel's mind. She tried to ignore it, but it burrowed in, like a hookworm through its host's foot. "Do you, umm, know how you got sick?"

Ashley nodded, then shook her head. "Apparently rat poison. I guess someone wants me dead."

Rachel froze. "Do you know who gave it to you?"

"Not yet, but they will figure it out." Ashley studied Rachel for a long moment. "It's not something that you need to worry about, Rachel. I'll be fine. I promise."

Now this was a promise that Rachel knew Ashley may not be able to keep. For she had her own suspicions. If *he* had anything to do with it, he would not stop until he got what he wanted.

"Be careful."

"I will," Ashley said, but Rachel knew better.

No woman was safe from *him*.

28

KATIE

45 days before trial

It was Friday, the last day of Katie's employment with the Brine Police Department. Her heart was heavy as she looked around the cubicle that had been her second home over the past six years. It was no longer hers, or it wouldn't be in another hour. She didn't recognize it now that she'd taken down and boxed up her things. The walls were barren, the computer screen dark.

Katie didn't know what she would do next. Where she would work. Who she was meant to become. Ashley had said that her termination was an opportunity to do bigger things with her life. Whatever those things were, they hadn't yet surfaced. When they did—if they did—they most certainly would require her to move. Her relationship with Brine had been love-hate, but it was the first place that had ever felt like home to her. She wasn't eager to leave.

Her cell phone began buzzing in her pocket. She picked it up and looked at the screen. The name *Josh Martin* filled the screen along with Josh's face, wide with a toothy grin. Katie shook her head, but a small smile crept into the corners of her lips as she picked up.

"Yes?"

"Is that how you always answer the phone or is that a special greeting just for me?"

Katie rolled her eyes. "Nobody annoys me quite like you do."

"So, you're saying I'm special."

"Is there something you wanted other than to waste my time?"

Truthfully, it didn't matter. Katie had thirty minutes left in her workday and only one task to complete. The rather dismal and depressing chore of briefing George on her ongoing work with Ashley's poisoning and the leads left to follow in Rachel Smithson's case. Neither were cases that she wanted to hand over to him. There was a good chance that he'd already screwed up Rachel's case. She wasn't eager to see what he would do with Ashley's poisoning.

"Yes. There's someone here who would like to speak to you."

"Who?"

Josh didn't answer. Katie could hear the rustle of the phone as it was passed to someone else.

A throat cleared, a deep, guttural sound. Then an unknown voice said, "Miss Mickey?"

"Yes. This is Katie Mickey."

"This is Chief Canterbury. I'm the chief of police here in Waukee. I hear that Brine has suffered some budget cuts and had to, for lack of a better term, cut you loose."

There were plenty of better terms, but Katie didn't correct him. "Yes. That's true."

"Would you like to interview with our department? We are always looking for good, diverse people. And our city council supports us."

Katie knew what he meant by *diverse*. Women. Less than one percent of the Waukee Police Department was female and most of them were secretaries, dispatchers, or office managers. Katie had already looked it up.

"I'd love to interview," Katie said, trying to force some excitement into her voice.

"Great. How about this upcoming Monday? Will that work?"

"Yes." Katie would be out of a job by then. "I'm free anytime."

"Let's say 11:00 a.m. See you then."

"I'll be there."

Katie hung up the phone before Josh could get back on the line. There wasn't time to do their usual song and dance—Josh flirting while Katie feigned annoyance. She only had twenty minutes left in her last day and she still needed to talk to George.

Procrastination. That was what she had been doing when it came to the task of briefing George. But now it had come to the end of the day and she couldn't put it off any longer. Katie stood and headed toward George's office. No other officers were around. They had been avoiding her since they learned the news. It was like they thought her termination was airborne. Contagious.

"George," Katie said. His office door was open, so she knocked on the frame three times.

"Come in. Come in."

Katie stepped across the threshold. It was far warmer in George's office than in the rest of the building. A shiver ran through her as her body acclimated to the temperature change. George remained seated at his desk, looking down at a document, his readers perched near the tip of his nose. Katie waited for several moments, but George kept on reading, ignoring her.

Screw him, Katie thought, marching further into his office and dropping into one of the two chairs directly across from his executive-style desk. She'd spent years standing in doorways waiting for men to invite her to take a seat at the table. But she didn't have to do that anymore. Those same men had fired her.

"I'm here to brief you on the final strings left to tie up in Rachel Smithson's case as well as the Montgomery attempted murder."

George kept his eyes on the document, then put up a finger in the universal *one moment* sign. Katie had no intention of waiting. Not anymore.

"I'll start with Rachel's case." If he wasn't going to pay attention, Rachel's was the less important case. At least to Katie. "I have emailed you the calls to service that Officer Josh Martin sent to me. I have also included a brief summary of them along with it. There are a few important things to garner from my follow-up investigation into the calls as well as Rachel's parentage."

"Parentage?" George finally looked up.

"Isaac Smithson is Rachel's putative father, but I don't believe he is Rachel's actual father. Lyndsay, Rachel's mother, gave birth to her in secret, in Brine."

"I don't see why that matters."

"It matters because he has physically and mentally abused Rachel Smithson her entire life. There is also a question as to whether that abuse extended to sexual abuse."

"I still don't..."

Katie cut him off. "I think Isaac is the father of Rachel's baby. You should get a DNA sample from Isaac and compare it against the baby's. I think you'll find that they match."

George removed his glasses and tossed them on his desk. "I don't see why I would do that. It makes no difference who fathered Rachel's child. It doesn't change the fact that she killed her baby."

Katie rolled her eyes. George had grown lazy and complacent in his detective role. "If you don't, Ashley will. She'll use the physical and sexual abuse to justify Rachel's choice to give birth alone in a hotel room. It will make Rachel look like a concerned mother, not a villain. Then we have the problem of the medical examiner's report."

"Yeah," George cut her off, "I was just looking at that." He gestured to the document he had been reading. "I'm not all that worried about it. It doesn't say that the baby was born alive, but it also doesn't say that the baby wasn't born alive. And if you recall, Rachel admitted that she heard the baby cry once before placing him in the bathtub."

"I recall Rachel agreeing with you that the baby cried. I don't think she ever said it in her own words."

"Same difference."

It wasn't the same. If George couldn't tell the difference, then that was his problem. Katie felt certain that a judge and jury would. And then there was Ashley's motion to suppress. If the judge ruled that interview inadmissible, they had no evidence of live birth. But Katie could see by George's uninterested expression that he didn't care. She shrugged. It wasn't her problem anymore.

"Moving on to Ashley's poisoning. We have preliminary reports from the forensic lab in Ankeny. Fingerprints found on both letters contained inside the boxes of chocolates match Tom and Ashley. There are no other identifiable fingerprints. The handwriting on the letters also matches Tom's. The report confirms that the package found in Ashley's car contained traceable amounts of rat poison. The chocolates in the box found in Ashley's trash can were also tested. There were ten chocolate peanut butter balls remaining in the package. All of them tested positive for rat poison."

"Great work," George said, flipping his pen around his index finger.

"The hospital sent a sample of Ashley's hair for testing, too. The lab was able to determine that Ashley had been exposed to the same poison multiple times, but they couldn't pinpoint exact dates. The criminalist did say that there is evidence that the first date of ingestion was within the last month."

"Wow. I never thought I'd be saying this, but poor Ashley."

Katie leveled him with a challenging glare. "You don't sound all that sorry."

"You're right," he said, chuckling. "I'm not. She sucks. But I'll start working on an arrest warrant anyway. It'll be good to get that one behind us."

"That's the problem, though. I think Tom was set up."

"Why?"

"I don't know." Katie looked down at her fingers. "It's a hunch. But I think there's more to this than we think."

George waved a dismissive hand. "Nine times out of ten the simplest option is the right one."

"Yes," Katie said through gritted teeth, "but that still leaves one time when it isn't."

"Katie, Katie." George stood and came around the desk. "I know it's hard for you to believe because Tom is your friend. But you haven't always been the best judge of character. You know, with your father and all."

If Katie had misjudged anyone's character it had been George's. She could hardly believe that she had once considered him a friend.

"Don't be a lazy ass," Katie said, unable to control her temper any longer. "Tom has no motive, and you know it. Tom's roommate, however, does. She's Ashley's former foster sister. You need to follow up on that angle before you go issuing arrest warrants. If you don't, Josh will, and Waukee will make Brine look like a lazy police department in a Podunk town."

"The good news, Katie, is that you don't have to worry about this police station anymore. Or either of these investigations. They are closed as far as I am concerned, and the guilty parties will be held accountable." George's nostrils flared as he spoke. He marched toward the door and motioned for her to leave.

She'd pissed him off. It was an unplanned bonus. "Fine," Katie said, balling her fists.

As she passed him, she had to fight a very real urge to punch him square in the jaw. She grabbed her box of belongings as she passed her former cubicle and marched out of the building. She didn't stop to say goodbye to anyone. In that moment, she hated that entire police station. It was full of misogynistic pigs.

Despite her anger, her mind still whirred. She needed to find a way to prove Tom's innocence. Throughout the entire investigation into Ashley's poisoning, she'd kept her distance from Tom because of her position as a police officer. For the first time in over six years, she no longer held that position. She was free to do whatever she wanted.

Katie pulled her phone out of her pocket, dialing Tom's number while balancing the box from her office in the other hand.

"Katie." Tom sounded exhausted, his voice on edge. "What's going on? I haven't heard anything from anyone. How is Ashley? What's happening with the investigation?"

"Oh, nobody told you. Ashley's out of the hospital and back to her usual shenanigans."

"Thank God. Can I talk to her? Call her?"

"Umm, I wouldn't just yet." Katie pursed her lips. "Listen, I don't know how else to say this so I'm going to come right out with it. George thinks you tried to kill Ashley. If we don't prove him wrong, and soon, he's going to issue a warrant."

Tom hissed through his teeth. "I didn't do it, you've got to..."

"I believe you, Tom. That's why I'm calling you. If I thought you had anything to do with this, I would have arrested you myself."

"Okay, then who do you think did it?"

"Let me send you a picture of the letters that were found with the poisoned candies. I have copies stored on my phone. Look at them and then call me back."

"Okay."

Katie hung up and sent Tom the photographs. A few moments passed before her phone started buzzing.

"Did you write those?"

Tom sighed heavily. "Yes..."

Shit, Katie thought. Maybe he was the guilty party.

"Except I didn't write them to Ashley."

That was news.

29

ASHLEY

42 days before trial

Ashley was at her computer reading through a recent Iowa Supreme Court decision when the email notification came through. She dropped what she'd been doing and clicked on Outlook. The clerk of court sent notifications of filings by email. The ruling for Rachel's motion to suppress was due any second now. Ashley had been on pins and needles ever since the hearing.

The subject line for the notification read *Courtesy NEF: FECR015987 State of Iowa v. Rachel Smithson*. It had to be the ruling. Ashley's heartbeat quickened. A bead of sweat formed along her brow as she logged into the electronic filing system and pulled up Rachel's case file. There it was. *Ruling on Defendant's Motion to Suppress*.

Ashley clicked on the document. Her hands shook with anticipation. This was it. The moment of truth. The entire case hung on this ruling.

The document populated the screen. Ashley didn't read the court's analysis including all the reasons for the decision. She didn't need to know all that information just yet. What she cared about was found at the end. She skipped forward, scrolling down through pages and pages of facts and cited case law. Then she began to read.

It is for the above stated reasons, Judge Ahrenson wrote, *that the Court FINDS that the Defendant's Motion to Suppress should be granted.*

"Yes!" Ashley jumped out of her chair and pumped her fist in the air. "Take that, Charles Hanson!"

With the suppression of this evidence, the State would not be able to prove that the baby was born alive. Without a live baby, there could be no child endangerment or murder. The State's case was dead. They could still proceed to trial, but Charles Hanson would look like a fool on a national stage. He couldn't present evidence to all elements of the offense, and Judge Ahrenson would direct it out before a jury could consider the evidence.

Charles Hanson, as an elected official, would never humiliate himself by losing so horribly and so publicly. It was bad for reelection. He would instead choose to dismiss the case. Rachel was as good as free. Not that it would happen immediately. Charles would wait to the last moment to file the motion to dismiss, ensuring that Rachel waited in jail right up until the trial date. That sucked, but Rachel would have an end date. Forty-two days until freedom.

Ashley skipped out of her office and to the front, where Elena sat, typing on her computer while humming a tune. She looked up as Ashley drew nearer.

"It's nice to see you smiling," Elena said.

It was true. Ashley couldn't remember the last time her lips had tipped up to form something other than a tight, forced grin. There had been a lot going on over the past few months, and very little of it positive. But that was all changing now. She could feel it in her bones.

"Look at this," Ashley said, handing a printed copy of the court's ruling to Elena.

Ashley would print another later and frame it. She'd put it on her wall of achievements, the section of her office dedicated solely to wins against the State.

Elena focused on the first page, reading slowly, carefully.

"Just flip to the end," Ashley said, taking the document and turning to the last page. She handed it back to Elena and pointed to the final paragraph. "There. Read that."

Elena did, then she looked up, her face blooming with happiness. "That's awesome, Ashley! When are you going to tell Rachel?"

"I'm on my way to the jail now."

"Oh, wow. I can't wait to hear how she reacts. This is good for her, right?"

Ashley nodded and headed to the coat rack. "Really, really good," she said, pulling on her coat.

It only took a few minutes for Ashley to walk to the jail. When she arrived, Kylie was out front waiting for her.

"I heard about the ruling." Kylie's smile spread all the way to her eyes. "The great Ashley Montgomery strikes again."

"Thank you. I'm pretty excited to tell Rachel."

"About that." Kylie paused, sucking in a deep breath. "Be cautious. She might not handle the news the way you think she will."

"What?" Ashley was shocked. "Why not?" Nobody wanted to go to prison for life. Rachel was going to be one of the few people to beat prison entirely. She was getting out in a little over a month. That wasn't a small thing. Plenty of inmates would kill for a ruling like this one.

"I don't know anything for certain," Kylie said with a shrug. "I just know that the girl has been enjoying herself here in jail. I mean that. She's completely changed. Rachel came in here as a wispy shell of a person. Now, she's a regular chatterbox. Smiles more often than she doesn't. Reads every free moment she gets. This may seem shocking, but I don't think she wants out."

"Oh, that's ridiculous," Ashley said. "Everyone wants out of jail. That's the whole point of it. Punishment."

Kylie grunted noncommittally and led Ashley into the attorney-client room. "I'll go get Rachel."

The room only had two plastic chairs and an old, worn desk that separated them. Ashley sat in one of the chairs, crossed her legs, then uncrossed them and stood up again. She was all energy. Filled to the brim with excitement. Telling a defendant they had won was one of her favorite parts of her job. It didn't come that often—rarely, in truth—but when it did, it almost made up for the devastation that came with all the other losses.

The lock on the door clicked and Ashley looked up in time to see Kylie ushering Rachel inside. Ashley took a moment to study her client. Rachel had undergone a transformation. She'd added fifteen to twenty pounds, transforming her face from sunken-in and haggard to a true beauty. It wouldn't matter what Ashley did with Rachel's hair now. The girl was stunning. Almost hypnotizingly so.

"Hi, Ashley," Rachel said. She gave a genuine smile that showed a small gap between her two front teeth, a flaw that only added to Rachel's beauty.

"I've got great news."

"Oh?" Rachel said, furrowing her brow. "Better than your full recovery? I can't imagine what could be better." Coming from anyone else, Ashley would have thought the phrase was meant to be sarcastic. But Rachel's voice was so small, so sweet, it couldn't be anything but sincere.

"Judge Ahrenson granted our motion to suppress." Ashley produced a copy of the court's ruling and set it on the desk.

Rachel's smile disappeared and her mouth dropped open.

"It means that we have won."

Rachel gripped the back of the other blue plastic chair, leaning against it like she might faint.

"You're going to walk."

A tear slid down Rachel's cheek as she pulled out the chair and sank into it.

"You're free."

Rachel was speechless for a long moment, then she shook her head. "No. This isn't how it was supposed to happen."

"I don't understand..." Kylie had said that Rachel's reaction might be odd, but Ashley was unprepared for the complete lack of joy.

Rachel traced little circles on the desk with her fingers, then looked up. "I want to plead guilty." Her eyes were hard and determined, an expression Ashley had never seen from her client.

"What?" Ashley leaned back in her chair, as though creating physical distance would give her the space she needed to find a way to change Rachel's mind.

"I said I want to plead guilty." Rachel set her jaw firmly.

"Why? You've won."

"I can still plead guilty, can't I?"

"Umm, yes," Ashley said, shaking her head. "But I don't know why you would. We are talking about life in prison here."

"That's what I want. Life in prison." There was no hesitation. "Thank you for your assistance. I truly appreciate it. But I don't want what you want. It is safe in here, in jail. It will be safe in prison, too."

"Safe from whom?"

"Isaac."

Ashley sucked in a long breath. She should have expected this. She had read the calls to service. It was clear that Isaac had been physically abusing his daughter for more than ten years. And hadn't Kylie tried to warn her? But she'd been too excited, too arrogant.

"I know Isaac has hurt you, Rachel, but we can keep you safe. There are options out there."

"Were you able to keep yourself safe?"

"I don't know what you…"

Rachel cut Ashley off. "Your poisoning. I don't know who the cops think did it, but it was poison in homemade chocolates, right?"

"Yes. But I still don't see what that has to do with you."

"My mom makes the homemade chocolates. Isaac adds the last ingredient. Rat poison."

Ashley shook her head, unable to fully process the information.

"That's one of the ways that he punishes me."

"What? Did he do that to you while you were pregnant?"

A tear slid down Rachel's cheek. She made no move to brush it away. "I tried to be good during the pregnancy. Not that I wanted to have a baby that was half *him*, but I thought that maybe he would turn out like me instead."

It was Ashley's turn to sit down. "But Isaac is *your* dad."

Rachel shook her head. "Not biological."

"So he raped you."

Rachel nodded. It was a gesture of resignation. Like her past was something she'd been unsuccessfully attempting to block from her memory.

"More than once?"

Tears threaded their way down Rachel's cheeks, leaving sparkling track marks in their wake. "Yeah. He wanted a son. He said he always wanted a boy, and my 'bitch' mom wouldn't give him one."

Isaac had raped his daughter. He knew she wasn't biological, so he also knew the baby would be healthy. Rachel was a victim. A very unexpected victim. Vilified by the world, but they were wrong. The poor girl had been abused her entire life.

"I don't understand," Ashley said. "How did the baby die?"

"He left me alone until the end. I thought I was safe since he seemed to want the baby so badly. I don't remember what he thought I'd done wrong, but apparently, I had done something to piss him off. That's when he did it. He had snuck some rat poison into my dinner. I knew he'd done it the moment I finished eating. The way he was looking at me and smiling in that cold, horrible way."

"Did the baby..." Ashley's voice trailed off.

"I got pretty sick that time. I think he gave me more than he had meant to. That, or my tolerance for the poison was low since it had been so long since the last time he had punished me."

The thought broke Ashley's heart. It meant that this poor girl had been poisoned so often that she'd developed an immunity to it.

"I missed a couple days of school. But when I went back, I left early and went to see a doctor. I was barely eighteen by then, so I could go without my parents knowing. They couldn't find a heartbeat. Labor started a couple hours later. It wasn't all that painful at first, so I came up with a plan. I'd have the baby, leave it in the hotel room for someone to find. Then I'd tell the cops that I had smothered him. They wouldn't know the difference so long as they thought he was born alive."

"Why?" Ashley said. She was stunned, but she had to admit it was a genius plan if Rachel did, in fact, want to spend life in prison. The doctor, bound by privacy laws, wasn't able to provide information to the State that the baby had died before birth. "Why would you do that?"

"You know why," Rachel said, her eyes flashing with anger. "He got to you, too. And he's getting away with it, isn't he? I doubt he's even on anyone's radar as a potential suspect. Someone will go down for your poisoning, but he's made sure it won't be him." She paused, pursing her lips. "Don't you see? You're not even safe from him. The only place that I'm safe is in here. That's why I want to plead guilty."

Ashley sighed deeply. Rachel had lived one fucked-up life. Ashley could have asked Rachel why she hadn't gone to the authorities—why she didn't report the abuse years earlier—but she didn't need to. There were years of calls to service that explained why Rachel didn't trust law enforcement or any other adult. They came, then they left. They never helped.

The revelation explained why Rachel had blossomed in custody. It was the only time in her entire life that she had been free. It wasn't true freedom, but it was something far better than what she had on the outside. But still, Ashley loathed the idea of letting an innocent person plead guilty. The thought made her stomach twist. Then, she had an idea.

"Rachel," Ashley said.

Rachel clenched her jaw, preparing for an argument.

"Just hear me out, okay?" Ashley spoke cautiously. She kept her voice low, soothing, a tone that one might use with a spooked horse.

"Okay."

"What if Isaac is arrested?"

"What for?"

Rachel was growing suspicious. Ashley couldn't blame her. All the adults in her life had lied to her, raped her, and abused her.

"Well, there are two potential possibilities. One, for attempting to murder me, and the second is for nonconsensual termination of human pregnancy."

Rachel was silent for a long moment.

"The termination of pregnancy is a ten-year sentence and attempted murder is a twenty-five-year sentence. If we can get the State to add a sexual assault charge or two, he's looking at the rest of his natural life trapped inside the walls of a prison."

Rachel chewed on her lip, then she nodded. "Okay. I'll give you a week. But if they don't charge him, then I want to plead guilty."

"Can I have two weeks instead?"

"No. I don't want them to dismiss my charges before I can plead."

"Fair enough." Ashley knew it was a long shot, but she had to try. She stuck her hand out and Rachel shook it. "We have a deal. If Isaac isn't in jail in the next seven days, you can plead guilty."

Rachel nodded, the smile reappearing on her face. "Deal."

Ashley left the meeting with a heavy heart. While she didn't understand

Rachel's position, she could sympathize with it. But Ashley was a defense attorney. Her goal was to get her clients released. Here she was on the precipice of a monumental win against the State and her client wanted to plead guilty. The two thoughts—winning at all costs and duty to her client —which had always been in sync, were now at war.

.Yet there was a way out. Isaac Smithson's arrest. Only one person could help Ashley with that. Someone who had an in with the Waukee Police Department, where the bulk of the crimes occurred. It was her old pal Katie Mickey.

30

KATIE

41 days before trial

Katie's interview with Chief Canterbury had gone well. Or at least she thought it had gone well. But that was yesterday, and she hadn't heard anything since then. It felt like an ominous sign. Wouldn't they have called her by now if they were going to offer her the position?

She'd spent the afternoon pacing across her living room, then pausing at the coffee table to glance at her phone, willing it to ring. But it hadn't. And she'd ended the night with a heavy feeling of dejection hovering over her.

By nine o'clock Tuesday morning, she'd all but given up. Then her phone began to buzz. She dashed across the room and picked it up.

"Hello?"

"Hey." It was Ashley. She sounded tired.

"Oh, hey."

"You sound like your day is going about as well as mine is."

"Why? What's going on?"

Ashley issued a heavy sigh. "I need your help."

"Okay. What's going on?" Katie didn't hesitate. She'd do anything for

Ashley. Especially since they were no longer working on opposite sides of the law.

"It's Rachel Smithson."

Then Ashley launched into a story about Isaac and Rachel Smithson and poison that was too fanciful to be untrue. Ashley's words tore at Katie in a way that no other case had aside from Ashley's wrongful arrest and near murder last year. Once again, law enforcement had gotten it all wrong. Rachel hadn't killed her baby, Isaac did. A dark sense of panic swelled within Katie's stomach, but it only grew worse the longer Ashley spoke.

"What do we do?" Katie said once Ashley finished talking. "We can't let Rachel throw her life away like that."

"We have a week, but aside from that, I'm out of ideas. That's why I'm calling you."

Katie thought for a long moment. "How quickly can you be at my place?" She lived in a small duplex at the outskirts of the Brine city limit. Ashley's office was nearby.

"I've got a hearing at ten o'clock, but I should be able to make it there by eleven. Why?"

"That should be fine. I've got to try to get one other person here anyway."

Ashley groaned. "Not that douchebag from Waukee."

"If you're talking about Josh, then yes. He is the lead in the Waukee investigation into your poisoning and it's important that he be present for what we are going to do."

"What *are* we going to do?"

"You'll see. Be here at eleven."

Katie hung up and immediately dialed Josh's number.

"Long time, no see," Josh said as a form of greeting. "Did you change your mind about my offer?"

When she saw him after her interview, he had asked her to meet him for a dinner date. She'd refused on the premise that they would soon be coworkers. Interoffice relationships were rarely seen in a positive light.

"No. But I need you to come to Brine."

"Sure thing, sweetheart. When?"

"Now."

Ashley and Josh pulled up to Katie's duplex within minutes of one another. Katie met them out front, jittery with excitement. She'd felt so useless over the weekend, knowing she wouldn't have a job to go to on Monday. Now, she had something to work on. A problem to solve.

"Come in, come in," Katie said as they both got out of their cars, eyeing one another suspiciously.

Katie motioned them to the front seating area. "Have a seat and make yourselves comfortable."

"What's going on?" Ashley said, choosing the old La-Z-Boy recliner that Katie had bought a few years ago at a local estate sale.

Josh sat on the sofa, as far away from Ashley as he could get, and Katie sat between them.

"First," Katie said, nodding at Ashley. "I want you to tell Josh what you found out yesterday."

"About Rachel?"

Josh winced.

"What?" Ashley said, frowning deeply. "You're *that* offended by the mention of Rachel's name. The law says she's innocent until proven guilty. You should know that. Cops..." She shook her head and crossed her arms.

"Actually," Josh said, "it's quite the opposite. I know at least some of what Rachel's been through. I feel sorry for her."

"Oh," Ashley said, but she didn't apologize.

"Can we cool the police officer-defense attorney hate dance and skip to the important details?" Katie asked. Because, really, it was a ridiculous waste of time. She hadn't brought them together so they could argue.

Ashley launched into the story about her meeting with Rachel, telling Josh about Isaac poisoning Rachel for punishment, that he was the father of Rachel's baby, and that he had killed the baby by "punishing" her in her last month of pregnancy. By the time Ashley was finished telling the story, Josh's face was red with rage.

"I knew it," he said, shaking his head. "I knew he was doing something to her. That bastard."

"Whoa, Officer," Ashley said, putting her hands over her ears. "My virgin ears."

Katie gave Ashley a hard look, then turned to Josh. "Don't mind her. She swears like a sailor."

"I'm just fucking with you." Ashley turned her attention to Katie. "Why are we here?"

"We need to get a recorded interview of Rachel telling her story," Josh said. "That's why I'm here, isn't it?"

"Nope." Ashley gave her head an emphatic shake. "She won't do it. We have to prove her innocence without her. She wants to get away from him, and her last-ditch effort is prison. She won't let us take that option off the table until Isaac is in jail."

"Then what are we doing?"

Both Ashley and Josh looked at Katie.

"Tom."

Ashley's mouth dropped open, and her eyes filled with hurt. "What about Tom?"

In that moment, Katie's phone started buzzing. She glanced at the caller ID. "Right on time," she said before pressing the green phone icon. "Hey, Tom."

Ashley gasped. Katie shook her head and mouthed, *just wait*, before pressing the speakerphone button and placing her phone in the middle of the coffee table.

"Katie," Tom said, his voice barely above a whisper. "I'm going to put my phone in my pocket and try to get Harper to confess. Are you somewhere that you can listen?"

"Confess?" Ashley hissed. "To what?"

Katie leaned toward Josh. "Turn on your body camera. We need to record this audio."

Josh nodded and pressed a button near his chest pocket.

To Ashley, Katie whispered, "Tom thinks Harper had something to do with your poisoning."

Ashley crossed her arms and harumphed in a way that indicated Harper's involvement had been clear to her from the beginning.

"Okay," Katie said. "We're ready on this end. Go ahead."

There was a rustling noise followed by the voices of Tom and Harper, muffled but audible. Katie, Josh, and Ashley all leaned forward to listen.

"Harper, I need to talk to you." Tom sounded hesitant, but his voice was clear.

"Then talk."

"Why didn't you tell me about your connection to Ashley?"

Katie glanced at Ashley to see if she would react, but her face was stone.

"I don't have a connection to Ashley. I lived with her for like six months when I was a kid. I'm new to the whole roommate thing, but I didn't realize you needed to know everything about me. Would you like to know the names of all my sexual partners and my favorite positions, too?"

"No." Tom's voice rose. "You know what I meant. Stop twisting my words. You knew Ashley was my girlfriend and you chose to live with me to get back at her."

"Yeah. That's probably true. You should have seen her face when she came to the door. Hilarious."

"But that's not all you've done to get back at her, is it?"

"I don't know what you mean." Harper's voice dripped with sarcasm.

"Katie showed me the notes sent with the poisoned candies. They are notes that I wrote you. One was from when I left dirty dishes in the sink and you flipped out."

"Yeah, well, that was gross."

"And the other note was one I left you after I forgot to wash some facial hair down the sink."

"It's so easy to turn the water on. That's all you had to do."

"I understand. That's why I apologized. What I don't know is how those letters that I wrote *you* got into packages sent to Ashley."

A short pause.

"Don't shrug. You know."

"Listen, Tom. You're right. I don't like Ashley. I did want to get back at her. I had planned to fuck with her by using you, but then this dude showed up one day. He had been following me around and I called the creeper out. Because, seriously, sneaking around behind a girl like that is weird. Anyway, he asked me if I was friends with Ashley. I laughed in his face. Then he asked if I had anything that he could use to mess with her.

The only thing I could think of were your letters. I'd been holding on to them. I was planning on using them myself to screw with the bitch, but I realized that this little weirdo was willing to do it for me. So I gave him the letters and that was that."

"Weirdo? Who?"

"He said his name was Thomas, but that was a lie. He must think I'm an idiot. His face is everywhere. On every news cycle talking about that girl of his who killed her baby, Rachel..." Harper snapped her fingers like she was trying to remember.

"Smithson?"

"That's her."

"What did Isaac Smithson do with my letters?"

"Don't know, don't care. Like I said, that was the end of my involvement."

The conversation deteriorated after that. Katie had never heard Tom lose his temper, but there was a first time for everything. Harper and Tom shouted at one another for a good ten minutes, but Harper didn't admit to any further involvement in Ashley's poisoning. So Katie ended the call. Harper had behaved childishly, but she hadn't violated any laws.

Isaac, on the other hand, was in hot water. This was what Katie loved about law enforcement. Getting to the truth. But that wasn't how all police officers saw the job. Some, like George, only cared about the power and the paycheck. And then there was the bureaucratic tape. Everything was political. Those who had power over their budget and control over the trajectory of cases, city council and the county attorney respectively, were all elected officials.

It gave her pause about potentially taking a job with Waukee. Not that it had been offered to her yet. But would she, should she, take it if the chief called her? Hours earlier, she'd been dying for an offer from Waukee, but now she was on the fence. She didn't know how she fit in with law enforcement anymore. But, then again, she didn't have any other options. To her, law enforcement wasn't about the paycheck, but she needed a paycheck to survive. It was a catch-22.

31

KATIE

40 days before trial

By the next day, Katie was once again sitting in her living room staring into empty space. Josh had the information from Ashley and Tom, but she had no control over what he did with it. She felt useless. No job, nowhere to go, and no way to help. Then her phone started buzzing. Katie jumped up and raced into the kitchen, snatching it off the Formica counter.

"You're not busy, are you?" Josh started talking before Katie could even form the first letters to the word *hello*.

"Umm, no. Why?"

"You need to come to Waukee."

"I don't *need* to do anything."

"All right, fine," Josh said with a heavy sigh. "*I need* you to come to Waukee."

"What for?"

"Do you really have to be this difficult?"

Katie did. Part of her liked challenging him. She wished she hadn't been so quick to say yes to everything while at the Brine Police Department. Maybe they would have appreciated her more. Maybe she'd still be there. Maybe it would have been George out on his ass rather than her.

The thought of her former friend made her blood boil. He'd betrayed her. It was the final nail in the coffin that once contained their friendship.

"Hello? Katie?" Josh said.

"Yes. I'm here."

"I've been staking out the Smithson residence, trying to find a window to talk to Lyndsay when Isaac isn't around."

"And…"

"And Lyndsay goes grocery shopping every Wednesday at ten o'clock in the morning. It is the only time she's away from her husband."

Katie glanced at her watch. "It's already 8:30. I'm not sure I'd get to Waukee in time."

"It's only a forty-minute drive. Come on, Katie. I need your help. She's a battered woman. She's far more likely to talk to you than me."

Katie didn't quite agree with Josh's characterization of Lyndsay Smithson. It had certainly seemed that way during Katie and George's original interview with Isaac and Lyndsay, but that could have been an act. For all Katie knew, Lyndsay was as guilty as Isaac when it came to the poisonings.

"Will you come?" Josh asked, cutting through her thoughts.

"Yeah," Katie said, pulling on a pair of jeans. She was already in her room, selecting clothes. She had given Josh some resistance, but they both knew she'd ultimately agree to come. "I'll be there in an hour."

Katie's phone rang a few minutes after she'd started her drive to Waukee. She glanced at the caller ID, saw George's name, and immediately silenced the call. But her phone immediately began ringing again, and she followed the same procedure. After the fifth call, Katie finally picked up.

"What do you want?" she snarled.

"I haven't seen you in a while," George said, his voice uncharacteristically sheepish. "I was just checking to see if you were all right."

"That's not why you called. You've had plenty of time to check up on me and you haven't. Cut to the chase or I'm hanging up."

"My wife left me."

Katie was silent for a long moment.

"Katie?"

"I'm here. But what the fuck do you want me to do with that information? I mean, that sucks. But we aren't friends anymore. You don't get to shit on me and then cry on my shoulder. That's not how relationships work."

"No. I mean, that's why I've been"—he paused, thinking—"off."

"Okay."

"She left nine months ago. She took the kids with her. They left the state and I've been unable to find her."

"Shit," Katie hissed through her teeth. She didn't want to feel any sympathy for George, but she couldn't help it. "Are the kids okay?" George didn't talk about his children much, but they were still young. There were two of them, one was eight or nine and the other was around five. Katie was never really good with children's ages.

"Yeah. Janine is *kind* enough to post pictures of them to social media, but she won't tell me where they are or what they are doing."

"Are you going to file for custody?"

"Yeah. But I have to find her to serve her." He sighed heavily. "I've tried everything, but she's avoided service."

"How can she do that?"

"My lawyer says that technically we both have one hundred percent right to them all the time since we are married. There isn't anything illegal about what Janine is doing."

"That sucks, man," Katie said, coldness creeping back into her tone. While she was sympathetic for his plight, it still didn't explain why he had thrown her under the bus.

"I just wanted you to know. I need this job to pay the lawyer and to keep paying the private investigator. That's why I…"

"Screwed me over?"

"Yeah. If that's what you want to call it."

"Yes. That most certainly is what I want to call it."

"Okay, well that's all I had. I hope you don't hate me."

"I don't hate you," Katie said. And despite her recent bout of fury toward him, the words did ring true. "I just need time to get over this."

"Okay. I understand."

"And you're going to have to stop acting like a total dick."

"Done."

"Okay, well, I've got to go," Katie said.

"You sound like you're in the car. Where are you going?"

"It's none of your business, George," Katie said. They had a tentative truce, but that didn't give him the right to ask questions about her life. "I don't work with you anymore. Remember?"

"Oh. Right, right," he said absentmindedly.

"Okay. Well, I'm going to go before you piss me off again."

"Okay. Yeah," George said awkwardly.

"Bye," Katie said, and hung up the phone.

Katie spent the rest of her drive to Waukee in silence, pondering the meaning behind George's call. Why had he even bothered? The last time they spoke was when she'd briefed him on her ongoing investigations into Rachel's background and Ashley's poisoning. His demeanor during that conversation had been aloof. Unemotional and uncaring. So, why the change? Why did he even care that she understood his behavior?

And then there was the question of how he had been able to keep such a big secret in such a small town. His kids were both school-aged. Their removal from school should have caused all kinds of rumors. But that hadn't happened. It made Katie wonder how many other people's secrets he was keeping. If he was using them in the same way he'd managed to keep his job.

Katie dispelled thoughts of George when she pulled into the parking lot in front of the gas station where she'd agreed to meet Josh. He was already there. Katie parked next to him, hopped out of her vehicle, and into the passenger side of his.

"Hey there, gorgeous," Josh said, flashing his characteristic smile.

Despite her best attempts, she could feel her face flushing. "Enough flattery. It's almost ten o'clock. We better get moving."

Josh drove the short distance to the grocery store, parking alongside the building so they could watch for Lyndsay from a distance.

"So," he said after a few beats of silence, "I heard Chief Canterbury offered you the job."

"He did."

The Waukee Police Chief had called at eight o'clock that morning. It was the call she couldn't wait to get Monday evening, but by Tuesday she was already questioning her desire to work for such a large department.

"But you haven't accepted yet."

Katie didn't respond. It wasn't a question, and she saw no need to elaborate.

"Why not?"

"I'm thinking about it."

"What is there to think about?"

"Lots."

"You'd get to look at this fine specimen of the male gender every day of the week. It's a no-brainer. Nobody can pass up that kind of opportunity." Josh flashed a winning smile and waggled his eyebrows.

Katie fought the urge to laugh. "It seems like I get to see your face every day as it is."

"That's just because I need your help."

"Men always need help from women."

Josh barked a laugh. "You would get along with my mama."

"Maybe," Katie said, staring out the front windshield. She doubted there would ever be cause for her to meet Mama Martin. "Hey, is that Lyndsay?"

A woman hurried toward the front door of the grocery store. She moved in jerky, shuffling steps. Her hood was up and her back remained stooped, like she was trying to make herself small.

"Sure is," Josh said, hopping out of the car.

Katie watched as Josh jogged over to Lyndsay. His legs were long and spry, moving in strong, even strides toward Mrs. Smithson. He reached Lyndsay just before she entered the front door. Lyndsay stiffened and appeared almost frightened, but she relaxed after Josh smiled. Josh's mouth moved rapidly, then he gestured to the police car. Lyndsay nodded and followed him as he led the way toward Katie.

Josh opened the back door to the cruiser. "It's a cold one today, isn't it?" he said to Lyndsay.

"Yes. Winter came early this year."

"Go ahead and get comfortable. Like I said before, you aren't under arrest. We are just using the police car to get out of the cold. The doors are unlocked. You can hop out at any time and go on your way. I'm not going to stop you. Okay?"

"Okay."

Josh shut the door and hopped into the front seat. "This here is Katie Mickey." Josh nodded at Katie. "She used to work for the Brine Police Department. I'm in the process of trying to convince her to come work with me."

Lyndsay nodded. "Yes. I remember you."

"So, I've just got a few questions for you, Lyndsay. Okay?"

"Okay."

"I want to know where in your house your husband keeps the rat poison."

"Excuse me?"

"Does Isaac keep rat poison at the house?"

"I don't know."

"If I tested a strand of your hair, Mrs. Smithson, would I find that you have been exposed to rat poison?"

Lyndsay was silent.

"Come on, Lyndsay," Josh said, turning to meet Mrs. Smithson's gaze. "I know what's going on here."

"What is going on?"

Josh quirked an eyebrow.

The interview was going nowhere, so Katie decided to cut in. "Isaac doesn't like Rachel's attorney much, does he?"

Lyndsay was taken aback by the change in topics. Shocked enough to actually answer. "No. He doesn't. Women are different than men. We aren't as smart. A woman's place is in the home. Not in a courtroom. And certainly not representing our daughter."

"But Isaac isn't Rachel's father, is he?"

Lyndsay chewed on her thumb nail for a moment, then answered. "Not biologically. But he is her father."

"A putative father who has disowned Rachel. He said so in his first interview at the Brine Police Department."

"He may have said that, but he very much wants Rachel to come home."

"Why?" Josh asked. "So he can continue raping her?"

Lyndsay stiffened. "I don't know what you mean."

"Come on, Mrs. Smithson," Katie said irritably. Her patience was running thin. "It doesn't take a rocket scientist to discover what's been going on. Isaac is the only man who had an opportunity to impregnate Rachel."

Lyndsay brought her purse close to her chest, hugging it. "That's not true. Kids get up to all sorts of things these days."

"We received the DNA test results, Lyndsay," Josh said, his tone almost apologetic. "Isaac is the father."

Katie shot Josh a questioning look. Was he bluffing? George was the lead of Rachel's investigation, and last she knew he had no intention of determining the baby's paternity.

"The good lawyer did the testing," Josh said with a knowing smile. "She got a court order to get Isaac's and the baby's DNA."

Ashley, Katie thought with a smile. She should have known. Ashley would have done the test so she could use the evidence to create sympathy for Rachel at trial. It had been the whole reason Katie had started digging deeper into Rachel's case.

A tear trickled down Lyndsay's cheek.

"But that's not why we need to talk to you," Josh continued. "We need to talk about the chocolates that were full of rat poison. Your fingerprint was on the box that somehow made its way to Ashley Montgomery's house in Brine. Do you know anything about that?"

"I..." Lyndsay's eyes widened with shock. Not the typical resignation that came with someone who had been caught, but genuine surprise. "I usually make homemade chocolates and Isaac takes them to church events. I recently made a batch for the church bazaar. But I didn't put rat poison in them."

"Do you know for a fact that the homemade candies went to the church?"

"No. I gave them to Isaac. He took them to the garage. I assume he put them in the car to drop them off at the church later that day."

"And where does Isaac keep the rat poison?"

Lyndsay was silent for a long moment. She pursed her lips, then after what seemed like a lifetime, she said, "In the garage."

32

ASHLEY

39 days before trial

Hearing Tom's voice last Tuesday had shaken Ashley more than she thought it would. Not that she had much time to prepare herself. Katie sprung the call on both Ashley and Officer Arrogant at the same time. Two days had passed since that call and Tom was still on her mind. Before hearing the cadence of Tom's melodic speech, she'd thought of him, but she had been successful at burying her emotions. Now, she was struggling. She was lonely without him.

Ashley was in a slump, a sadness that was growing heavier with each passing day. She needed to snap out of it. The best way to do that was to keep busy, never allowing her mind to wander. So that's why she picked up her phone and called Katie at the end of the workday.

"Hello?"

"You're meeting me for drinks," Ashley said.

"I am?"

"Yes. Meet me at the Corkscrew in ten minutes."

The Corkscrew was a new wine bar in town. Ashley loved wine, but Brine was more of a Bud heavy type of town. She gave it two months before the place shut its doors.

"Fine. But I'm not getting ready."

Katie had been feeling sorry for herself lately, growing more and more depressed by the day. Ashley suspected that the other officers in town had something to do with Katie's dark moods. They seemed to be everywhere now, visible in a way they had never been before. Probably with the intention of giving Forest Parker the middle finger without actually displaying any fingers.

"I don't care what you look like. Just meet me."

Ten minutes later, the two women were seated across from one another at a table made from a wine barrel with an open bottle of dark red wine between them.

"So," Katie said, swirling her wine, "why did you want to meet?" She wore no makeup and had pulled her bright red hair up into a messy bun. The smattering of freckles across her cheekbones were on full display. Katie wasn't a stunner like Rachel, but she was beautiful in her own way. Especially in such a natural state.

Ashley was silent for a long moment, considering whether to tell the truth or make up some bullshit reason. She decided on the former. With Katie, honesty was always the best policy. "I didn't want to be alone. I miss Tom."

Katie nodded solemnly. "I figured as much." She took a large gulp of wine. "He's been calling me nonstop. He wants to talk to you, but he's afraid to call."

It was ironic that Tom spent weeks ignoring her while they were together, but now that their relationship was over, he was dying to get in touch. "I don't think I'm ready yet."

"I get it. He lied to you. I'd feel the same way." Katie pursed her lips, then took another drink. "Do you think you'll give him another chance?"

Ashley shrugged. "Maybe. But not now. I need time."

Katie tipped back her glass and drained it of wine. Ashley stared at her, dumbfounded. She had barely taken a sip of hers. She shrugged and picked up the bottle, pouring Katie another generous portion.

Ashley eyed her friend suspiciously. "What's going on with you?" Something was off about Katie these days. A missing edge that had always been there. "I've never seen you drink like this."

Katie shrugged. "I'm not a cop anymore. At least not at the moment."

"What does that mean? Did Chief Carmichael find the money to hire you back?"

"No," Katie said, shaking her head. "Chief Canterbury at the Waukee Police Department offered me a job. Same pay, but I'll have to move there."

Ashley's heart dropped. Somewhere deep down she had known that Katie's layoff could lead to her moving away, but she'd intentionally ignored it. She couldn't bear the thought of losing both Tom and Katie.

"Did you take the job?" Ashley asked.

"Not yet. I told him I wanted to think about it."

Ashley's mind whirred. She didn't want Katie to leave Brine for personal reasons, but there were also potential business-related incentives for Katie to stay. "When do you plan to give him an answer?"

Katie shrugged.

"Can you hold off for another few days?"

"Why?" Katie cocked her head to the side, confused.

"Just, please. I have an idea, but I need to talk to a couple people before I'm ready to discuss it."

Namely, Ashley needed to talk to Carley at the *Des Moines Register* and Forest Parker down at city council. She didn't dare mention Forest's name, though. Katie would blow a gasket. She blamed Forest for the loss of her job, and her anger wasn't entirely misplaced. Although Chief Carmichael had made the decision as to who would get the ax, it was Forest who had handed him the weapon and demanded that he cut someone, anyone.

"Fair enough."

They fell into a companionable silence, each sipping their wine. The bottle was nearly empty already. Ashley was considering ordering a second when Katie spoke.

"How are things going with Rachel? Do you think she'll sign a release to let Josh talk to her doctor about the miscarriage?"

Ashley sighed heavily. How were things going? Not well. Rachel wouldn't even tell Ashley the name of the doctor who had treated her. There was no other way to track the doctor down either. Without Rachel's permission, Ashley couldn't even call around randomly, trying to find the OBGYN by chance.

"I know you are trying," Katie said, "but Josh is getting anxious. He's wanted to get something on Isaac Smithson for years. Now that it's a real possibility, he's champing at the bit."

The poisoning that led to the miscarriage had occurred at the Smithson home, which was in Waukee. Officer Arrogant territory. Josh was annoying, but Ashley was starting to warm up to him now that she knew he wanted to help Rachel.

"The problem is that it is Rachel's last card. It proves her innocence. If that information gets out and Isaac is never charged, she won't be able to plead guilty anymore. The court won't let her. Then she'll return to society, where Isaac will be able to get to her. It's the worst-case scenario in her mind."

Katie shook her head. "That's so weird. Who would choose prison just to get away from a guy?"

"It's not *that* strange."

After hearing some of Rachel's horrific stories from her childhood, Ashley no longer questioned her decision. Prison was full of women who, for the most part, were nonviolent. Many of the prison guards were also women. If Ashley had a background like Rachel's, she'd see a women's prison as a pretty safe place too.

"What I don't understand is why Isaac would want to poison me. Doesn't he want Rachel to be acquitted so that he can go back to playing house with her?"

"Have you met Isaac?" Katie said incredulously. "He would never believe that a woman could achieve anything. He thinks we are all idiots. He wanted you out of the way so that a man could do the job 'properly.'" She made air quotes around the word.

Katie had a point. Isaac was a real bastard. She hoped with all her heart that Officer Arrogant and his goon squad would find enough evidence to lock him up for the rest of his natural life. Because if anyone deserved freedom, it was Rachel.

33

KATIE

Three days before Rachel's plea hearing

"You are not going to believe what we found." Josh's eyes flashed with excitement, but his tone remained solemn.

Josh had called Katie last night, shortly after she and Ashley had finished their last drink and parted for the evening. He wanted her to drive to Waukee immediately, but she had been drinking, so driving any distance was out of the question. She wasn't an active police officer at the moment, but that didn't mean she was willing to break the law.

Instead, she had agreed to meet him in Waukee the following morning. That's how she found herself seated in a small, rectangular office tucked into a back corner of the Waukee Police Department on a Friday morning, tired and irritable.

"I'd be more inclined to believe it if you told me what it was." Katie leaned forward and rubbed her temples. She had a headache, and her eyes were extra sensitive to the florescent lighting.

"Right, yes." He paused, tapping a finger against his lips. "You know, it may be easier if I show you."

"Okay."

Josh stood and motioned for her to follow him. She did, moving robotically, her head pounding with every step.

"Where are we going?"

"The evidence room."

"You know," Katie said as they weaved their way from one identical hallway to the next, "I'm really tired of following you around."

"Impossible." He glanced over his shoulder and waggled his eyebrows. "Women never tire of my backside."

Katie snorted, but it was an exaggerated expression. She had to admit the view wasn't all that bad. "I mean I'm tired of having to drive up here over and over again."

"You rarely invite me to Brine. And when you do, you send me packing the moment business is concluded."

"Yeah, well, it was a *business* meeting."

They turned one last corner and Josh approached a window.

"It doesn't matter for today's purposes anyway. The evidence is all here in Waukee," he said before knocking on the large glass window.

A man best described as bear-sized slid open the window and leaned out.

"Hey, Dakota," Josh said.

"What's up, little dude?"

Dakota and Josh exchanged a weird handshake that could only exist between two people who were friends from childhood. It involved some strange hand movements, fist and wrist bumping, followed by a goofy thumbs-up.

"Dakota here is the evidence custodian," Josh said, nodding toward the giant man. Dakota had long, dark hair slicked back into a sleek ponytail. "This is Katie Mickey. She used to be a Brine police officer, but she's going to be working here soon."

Katie narrowed her eyes. He was placing her in an impossible position. She didn't want to contradict or agree with him. You never knew who was watching at a police station. Cameras were everywhere. She decided the best tactic was to change the subject.

"Why are we here?"

"Right, yes," Josh said, turning to Dakota. "We need to look at the evidence seized from the Smithson residence."

"Sure, come on back." Dakota pressed a button on the wall.

The door beeped and Josh pushed it open. Katie followed the two men through a maze of lockers. They curved around before finally stopping at a tall blue locker near the end of the last row. Dakota handed Josh a box of nylon gloves, and Josh gave a pair to Katie before snapping on his own. Dakota already had the locker open.

"Go ahead," Dakota said, taking a few steps back. As evidence custodian he would remain on scene, ensuring that the contents of the locker remained unaltered.

Josh removed a large, clear plastic bag. Inside was a red, rectangular box that read, *Ratsak, kills rats and mice.* "We found this in the garage next to a small dropper." He held up a second, much smaller plastic bag containing a dropper small enough to fit inside an iodine bottle. "We sent both off to the criminalistics lab in Ankeny. They confirmed my suspicion that the dropper was used to mix rat poison with water, then inserted into something chocolate. All three compounds were found on the tip of this dropper."

"That fits the narrative." Lyndsay had admitted that she made the chocolates but denied using rat poison as an ingredient. "What about fingerprints? Any found on the dropper or the box?"

"The dropper was too small to get a full print. The box, however, was a different story."

"Isaac's?"

"Yup."

"What about Lyndsay?"

"None of the prints matched hers."

"Good."

They were finally getting somewhere. With Rachel's testimony, the poison, the fingerprints, and Harper's recorded confession that she'd given Tom's letters to Isaac Smithson, they would likely get a conviction for Ashley's poisoning.

"What about sexual assault? Did you find any evidence of that?" They had the DNA match between Isaac and the baby, but they would likely need more if Rachel decided not to testify. Since Rachel wasn't cooperating now, Katie doubted she would in the future.

"That, my lovely lady, is right here." Josh reached into the locker and removed a spiral notebook.

"What's that?"

"Isaac's confession."

"What do you mean?"

The notebook was sealed inside the bag. They'd have to break the evidence label for Katie to read any of the pages, but she suspected that she didn't want to know in Isaac's words what he had done. She couldn't stomach it.

"He talks about what he did to Rachel. The psycho wrote it all down in detail. Like it was normal or something. He claims that their family is polygamous, and Rachel was his second wife."

"Are the journal entries dated?"

"Yup."

"How far back?" Katie hated to ask, but she had to know.

"Six years."

"Jesus Christ," Katie said, rubbing a hand over her face. That meant Rachel was only twelve years old the first time Isaac assaulted her.

"Right. We have a solid statutory rape case with the baby's DNA and this journal." Josh held it up, but Katie didn't want to look at it. The very thought of Isaac writing in it disgusted her.

Statutory rape was an understatement. The best-case scenario for Isaac. If Rachel agreed to testify, he would go down on actual forcible rape charges. Not that it mattered. With the six years of sexual assault, Isaac would be charged with enough counts that he'd spend the remainder of his natural life in a prison cell.

"That's not all."

"Seriously?" Katie wasn't sure if she could take more.

"We seized two hairbrushes. One from the master bathroom, the second from Rachel's bedroom."

"Why?" Katie wasn't sure where this was going.

Josh shrugged. "If Isaac was willing to poison Ashley, it's possible he was also poisoning Rachel and Lyndsay."

"Was he?"

"Rachel. Not Lyndsay. The criminalist analyzed three months of

Rachel's hair. We can't tell for sure when the poisoning occurred in those three months, but it definitely happened."

"What. The. Literal. Fuck."

Katie supposed that she shouldn't be shocked. After all, that's how Rachel had said she lost the baby at the end of her pregnancy. But there was something about the cold hard numbers that came from a hair stat test that sent a chill up her spine.

"That's what I thought," Josh said as he placed the journal back into the evidence locker.

"Wow." Katie paused, digesting all the information. "What's next?"

Josh flashed his winning smile. "The judge has already issued an arrest warrant for Isaac Smithson listing thirty counts of sexual assault and one count for the attempted murder of Ashley Montgomery. All we need is Rachel's doctor to provide proof of miscarriage prior to birth, and we can add the involuntary termination of a pregnancy to the list."

Katie shook her head. "I just talked to Ashley about it last night. Rachel won't sign any releases until Isaac is in custody."

"But that means she could end up going down on a murder charge when she didn't do it."

"Ashley can't stop her from pleading. It's Rachel's right. And there's no convincing the county attorney to drop charges early."

"What if we show him all this evidence?"

Katie shook her head. "Rachel's case is too political. He won't make any rash decisions. I doubt he will do anything until after Isaac is in custody and the public is screaming for Rachel's release."

"Right, well, there's the problem," Josh said, rubbing a hand over his face. "Nobody can find Isaac. There's a couple of guys stationed outside his house, but he hasn't come back since we executed the search warrant. He must have known that we'd find damning evidence and decided to skip town."

"Shit," Katie said.

She turned on her heel and began walking down the rows of lockers toward the evidence room door.

"Where are you going?" Josh had to jog to keep up with her.

"To find Ashley. We have to talk some sense into Rachel."

34

ASHLEY

Two days before Rachel's plea hearing

"I don't know if this is going to work," Ashley said as Kylie led her and Katie down the hallway toward Rachel's cell.

After Katie left her meeting with Josh, she'd called Ashley and they scheduled a time to see Rachel. It wasn't conventional, but Ashley wanted Kylie and Katie present for the discussion. Maybe one of them could talk some sense into the girl.

"It won't work," Kylie said darkly.

"You're positive today," Ashley said.

"I'm not negative, I'm realistic. You know the things that Rachel has been through. At least some of them. As bad as that is, I bet it isn't even the tip of the iceberg. I don't blame her for her decision one bit."

"I get that," Ashley said as they rounded a corner, "but I can't just sit by and let an innocent person go to prison."

"Me neither," Katie chimed in.

"Why?" Kylie stopped suddenly and turned to face Ashley and Katie, her hands on her hips. "Why do you think you know what's good for this girl? If she goes to prison, she'll get medical treatment and mental health therapy. She can even get her GED and go on to college. Do you think Rachel has ever thought college was a possibility for her?"

Kylie eyed Ashley, giving her a long accusatory glare before jumping over to Katie and doing the same. Neither of them answered.

"Well, I know the answer to that. No. Rachel never thought she would live a life other than torture, abuse, and misery. An existence that neither of you could possibly imagine."

"Can you?" Ashley asked, genuinely growing concerned about Kylie's upbringing. She'd never thought to ask her.

"No. I can't," Kylie said, shaking her head and turning around, "but I'm not arrogant enough to believe that I know what's best for someone like Rachel."

Apparently, we aren't getting any assistance from Kylie, Ashley thought. But she didn't begrudge the jailer. Of the three of them, Kylie had spent the most time with Rachel. She had, no doubt, developed a bond with the girl. And she was protective. That trait warranted admiration, not condemnation.

Kylie led them down two more hallways, then they were outside Rachel's cell. A momentary flash of déjà vu struck Ashley. The cell had once been her home. It was also the place where former officer John Jackie had almost strangled the life out of her.

Rachel was reading in the corner, seated on top of several ratty-looking blankets, leaning against the cement wall. She didn't look up as they approached, which was a testament to her growth. When Ashley first met Rachel, she'd been like a skittish street cat. Eyes always open, darting back and forth in search of danger.

After several beats of silence, Rachel finished her page and placed a bookmark in her book. She stood, stretching, then came over to meet them. "Hello," she said, smiling broadly. Her gaze settled on Katie and her expression grew wary. "I didn't think I'd see you again until trial."

"I don't work for the Brine Police Department anymore. I'm just here as Ashley's friend."

"Oh?" Rachel turned back to her attorney. "Moral support?"

"Something like that," Ashley said. "Listen." She ground the toe of her shoe against the cement floor. "I need to talk to you about something."

"I'm not changing my mind about pleading. Not until he's in jail."

"That's the thing," Katie cut in. "The warrants are out. The Waukee police issued a bunch of them. There is no way he is getting out of the charges. Isaac Smithson will go to prison for the rest of his life."

"That's good news," Rachel said, her smile widening. "When will he be in jail?"

"That's the thing," Ashley said. "It could be seconds, hours, or even days."

Rachel furrowed her brow. "How long can a person be on the run with active warrants?"

Ashley didn't want to answer, but she had to. She wasn't going to be one of the long list of adults who had lied to Rachel. "Sometimes it can be years. But that's usually only when the defendant has skipped town. Considering the amount of celebrity that came with your case, coupled with Isaac's visibility throughout it, I think they'll track him down pretty quickly."

"Well, then," Rachel said with a shrug, "there shouldn't be any problem with us keeping the same plea date. Two days is plenty of time."

Ashley groaned. "Come on, Rachel. Can you at least give me the name of your doctor? Please, I'm begging you."

"I can't take the risk." Rachel's gaze grew soft. "I know you are trying to help me, Ashley, but I've gotten this far by instinct. I'm not about to throw away my best weapon if it means that there is any chance, no matter how minute, that my abuser could touch me one more time. At least in here"—she gestured around her—"I know for certain that he won't get to me."

Ashley turned to Kylie, pleading with her eyes, but the jailer didn't offer any assistance.

"I get it, Rachel," Katie said, "but we can't let you become a martyr."

"Why not?"

"Because..." It wasn't much of an explanation, but Ashley assumed that it was all Katie could come up with.

"I've never had a chance to make my own choices," Rachel said. "Adults have always done that for me. They've done a pretty terrible job at it, too. This is my decision. Not anyone else's. If I want to make myself a martyr, then I can. Whether you two like it or not. But my life is mine to do what I want with. For the first time, I am realizing that."

She's right, Ashley thought. A sudden weight had landed on her shoulders, so heavy it was suffocating. Could she really allow this to happen? She supposed that she must. If not for any other reason than to let Rachel rule her own destiny.

"Okay," Ashley said, motioning to Kylie and Katie. "I will stop trying to change your mind. Your life is your own. I'll see you at your plea hearing."

Never in Ashley's life had she felt more dejected than she did in that moment. She followed Kylie out of the jail, trudging behind her without paying attention to her surroundings. There was nothing she could do to save her client. The thought filled her with hopelessness. This wasn't how the criminal justice system was supposed to work. Her only hope was for Josh to find Isaac and bring him into custody.

35

KATIE

The day of Rachel's plea hearing

"Have you found him yet?" Katie said into her phone.

She was at Ashley's office, sitting in a rather uncomfortable chair. The room was a complete disaster, with stacks of documents all over the place. So many covered the floor that she had to hop over them like an odd game of hopscotch in order to get to her current seat.

"No," Josh said. He sounded as frustrated as Katie felt. "And I feel like we've tried everything. Still no Isaac Smithson. I'm afraid he might have skipped the state."

"Shit," Katie hissed through her teeth.

"What?" Ashley whispered. She was sitting at her beat-up executive desk, squeezing a stress ball in one hand, then tossing it to the other and squeezing again.

Katie gave her the *one moment* signal, then pressed the speakerphone button. "Josh. Can you hear me?"

"Yeah."

"I just put you on speakerphone. Ashley Montgomery is here with me." Katie paused to allow time for the defense attorney and officer to exchange pleasantries, but neither said anything, so she continued. "What happens if Isaac has left the state?"

Josh sighed heavily. "I'll put out a BOLO for him. Hopefully, someone will recognize him. I don't have a lot of hope it'll happen today, though."

"It has to happen today," Ashley said. "Rachel's plea hearing is in one hour."

Katie leaned forward and rubbed her temples. It was maddening, the thought that an innocent person would go to prison for something she didn't do. What made matters worse was that Rachel wasn't just innocent, she was a victim.

"Can't you put it off?"

"No," Ashley growled. "She won't agree to a continuance and I'm not going to force the issue. I lose credibility with Rachel every time I ask for more time. One hour. That's all we've got."

"Fine. But I'm telling you now, we aren't going to find him."

"You'll have to try harder," Ashley said. Then she leaned forward and clicked the button on Katie's phone to hang up the call.

"Hey," Katie said, "that was rude."

"He doesn't have time to talk to us. He's got sixty"—she glanced at her watch —"no, fifty-four minutes to find Isaac. He needs to spend his time wisely."

Katie leaned back in her chair, groaning. "I wish I could be out there with him. I feel so useless sitting here twiddling my thumbs."

"Who says you can't be out there?"

Katie sat up and gave Ashley a hard look. "Chief Carmichael. When he fired me."

"Ha! You think the only people who can look for criminals wear a blue uniform?"

Katie frowned. The answer was yes, but Ashley was making it clear that she believed the opposite.

"What about bounty hunters and bondsmen?"

"I'm neither of those. And bonds*men*. Women can do that job, too."

"Bondspeople."

"Well, I don't work for a bail bonds company and I'm not a bounty hunter, so..."

"Private investigators also look for people."

"I guess that's true," Katie said with a sigh. "But I'm not one of those either."

"Do you want to be?"

Katie sat forward. "What do you mean?"

A smile spread across Ashley's lips. "I recently came into some money. A friend of mine at the *Des Moines Register* raised some donations for my office. I'm going to use it to hire an investigator. I thought you would be a nice fit for the job."

Katie's jaw dropped. Her? Working for the public defender's office? She had once hated Ashley for representing defendants. Over the past year, her opinion had greatly changed, but was it enough to stomach investigations on the defense side?

"Well?" Ashley's expression was open, excited.

"How much money are we talking?"

"I'll match the salary you had at the Brine PD. You won't have to move, and you'll get to see my smiling mug every day of the week."

"You don't smile that much."

"Details," Ashley said, waving a dismissive hand.

"How long is the position funded?" Ashley had said that she had come into some money, but she didn't say how much. If this was only a one-year position, she shouldn't choose it over the position in Waukee. It wouldn't be responsible.

"I have enough to pay you for two years."

Katie opened her mouth to respond, but Ashley cut her off.

"And I have something set up for you after that. But for those details, I'll refer to my good friend Forest Parker."

"Forest Parker?" Katie said with disgust. "I don't want anything to do with him."

"Just give him a chance to explain." Ashley picked up the receiver on her desk phone and pressed a button. "Yes, Elena, will you send Forest back?"

Katie stood, ready to leave the office, but then she realized there was only one way out. If she left now, she'd have to pass Forest. She was trapped. *Checkmate*, Katie thought as she glared at Ashley.

A moment later, Forest was in the doorway. There was another open chair, but because of all the stacks of documents, Forest wouldn't be able to reach it without Katie moving first. She didn't.

"Hello, Ashley." He paused, then nodded at Katie. "Katie."

"Let's cut to the chase," Ashley said, glancing at her watch again. "I don't have much time before Rachel's plea hearing. And, quite frankly, you have about five minutes to explain yourself before Katie here loses her patience."

"Right," Forest said, swallowing hard. Katie had never seen him so nervous. "Remember when you told me that I needed a plan if I was going to start dismantling the police department?"

Katie snorted. "I don't remember saying it so nicely, but yeah. I do believe I told you something along those lines."

"Well, I've had a plan all along. That's actually how I finally got the rest of the council on board."

"And that plan is..." Katie wasn't amused. His actions had destroyed the career she'd spent years building. It would really have to be one hell of a plan to convince Katie to forgive him.

"I want to create a mental health response team to join the police department on their calls. I've spent many hours discussing cases with Ashley here, and I think everyone could benefit if a trained mental health officer was present at the time of an arrest. To deescalate the tension and to keep the peace using a tactic other than brute force."

Yeah, Forest was right, almost every crime had some form of mental health component. Most people didn't commit crimes because they were evil—the exception being Isaac Smithson—they often were suffering from substance abuse and mental health issues.

"I have applied for and received a grant from the federal government to start working on forming the new team," Forest continued. Then he looked up, meeting Katie's gaze. "And I'd like you to lead it."

"Me?" Katie looked from Forest to Ashley. "But I don't have a degree in mental health."

"That's why you would work for me for two years," Ashley cut in. "Investigation work is flexible hours. It should give you the time to take some courses."

"And the grant will fund the classes, of course," Forest said.

"Let me get this straight," Katie said, turning all the way around so she was facing Forest. "You cut the police department's budget, forcing them to fire me so that you could offer me a different job?"

"A better job," Forest said, smiling. "Also, we really do need to start saving some funds to allocate to the new team. It's going to be completely separate from the police department, so you will need all your own equipment and an office. But that's all logistical. We can figure it out later."

"What do you say?" Ashley said, her eyes sparkling.

"I say I'll think about it." Katie's eyes darted toward the clock mounted on the wall. It was 9:30. Rachel's plea hearing was in thirty minutes. "But shouldn't we be getting over to the courthouse?"

"Shit." Ashley looked at her watch and jumped up. "You're right. We've got to go, Forest. We'll circle back to this later." She began shoving items into her computer bag. A laptop. Several pens. A notepad. A large file folder that read *Smithson, Rachel* on the tab.

Katie picked up her phone and stared at it, willing it to do something. Ping with a message, buzz with a call, but the screen remained dark. Josh hadn't found Isaac yet, and they were nearly out of time.

36

ASHLEY

The courtroom was stuffy, full of anxious onlookers. There were no empty spots in the gallery and the hallway had been packed with people. Everyone wanted the chance to set eyes on Rachel. To bear witness to her confession. A lie, but they didn't know that. They believed she was a killer. Someone undeserving of sympathy.

The trek from the jail to the courthouse had been horrible. It was like what Ashley imagined it felt like to walk the Green Mile. *Dead man walking.* Or woman, in this case. The death penalty was not an option in Iowa, but the phrase applied in an abstract, theoretical fashion. Ashley had spent months proving to Rachel that she would not betray her. But today, she would, and it would lead to the death of the trust they had built between them. A tenuous bridge that was sturdy, up until today.

For Ashley could not allow Rachel to plead guilty. It was completely against everything she stood for. Ashley had one last trick up her sleeve. A final delay tactic. She couldn't prevent Rachel from pleading, but she could withdraw as Rachel's counsel. As an attorney, she was an officer of the court. One of the cannons of legal ethics was to never allow a witness to testify falsely. To enter a guilty plea, Rachel would have to form a factual basis, meaning she would have to tell the judge that she murdered her child. Ashley knew with absolute certainty that Rachel did not kill her baby.

Since Ashley couldn't prevent the guilty plea or control her client's statements, the rules of ethics only allowed one option. Withdrawal. It wouldn't stop Rachel, but it would buy some time. Judge Ahrenson would have to stop the hearing and appoint new counsel. The new attorney would require weeks to get up to speed on the case in order to properly advise Rachel about her plea. It wasn't a perfect solution, but it would buy law enforcement some time to find Isaac.

Ashley looked at her client and Rachel met her gaze. The girl's eyes were no longer dull and lifeless. They sparkled. She smiled, the gesture lighting up her entire face, and patted Ashley on the hand.

"Don't look so sad," Rachel whispered. "I know what I'm doing."

The words cut Ashley deep. Rachel had no idea that Ashley intended to deceive her. They'd been strangers a few months ago. Rachel a tiny shell of a woman, closed off from the world. But now, after time in warmth and safety, she was a whole new person. Ashley's actions would soon destroy that progress.

"All rise," the bailiff shouted.

Everyone in the courtroom rose. Ashley took the opportunity to scan the room. Charles Hanson, wearing his typical smug expression, was at the prosecution table. One of his assistant county attorneys stood next to him, wringing his hands nervously. Katie stood directly behind Ashley. She, too, looked nervous, but for a wholly different reason. Ashley made eye contact with her, begging for some good news. Katie's frown deepened and she slowly shook her head. No sign of Isaac, then.

"You may be seated," Judge Ahrenson said as he took his seat at the bench.

Ashley's heart sank.

"We are convened today in State of Iowa vs. Rachel Smithson, Brine County Case Number FECR015987. Today's hearing has been scheduled after motion made by defendant's counsel for a plea hearing. Is everyone ready to proceed?" Judge Ahrenson paused, his eyes settling on Charles Hanson.

"Yes, Your Honor," Charles said.

The judge's cold gray eyes shifted to Ashley.

Ashley swallowed hard. She opened her mouth to speak, but no words followed.

"Ms. Montgomery?"

"I..." Her throat was dry, scratchy.

Rachel placed a hand over Ashley's. "You can do this."

Oh, how times had changed. It was Ashley who now needed Rachel's support. It was too bad that she was about to burn that bridge to the ground.

"Ms. Montgomery," Judge Ahrenson said. "Are you ready to proceed?"

Ashley cleared her throat. "Yes, Your Honor." Her voice was raspy and quiet, completely lacking its typical booming confidence.

"Very well then. I see no amendments on file. Or plea agreements. Am I right to assume that Ms. Smithson will be pleading as charged?"

"Yes, Your Honor," Charles Hanson said. "She will be pleading to both counts. Murder in the first degree and child endangerment causing death."

"Is that so?" Judge Ahrenson narrowed his eyes, meeting Ashley's gaze.

Ashley had been working with this same judge for the better part of ten years. He knew something was up. She had never willingly pled a client to a life sentence. Nor had she ever pled something without the promise of a lighter sentence.

"Um, yes. But first, before we get into the merits of the plea, I have one issue that I'd like to raise."

Ashley could feel Rachel stiffening beside her. This was not in the plea hearing script they had discussed. Ashley hoped against hope that Rachel would forgive her for what she was about to do.

"Go ahead," Judge Ahrenson said. "You have the floor."

Ashley struggled to her feet. "I, um."

There was a buzzing noise behind her, followed by a gasp.

"Yes?" Judge Ahrenson said.

"I need to..."

"Stop!" Katie's distinctive voice rang out in the silence of the chamber.

Ashley swung around to see Katie holding up her phone. It was open to text messaging, but Katie was too far away for Ashley to read it.

Judge Ahrenson's gaze grew stormy as it shifted toward Katie. "What is this outburst all about, Ms. Mickey?"

Katie ignored the judge, speaking only to Ashley and Rachel. "They got him!"

"They got *him*? Meaning Isaac?"

"Yes!" Happy tears streamed down Katie's face.

Ashley swung around. "Your Honor." All confidence had returned to her voice. "The defense would like to withdraw its motion. Rachel will no longer be pleading guilty."

There was a gasp from the prosecution table.

"Very well," Judge Ahrenson said. "The court is now in recess."

It was over. Isaac was in jail. They had won. Rachel would finally be free.

Ashley stood and pulled Rachel to her feet. She hugged her tightly, pulling her so close that she could feel the younger woman's heartbeat. Rachel's wrists were still in chains, so she couldn't return the gesture, but neither seemed to care.

Tears spilled down Rachel's cheeks, and Ashley's collar grew wet as Rachel tucked her face into Ashley's shoulder and began sobbing. Cameras clicked all around them, but Ashley paid them no attention. She looked up at the gallery of onlookers. They all wore similarly confused expressions. Nobody knew about Isaac and the baby. Not even Tom, who was seated near the back of the courtroom.

Ashley's heart leapt at the sight of him. He had come to support her. It didn't even begin to make up for his mistakes, but it was a start. She wondered if, like Rachel, she too could have a future.

EPILOGUE
RACHEL

Six months later

Winter melted into spring and spring shifted into summer. Rachel wasn't carefree—she probably never would be after the trauma she had suffered—but every day she grew a little lighter. Therapy was helping, but it was a slow, arduous process. She would never be normal, she knew that with absolute certainty, but what was *normal* anyway?

The sun shone on Rachel's face as she made her way down Central Avenue, toward Ashley's office, with a bundle of flowers purchased at the small downtown farmers' market. They were bright with color—vibrant pinks, yellows, and greens—and left a fragrant trail behind her. Rachel had never felt so untethered. She didn't know it was possible.

It was Saturday, but the door to the public defender's office was unlocked. A bell jingled as Rachel stepped inside. It wasn't dark inside, but only half the lights were on. People were here, but they weren't doing business. Nobody was at the receptionist's desk. Elena had the day off.

"Hello?" Rachel called. "Is anybody home?"

"Back here." Ashley's voice echoed down the long hallway. "Come on back."

Rachel found Ashley, Katie, and Forest all crammed in Ashley's tiny

office. It was cleaner than usual, though, with only a few stacks of documents on the floor.

"Hello there, Rachel," Forest said.

"Hello," Rachel said.

She didn't meet his gaze. Not because he was unkind, but because she
hadn't learned to trust men yet. She was working on it, but her therapist
said that she may never fully get there and that was okay. Men had done
some horrible things to her.

"What do you have there?" Ashley said, nodding to the flowers.

"They're for the house."

After her release, Rachel had moved in with Ashley. Ashley had
insisted, saying that she had a four-bedroom farmhouse with plenty of
room to spare. Rachel wasn't paying room and board yet, but she would
soon. Once her civil suit against Isaac and her mother settled. As Isaac's
victim, she was entitled to compensation, restitution for all that she had
endured. Isaac would spend the remainder of his days in prison, but
Lyndsay had gotten off scot free. She'd known what was happening, was in
a position to protect her daughter, but she didn't. For that, Rachel intended
to take every last dime from her mother.

"They are beautiful," Ashley said.

"Now that you're here," Katie said, leaning back in her chair, "we need
to talk."

"Wait a minute," Ashley interjected, "you were filling me in on Indigo
Brown's case."

Katie now worked for Ashley as an investigator. Everyone in town had
taken to calling them the *dynamic duo* because they were rarely seen apart
anymore.

"We can talk about that in a minute. We need to discuss the mental
health response team while Forest and Rachel are here."

Forest had recently offered Rachel a job on the team. It would require
her to get her psychology degree, but she didn't need it when she started
her job. She only had to be working toward it. She had plenty of real-life
trauma experience anyway.

"Do you plan to accept the job?" Katie asked.

Katie would be on the team as well. The leader, in fact. But she would only work part-time. In the six months she'd been working with Ashley, she had discovered that she loved working from the defense side. Katie seemed surprised by this, but Ashley had told Rachel that she wasn't the least bit shocked. Ashley had said that defendants were people with complicated stories. Once Katie got in there and started working with them, she saw them as people rather than defendants. But Ashley didn't have to explain it to Rachel. She understood all too well.

"I will accept the job," Rachel said.

And that was when the next stage of her life began.

UNFORGIVABLE ACTS
ASHLEY MONTGOMERY LEGAL THRILLER #3

Nobody is surprised when a fire erupts on a property owned by Frank Vinny, who's been using the wooded lot for the highly flammable process of meth manufacturing—until two bodies are pulled from the wreckage.

One is Frank Vinny himself. The other is a teenage girl that can't be identified.

As law enforcement targets one of Ashley's clients with ties to Frank as the arsonist, Ashley joins forces with PI Katie Mickey to get a jump on her defense.

Katie and Ashley discover that Frank's involvement in the criminal underworld goes beyond cooking and distributing meth. They uncover a trail of missing teenagers, all of them linked to a series of unforgivable acts that begin and end with Frank Vinny.

In their search for the missing girls, Ashley and Katie discover ties that could implicate their client, leading them to an impossible choice: help the girls, or protect their client.

With so many lives on the line, Ashley and Katie must navigate a tangled web of high-profile lies and dangerous secrets...even if that means putting their own lives at risk.

Get your copy today at

ACKNOWLEDGMENTS

First and foremost, I want to thank all the wonderful people at Severn River Publishing for choosing to publish my stories. Especially Catherine Streissguth and Amber Hudock who have spent many months answering my seemingly unending list of questions.

I also want to thank my content editor, Randall Klein, and my copy editor, Kate Schomaker. This book would be a complete mess without the two of you. Randall with your guidance on plot points, and Kate with your attention to detail.

To Stephanie Hansen, my amazing agent and all the good people of Metamorphosis Literary Agency, I am endlessly grateful that you took a chance on me. You receive thousands of manuscripts daily, all from other undoubtedly talented authors, yet you chose to represent my work.

A special thanks to Brooke Johnson Wright, DO, for all your assistance with the medical portions of this book. They would have been a disaster without your guidance. The book would also have a different name because it was you who suggested *Undetermined Death* to me when I was completely stumped on a worthy title.

Last, but not least, I want to thank my family. My sisters, brother, and parents, who have been at my side, encouraging me from day one. I especially want to thank my husband and our three children, H.S, M.S, and W.S, for bringing so much joy to my life.

ABOUT THE AUTHOR

Laura Snider is a practicing lawyer in Iowa. She graduated from Drake Law School in 2009 and spent most of her career as a Public Defender. Throughout her legal career she has been involved in all levels of crimes from petty thefts to murders. These days she is working part-time as a prosecutor and spends the remainder of her time writing stories and creating characters.

Laura lives in Iowa with her husband, three children, two dogs, and two very mischievous cats.

Sign up for Laura Snider's newsletter at
severnriverbooks.com/authors/laura-snider

Printed in the United States
by Baker & Taylor Publisher Services